MW01045564

JANET KELLOUGH

THE BATHWATER CONSPIRACY

A tightly-plotted mystery and fascinating

glimpse of the future run amok.

EDGE SCIENCE FICTION AND FANTASY PUBLISHING
An Imprint of HADES PUBLICATIONS, INC.
CALGARY

The Bathwater Conspiracy

Copyright © 2018 by Janet Kellough

EDGE SCIENCE FICTION AND FANTASY PUBLISHING
An Imprint of HADES PUBLICATIONS, INC.
P.O. Box 1714, Calgary, Alberta, T2P 2L7, Canada

The EDGE Team:
Producer: Brian Hades
Acquisitions Editor: Michelle Heumann
Edited by: Heather Manuel
Cover Design: Rena Hoberman
Book Design: Mark Steele
Publicist: Janice Shoults
Copywriter: Myles McDonough

ISBN: 978-1-77053-164-2

EDGE Science Fiction and Fantasy Publishing and Hades Publications, Inc. acknowledges the ongoing support of the Alberta Foundation for the Arts and the Canada Council for the Arts for our publishing programme.

Canada Council   Conseil des arts
for the Arts   du Canada

Library and Archives Canada Cataloguing in Publication
CIP Data on file with the National Library of Canada
ISBN: 978-1-77053-164-2
(e-Book ISBN: 978-1-77053-163-5)

FIRST EDITION
(20180209)
Printed in USA
www.edgewebsite.com

Publisher's Note:

Thank you for purchasing this book. It began as an idea, was shaped by the creativity of its talented author, and was subsequently molded into the book you have before you by a team of editors and designers.

Like all EDGE books, this book is the result of the creative talents of a dedicated team of individuals who all believe that books (whether in print or pixels) have the magical ability to take you on an adventure to new and wondrous places powered by the author's imagination.

As EDGE's publisher, I hope that you enjoy this book. It is a part of our ongoing quest to discover talented authors and to make their creative writing available to you.

We also hope that you will share your discovery and enjoyment of this novel on social media through Facebook, Twitter, Goodreads, Pinterest, etc., and by posting your opinions and/or reviews on Amazon and other review sites and blogs. By doing so, others will be able to share your discovery and passion for this book.

Brian Hades, publisher

Dedication

For the boys

CHAPTER 1

A murder? Unusual. We didn't see many of those, and they were seldom very interesting, but I waited politely while Inspector Trent jogged some papers into a tidy pile and retrieved a stray paper clip that had gone skittering across her desk.

"This is little more than a courtesy request, Mac," she said. "The crime occurred in our jurisdiction, so we need to sign off on it, but it's a Darmes case, and they're handling the investigation. The only reason you're at the postmortem is as a witness. All you have to do is sign whatever they ask you to sign."

I glanced at the clock. It was ten-thirty already and I still hadn't had enough caffeine to jumpstart me into the morning.

Trent had been steeping tea in the ceramic pot that sat on a corner of her desk blotter. I could smell it when I'd walked into her office. I'd have liked a cup just then — I was feeling a little bleary-brained — but I knew none of it was coming my way, not even if I offered to drink it out of my old office mug instead of from one of the thin porcelain cups she kept for visitors. Oh well. I consoled myself with the fact that it was mid-morning and she'd probably already switched to decaf by now anyway.

She frowned at me. "Have you got that? Rubber stamp whatever they want."

Oh, cazzo crap, I thought. Just one more tick on the day's list of Tiresome Tasks.

— «» —

"Hey, MacHenry! Pulled in to see Boss Tweed, huh?" Detective Garin Davis smirked as she threw a pile of papers on top of the pile of papers that was already threatening to slide off my desk. "What have you done now? Or not done, more to the point."

"Thank you, Detective Diva," I said in a singsong school-girl voice. Diva hated her nickname. I used it whenever I could.

"Somebody run away from home? Dirty words sprayed all over the front door of City Hall?"

Detectives like Diva were usually assigned to the high-profile crimes, like kidnapping, because they could talk to the newsfeeds without the use of highly descriptive and borderline offensive language. Inspector Trent liked her officers to be polite and presentable at all times. I wasn't. Or wasn't often, anyway. Instead, I worked a lot of Tiresome Tasks. TT's were a grab-bag of cases that were high-labor and low-resolution, like missing persons and vandalism — everything the uniformed cops didn't have time to investigate. They were a pain in the ass for any number of reasons, not least because they generated enormous piles of paperwork. There weren't a lot of us in Detective Division to begin with, and just then several of the regulars had been pulled off to provide extra security for the election, so there was a giant backlog of these nuisance cases, and a distressing number of them had ended up on my desk.

Having had her fun with me for the time being, Davis went off to impress the junior officers who had been assigned to trail after her. She was making the most of it, regaling them with all the cases that she'd solved, single-handedly to hear her tell it. I stared at the reports I was supposed to be filling out and drummed my fingers on the desk for a minute. I had a half-hour to kill before it was time to leave for the morgue.

Murder, huh? Strange sort of case for the Darmes to be involved in. Most murders occurred as the result of domestic disputes that got out of hand, or as accidental killings in the course of other crimes. Once in a long while, somebody was bumped off for the insurance or some other kind of financial gain. Cause and effect was generally pretty clear-cut, and the cases were sewn up quickly. Fraud and forgery were a lot more interesting. In those, motive was evident, but method was frequently convoluted, elaborate and inventive. I loved those cases.

I glanced at the clock. If I left right then, I would have time to stop and grab a take-out tea from the shop at the corner. The Tiresome Tasks could wait until I got back.

— «» —

The only person I knew at the autopsy was the medical examiner. The rest of the people present were grim-faced agents in supremely unmemorable suits. You could tell just by looking at them that they were federal law enforcement, from the Gendarmes National Security Corps — "Darmes" in general parlance. City cops like me don't usually have much contact with Darmes, and, when we do, we find them a little spooky.

I took a position on the opposite side of the body from them. No introductions were made, but one of them did glare at the cup of tea I was cradling in my hands. I smiled at her and took a sip. After that she joined her companions in ignoring me.

Dr. Jo Norris Hines, the medical examiner, was a small woman who always reminded me of a bird — a wren or a chickadee or something — one of those little jittery ones you see in the park. She flitted around a corpse, swooping at it with an instrument, then retreating and circling, and closing in again with a different instrument in hand. The fluttering was deceptive. She was fussy, but that wasn't a bad trait in a pathologist, and her attention to detail was legendary, her testimony in court unassailable. I'd always had a bit of a thing for Hines, in a theoretical, remote, fantasy kind of way, not the least because she sort of reminded me of my ex-girlfriend, only classier.

Hines removed the sheet that covered the body, quickly and precisely folded it, then placed it on a shelf under the instrument tray.

The victim was in her early twenties, I figured, and had been quite pretty, if you could look past the facial bruising and the wound at the side of her head. There was quite a lot of bruising to look past. Somebody had whaled on this girl. Repeatedly.

Besides the ugly trauma to her head, the girl's arms showed a mass of livid bruises, as did the lower part of her legs, but it was the damage between her legs that shocked me the most. Her whole vaginal area was pulpy, bloody, and covered in shit. Suddenly the tea was leaving a sour taste in my mouth.

Hines worked methodically, dictating descriptions of the injuries and carefully noting their locations on the body.

Any unexplained death warranted a full autopsy, and, as far as I could judge, the damage done to this poor girl's body was inexplicable, but when Dr. Hines reached for the scalpel to begin opening the chest cavity, one of the Darmes stepped forward.

"That will do," she said.

Hines looked up, startled. "But I haven't finished yet."

"I think we've seen all we need to see."

"No, we haven't," Hines protested. "I can't determine the cause of this death solely on the basis of a cursory body exam."

"I think it's clear that the victim died as a result of being accidently pushed from the third floor of a building onto a paved surface," the Darme said. "Probably by a fellow student."

"No, that's not clear at all. The condition of the body isn't consistent with that conclusion."

"We believe it is," the Darme said. "Please wrap her up again and we'll arrange for the transfer of the body to the family."

Open-mouthed, Norris Hines did exactly as she was told, but I could see how angry she was by the set of her shoulders.

The Darmes waited until the corpse was fully contained and deposited into the coffin-like vault, and then they sealed the edges of the drawer with police tape.

I'd never seen anything like this. Just for starters, there are few areas more secure than a morgue. Who were they expecting to break in, and why would anyone want this dead body other than to mourn over it? Then I realized that it wasn't outside intruders they were worried about. They didn't want Hines to look at the body again.

I was handed a sheaf of papers with x's marking the places where I was supposed to sign. I did what I was supposed to — I signed them — but I did it slowly so that I could take note of any recorded details before I handed the report back to the Darmes. There weren't a lot of them to note. Most of the spaces had been left blank. I wasn't sure why I even bothered trying to see what was there, since it seemed that this case was being buried in a deep, dark place somewhere, but the whole thing was just weird, and I wanted as much ammunition as I could muster, in case, at some future point, I might have to cover my ass.

— «» —

Inspector Trent was out of the office when I returned. She hadn't requested that I report back to her after the autopsy — after all, it was simply a matter of, as she had put it, "rubber stamping" — so I wasn't sure why I went looking for her, other than the fact that I was so puzzled by what had occurred. That, and the fact that Davis was in full-blown obnoxious mode, loudly reiterating evidence and making unfounded pronouncements about the Tanaka Tyler kidnapping.

As far as I was concerned, it was the same old story — an infant in a shopping mall with her parents, who turned their heads for a second or two, only to discover an empty stroller when they turned back again. In my experience, if these cases weren't solved in the first week or so, there was little chance of ever finding the kid. She'd been snatched by some baby-starved couple with just enough counterfeit paperwork to pass in a far-off town, or worse yet, by a black-market ring who could smuggle a child across a border somewhere. Fortunately, there are a lot fewer kidnappings than there used to be, thanks to the Insemination Registry. Snatching a kid used to be dead easy and extremely lucrative. It's not so easy anymore, but it's still lucrative if you can get away with it.

Every once in a while, a snatchee from the old days will turn up as a teenager, when her papers aren't good enough to get her into university or something, and she's tracked down the truth of her parentage. By then it's way too late. These kids have no memory of their real parents and it's not like they've been mistreated by their new families or anything. In fact, most of them have been given everything they could possibly want. The reunions are nothing but sad and awkward. Honestly, if you can't get the kid back to the old family right away, you're probably better off leaving her with the new one.

All enforcement agencies have an obligation to make it look like they're doing everything they can however, especially in an election year, so even though the Tanaka Tyler case was spearheaded by the Darmes, Davis had been seconded as City Police liaison. Whoever else not working political rally mob control had been left with the scut work.

Capital City Detective Division is jammed into a small space on the second floor of the Police Services building and my desk was shoved way over in the back corner of it. I had to shoulder my way past the crowd of juniors clustered around the evidence wall in order to reach it. Most of them ignored me, but one of them — the perky one with the reddish hair, Detective Nguyen — smiled at me and politely stepped aside to let me pass. Nice to know that at least one of the juniors had manners. No doubt Davis would grind that right out of her.

I ignored the delinquent paperwork on my desk and tried to shut out Davis's braying voice as I slumped in my chair to think about the strange autopsy I'd just seen. If it was an accidental death, as the Darmes claimed, or even a simple murder, it should have come to City. That would be the protocol except in cases that somehow affect national security. But a student shoved off a building? There was a big, stinky smell all over this one.

For some reason, the Darmes had swooped in on the case and shut us out, but I figured there had to be a rudimentary report available somewhere in-house. We'd been called in only to keep the paperwork tidy, so there wouldn't be much of a trail, I knew, but surely there was something, if only a notification and a request for a waiver of interest.

Curious to see what I could find, I keyed in the autopsy date and time and Dr. Hines's name as the presiding medical officer. It was there, all right, but access to it had been blocked. That happened sometimes, if it was a sensitive case. I knew that there was no point in asking Trent for an override. The inspector had been clear — sign off, don't ask questions.

I had too many questions not to ask them and I had lingered over the paperwork long enough to pick out a few details, so at least I was armed with a starting point. The girl's name had been Alfreda Lucas Longwell. I hooked onto the Wire and typed the name into search, but nothing came up. I tried *IMeMine*. The girl had been young, only twenty-three according to her death certificate. She probably used the popular network to keep up with her friends. To my surprise, there was nothing.

I drummed my fingers on the desk as I tried to bring to mind what else I had seen. It was a nasty habit that bugged the hell out of people, especially people like Inspector Trent, but it helped me focus. There had been a downtown address at the top of the form — 91 Victoria Street — near the city center. And near the university. I found the school's website and accessed the student enrollment files, but there were no Lucas Longwells listed. And yet the Darme had referred to a "fellow student" when she had directed Hines to discontinue the autopsy. There really wasn't any other school close by, just a high school, and a couple of public schools. Alfreda had been too old for either.

I scrolled through the rest of the uni site, but it was mostly descriptions of courses and bios of faculty members. There was a link to the student council page. I clicked it. Their WirePage consisted of listings of club meetings and upcoming social functions — dances, rallies, the Chess Club, the hockey team. And then I found it. The contact for the student choir. Alfi Lucas Longwell. The link was inactive though. When I clicked on it, I got a message saying the page couldn't be found. I looked through some of the other student activity pages, but that one listing seemed to be the only mention of the girl.

I was really puzzled now. I would have thought that anyone who was an organizer of a student function would be a student, but maybe it wasn't a given. Still, it was beginning to look as though Alfreda Lucas Longwell had been virtually erased. I supposed the Darmes would have that kind of power, although the Wire is notoriously difficult to control. But why would they do that? Longwell was not a public figure, otherwise her name would have been all over the Wire. As far as I could tell, there was no notoriety to attach to her death, no reason to hush up whatever had happened to her. At least, not on her own account. I wondered about the "fellow student" who had supposedly pushed her from the building. Was there some connection there that needed to be protected?

I sat, staring at the Vu screen, my fingers drumming faster and faster as I tried to think the thing through. Trent had specifically warned me off, told me to cooperate with whatever the Darmes wanted. The shit would surely fly if I went snooping around in light of such a specific warning. And even if I found something, I wasn't sure what I could do with it anyway. I had no official status in the case. Maybe, for once, I should just leave well enough alone. I closed the page I had been staring at, blitzed the files and rebooted the terminal. Best not to leave too-obvious a trail behind.

CHAPTER 2

I spent the next day trying to clean up the paperwork from a rash of bike thefts and a final report on three missing teenagers, who, predictably, had decided to take a long weekend to go clubbing without informing their parents. They had turned up, hungover and sheepish, on the Tuesday morning. The bikes, on the other hand, had completely disappeared and I knew there was little prospect of them ever finding their way home.

Forms, however, are made to be filled out, and I'd slogged through nearly half of the cases that had accumulated in my inbox when the numbers on the office clock flipped over to eight and I decided to pack it in for the night. Keeping irregular hours was one of the things that had driven my girlfriend crazy. Just one of them, mind you, and I supposed her departure was the result of a cumulative effect and not directly attributable to a single cause. Or so I liked to tell myself.

I was just shrugging on my coat when my Fone buzzed. Just for a moment I hoped that maybe it was Georgie. She sometimes used to call when I was working late, just to say hi. But then I checked myself. That wasn't going to happen again, was it? The ID was blocked on the incoming call, so I figured it was a complaint of some sort that had been routed up to me by the main desk.

"MacHenry." Trent liked us to state the name of the department, our rank and full names when we answered the Fone, but this was after-hours and nobody else was in the office, so I didn't bother.

"Detective MacHenry? This is Jo Hines."

"What can I do for you, Doctor?" I had no idea what the answer to that particular question might be. It was highly unusual for someone like a medical examiner to communicate directly with a detective. Trent was a stickler for having everything go through the correct lines of communication, and those lines ran from the top down.

"I wonder if you could meet me tomorrow? For lunch?"

I was so flabbergasted that I had to take a long pause before I could find the words to reply. Direct communication was unusual. Social contact was unheard of. Just for a moment, I wondered if Hines was asking me out, then I shoved the thought away. I hadn't picked up on any of the subtle clues that signal sexual interest, certainly not on her part anyway. There had been no over-long glances, none of that slight leaning in that happens when someone thinks they want to be close. Besides, much as I might welcome such a development, I knew perfectly well that Jo Hines was way out of my league.

"Sure," I finally replied, then mentally kicked myself for the inelegance of the reply.

She named a trendy bistro near the station and asked me to meet her there at one-thirty. That was past the usual lunch hour. Most diners would have eaten and gone back to work by then. I agreed and rang off.

When I'd had time to get over any little fantasy I had about dating someone like Jo Hines, I realized there could be only one reason why she would want to meet with me away from the prying eyes of our colleagues. The Longwell murder case.

—— «» ——

I was acutely and embarrassingly aware of my shapeless jacket and scuffed boots as I approached the reservations desk the next day. I should have spiffed up a little, but it had been pretty clear that Hines hadn't wanted attention drawn to our meeting. Someone would have commented if I'd shown up for work that morning as anything but my usual rumpled self. There were two people ahead of me and they were seated immediately by the stylish hostess. As I expected, most of the lunch crowd had eaten and gone, the majority of the tables empty and reset for the dinner service. Each table was covered with a snowy white cloth, the place settings splayed out around fussy floral centerpieces. Parts of the room were sectioned off by delicate brass screens which diffused the sunlight pouring in through the massive front window, making odd, filigreed patterns on the walls and floor. Slender young women with tight black dresses and perfectly cut hair floated here and there, languidly piling coffee cups and dessert plates onto trolleys. Bijou girls, on the look-out for someone important or famous, hoping to find a mover and a shaker who might whisk them away, at least for a time, from the tedious necessity of earning a living.

When the hostess returned to the front desk after seating the other late lunchers, she looked me up and down with a barely disguised air of disdain, her eyes making a brief stop at the unruly mop of hair I'd scraped back into a ponytail, and at the stain on my jacket sleeve that I hadn't noticed until just then.

"I'm supposed to be meeting with Dr. Norris Hines," I said.

The woman's iciness thawed a little at the mention of the name. "Dr. Hines has already arrived. Please follow me."

Hines had chosen a small table at the rear of the restaurant, near the kitchen and against the wall. Without a doubt the lousiest seat in the place. She most certainly did not want us to be seen together. As I approached the table, I was once again struck by the doctor's resemblance to some small, fragile bird. Forensics was a tough business and I wondered what made her go into that field. But then, I reflected, sometimes these tiny women are the toughest customers.

She smiled as I sat down across from her. "Glass of wine?"

I hesitated. Drinking at lunch time was never a good idea for me. I'm the quintessential cheap drunk. Even a little booze makes me sleepy and befuddled. But it felt unsociable to refuse.

"Sure. Something red?"

The doctor lifted a hand and a young woman was there almost immediately to take the order, leaning down and simpering at Hines as she did so. Me, she ignored.

I opened the heavy, leather-bound menu. Nearly every entree was some sort of salad — the restaurant catered to professionals and government bureaucrats, who are notoriously obsessed with remaining svelte, their determination failing them only when it comes to the dessert menu. Everything listed under "Afters" included some form of chocolate, and I wondered how the restaurant managed to get so much of it. Recent trade talks between the Northwest Zone and the South Central Zone had stuttered to a halt, with the result that the SoCens had, in a fit of pique, cut us off entirely. Chocolate and, even more importantly, coffee were in short supply here in NowZo.

I gulped a little at the prices. There was certainly nothing slim about those.

"This is on me, by the way," Hines said as she scanned the specials. "The pasta salad is excellent."

I'd accept her generosity. I knew that in spite of the cost of this meal, as soon as I was out the door I'd be looking for a hamburger stand. It was just that kind of place.

"Sounds good." We gave our drink orders and Hines waited until the waiter was well out of earshot.

Then she leaned forward. "You've probably already figured out what this is about."

"The Longwell girl. The Darmes were shutting the case down real tight weren't they?"

"Yes, they were. But not quite tight enough."

"You got a good look at the file?"

Hines nodded. "None of the injuries were consistent with the story that was given. The head injuries were caused by blows, not by a fall. And the rest of the damage…"

"What did you make of it? I've never seen anything quite like it."

"Neither have I. I wasn't sure what I was looking at. I've never seen vaginal tearing like that."

"Something gone sadly awry with sexual appliances?" I ventured.

"There was no indication that any sort of … tool … was used. Just physical force. And the other injuries wouldn't be consistent with that theory."

I leaned forward. "So just what theory were the findings consistent with? In your opinion?"

She took a moment to answer, marshaling her thoughts with a wrinkling of her forehead. "An unbelievably brutal attack, without the use of any kind of weapon. Someone beat her to death with their fists and their feet, and they kept at it long after she was dead. For example, one arm was obviously broken, but I think that happened after she died. She was held down, but there were no signs that restraints had been used."

"And the vaginal injuries?"

"I'm not entirely sure. I think she was assaulted repeatedly, though. It's hard to tell which came first, that or the gash in the head."

"Whoa."

Our wine arrived, and the conversation came to a halt. I sat back and tried to digest what the doctor had said while the waiter fussed with napkins and cutlery. Alfreda Longwell's death was a whole lot more than an accident.

"So you're saying that more than one person was involved?" I asked as soon as we were alone again.

"That's exactly what I'm saying. Someone did the holding, while the other, or others, did the damage. And then maybe they traded places."

"Someone with a giant-sized grudge and an accomplice?"

"Big enough to commit brutal murder?"

She had a point. Generally speaking, revenge attacks took place on inanimate objects that held an association for both parties. You see a lot when you're a cop — I've seen women shred their ex-girlfriends' clothes, trash their apartments, empty their bank accounts, steal their cars and even, in one case, set fire to a life-sized effigy in a public park — but those kinds of attacks seldom involved physical injury to either party. Down and dirty cat-fights, on the other hand, involved liquor, hair-pulling and verbal abuse, but not much else.

"What about a group vengeance thing?" Hines said. "Somebody trying to teach someone a lesson?"

"Like bully bopping? A group of teenagers ganging up on somebody they don't like? I don't think so. That's about humiliation, more than harm. I can't imagine that kids would go that far. I mean the whole point of it is so they can psychologically torment the victim afterwards. They wouldn't kill her. That would take all the fun out of it."

Our waiter reappeared to take our food orders. I followed Hines's advice and ordered the pasta. It was the most substantial-sounding thing on the menu.

"Any other theories?" I asked when we were alone again.

"A sadomasochistic ritual, maybe? There are women out there who get their kicks out of that kind of stuff."

I shook my head. "That kind of sex is consensual. Any injuries that result from it are relatively minor and the result of somebody getting carried away or someone having second thoughts. Both parties tend to be extremely contrite after it happens. And, as far as I know, no one has ever died from it."

"As far as you know."

"I suppose it's possible," I said, trying to think of any case I'd run across where things had spun that far out of control. "If somebody with a really nasty streak was cruising that circuit, it would be easy enough to find a victim. She'd go along willingly, wouldn't she? But why kill her? You could get whatever you wanted just by asking for it."

"Unless what you wanted was to kill somebody."

"A monster? Is that what you're saying?"

Hines shrugged. "I don't know. All I do know is that there's something very strange going on, but I have no idea how to go about finding out what it is."

"So why have you come to me? Why not take your questions to the inspector?"

"I think it's pretty clear that there's a lot of pressure from the top to keep this case quiet. I doubt the good Inspector Trent would be interested in bucking direct orders from the Darmes." The doctor looked at me and grinned, an action that animated her narrow face. "Besides, you have a reputation for getting good results in an unconventional kind of way. And this is the most unconventional case I've ever run across."

"I must admit, I'm a mite curious about why the case is being handled by the Darmes," I said. "If it's murder, pure and simple, it should have come to us in the first place."

"Are they protecting someone?"

"That would be my guess. And it would have to be somebody pretty important to justify the steps they've taken to hush it up."

Our lunches arrived just then, and again we were both silent while the waiter slid the plates onto the table. There were six smallish pieces of gnocchi, two lettuce leaves and a long, slender stalk of celery on the plate in front of me. I'd definitely be looking for a burger later. I pushed the pasta around a little with my fork, just to use up some time. Once I started eating, I knew the food would disappear in about three bites.

"So why are you bothering with this at all? I asked. "Why not just accept whatever the Darmes have decided and get on with your life?"

She hadn't tasted her food yet either. She took a long, slow sip of her wine before she answered.

"Because it offends me. I worked hard to get to where I am and I'm good at my job. I pride myself on being meticulous and thorough. I don't rule on a cause of death until I'm one hundred percent certain that I've collected all of the evidence and that I've considered all of the possibilities. By participating in a cover-up, I'm putting a permanent stain on what has been, up until now, a sterling record. I won't stand for it."

My respect for this tiny doctor, already considerable, cranked up another notch. "Fair enough. So ... what information did you manage to get before everything was snatched away?"

"She was twenty-three years old. She was supposedly pushed off a building. Other than the fact that she was a student and lived on Victoria Street, the official record wasn't much of a record. There wasn't even an address given as the scene of the crime."

"She was a member of the student choir. She was the official contact. I did a little snooping already," I confessed, in response to Hines's look of surprise. "Other than that, her record has been wiped. I couldn't even find her on *IMeMine*. There aren't a lot of loose strings that have been left dangling for us to tug on."

"So where do you start when there's so little to go on?" Hines asked.

"I start with what I know for sure," I said. "She was a student at the university and she lived on Victoria Street. We'll see what I can find out from there."

"I knew I came to the right person."

And with that encouragement, I finally lifted my fork and dug into my lunch. As I had feared, it disappeared quickly. The chocolate cake I ordered for dessert was far more substantial, but it was a little too sweet and had that peculiar texture that's a dead giveaway that they used carob instead of chocolate. And to my profound disappointment, they didn't have any coffee either.

CHAPTER 3

The south end of Victoria Street is almost entirely given over to student housing, row after row of once-handsome three story brick houses that have been chopped up into cheap apartments. I know the street well. It's only a block from where I rented an apartment in my final year of school and I had gone to many a good party on Victoria. I rode along the street and pulled my bike up in front of number ninety-one. Oh, luck and lux. There was an "Apartment for Rent" sign in the window of the front door, with a Fone number listed, and an instruction to contact someone named Martha Chin Beliveau. I made a note of the details, turned my bike around and rode toward the campus.

I knew that the most likely place to shake something loose would be at Rosie's, the café that caters to the student population. I checked the time on my Fone. I was disappointed to see that it was quarter past three. Rosie's would have finished their lunch service already.

The café was still half-full of students, however. It always was, at least when I'd hung out there. No more food till five, but lots of tea and coffee. Except for the current scarcity of coffee, nothing much had changed from my time. Battered wooden chairs were pulled here and there into groups around scarred tabletops, and a row of fixed stools marched along the counter that separated the grill from the rest of the room. The walls were covered with posters, most of them announcing student concerts, or study groups, or rooms for rent, and here and there the sulky head of a popular singer, or a reproduction of a famous painting.

Heads swung in my direction as I threaded my way through the sprawl of chairs to a stool half-way along the counter. The animated conversations that had been taking place as I walked in ceased immediately. I knew that I was already marked as a cop. I ordered a mug of tea and stirred the sugar in slowly as the café emptied two and three students at a time. Every one of them was probably in violation of at least one of the myriad of statutes, bylaws and ordinances that had been enacted for their protection and well-being. No one bothered enforcing many of these nanny laws anymore, unless it was in the course of busting someone for something more important, but there was still nothing like a cop to clear a place out in a hurry.

There was an older woman mopping the floor at the back. She worked her way toward me, swishing under the tables and pulling chairs back to their proper places. When she reached the stools, I pulled my feet up out of the way so she could reach under the counter. She glared at me. "Whaddya want in here? You drive all my business away."

"I'm just curious."

"About what?" She slapped the mop against the floor, spattering gray water across the linoleum. "About the students? You have dreams of being young and foolish again? Wanna go back to when you were carefree and happy and had nothing to worry about except grades and other girls? Pah!"

She slapped the mop again and the water shot sideways like spit.

"Nah, it wasn't that great the first time around."

The woman snorted. "You got that right."

"I'm only after a little information, that's all."

"I don't know anything about anything."

"You ever hear of a student named Alfreda Lucas Longwell?"

The woman shrugged. "There are lots of students. Most of them come here at least once. I'm supposed to know all their names?"

"You hear about one of them that died recently? From a fall?"

The woman's eyes flicked towards the hall that led to washrooms at the back of the café, but she didn't say anything, just shrugged.

"Well, thanks for your time anyway," I said.

She grunted and continued mopping with aggressive swipes, working her way toward the front of the café.

I pulled out my Fone and punched in the number I'd retrieved on Victoria Street.

"Is this Martha Chin Beliveau?" I asked when a voice said hello.

"Yes," the voice allowed.

"My name is Carson MacHenry," I said. "I'm a lawyer calling on behalf of Alfreda Lucas Longwell's family."

"I already told the police, I don't know anything about the Longwell girl," Beliveau said. "She just rented an apartment from me."

"Is that the apartment that's currently for rent again? At 91 Victoria?"

"Yes. The police took away all her belongings. In fact, they took some things that didn't belong to her. You're a lawyer, you say? Maybe you could get them back for me."

Oh sure, Martha Beliveau, I'm sure you're missing all sorts of things.

"Actually, I'm not that kind of lawyer," I said. "You should probably contact your own solicitor if there's property gone astray."

"Oh, well. They weren't that important. So why are you calling me? The police told me not to talk to anybody."

"I've been charged with tidying up the estate for the Lucas Longwell family. I was just calling to find out whether or not there is still any rent owing on the apartment."

"I'll have to check my records. Just a second…" It was no surprise when, a few moments later, she said, "Well, yes, as a matter of fact, the girl hasn't paid for the last two months."

"I see. That's just the sort of detail I'm here to deal with. Could you possibly send an invoice to her home address? Just so I have a record of disbursements, you understand."

"Of course," she said. "That's her address in Cedar Lake, is it?"

Lux. Lux and luck. "That's correct. You send it right off and I'll make sure you get the monies you deserve."

"Well, thank you, thank you very much. I'll do that right away. Thanks for calling."

"My pleasure," I said and disconnected. Cedar Lake, huh? Where in the back of beyond was that?

I gulped down the rest of my tea and threw a credit on the counter. "If you hear of anything I might be interested in can you give me a call?" I said to the mop lady, who didn't even bother looking up. I put my card beside the credit, even though I knew it was a waste of good paper. You didn't win students over by spilling all their secrets. Then, just as I turned to go, I happened to glance at the hallway at the back and caught a glimpse of a girl with long brown hair leaving through the back door.

I knew there was little point in trying to talk to university administration — the Darmes would have sewn them up tight and bureaucracy doesn't budge. They wouldn't have been able to keep students from talking, though. I figured if I hovered around on campus for a while I might overhear some useful piece of information. The death of a fellow student would be hot news. Even those who hadn't known her would be trying to place her. Unless they hadn't heard about it, which I supposed was possible. The Darmes had moved real fast.

I knew it wasn't the most inspired investigative strategy, but at the very least I might be able to get a sense of what was being said about Alfreda's death.

I sauntered toward the library, catching a whiff of tobacco smoke as I rounded the corner of the building. Smoking on school property — definitely a fineable offence, and one that was beloved of a certain type of rule-breaker. Like me, except that during my student days I had often added a little wacky-weed to the mix as well. But like I said, most of these laws are archaic anyway, and have long been overlooked by authorities who realized that sooner or later you have to let children make their own stupid mistakes.

I was crossing the west lawn when I saw what I'd been looking for — a group of girls sitting together under a tree. Unlike the other knots of students here and there, who were taking advantage of a sunny afternoon to study outside, they did not have their eyes glued to Fones and Porta-Vus. One or two of them were crying and the others looked distinctly unhappy.

I shoved my Fone deep into my pocket and pushed the sleeves of my jacket up around my elbows in an attempt to mimic the latest fashion. I wandered this way and that for a few minutes, as if I was looking for something and was unsure where to go. It wouldn't fool anyone for long, but at least I wouldn't immediately spook the group under the tree. Finally, I ambled over to them.

"Excuse me. Did any of you know Alfreda Lucas Longwell?" I said.

They looked up, startled, and one of the criers gave a gasp and cried all the harder. That was the one I wanted to talk to.

"Excuse me, who are you?" A girl with long brown hair walked up behind me. I couldn't be absolutely sure, but she looked like the girl who had slipped out of Rosie's back door. I wondered if she'd been following me.

"I'm a friend of the family," I said. "Her parents asked me to come along and collect her things, but I discovered they've been taken away and no one will tell me where."

The crier wailed. "The Darmes took them. Everything. Even her photographs."

The brunette poked the other one with her toe, as if to shut her up, but the statement had opened a floodgate.

"They even took all her textbooks and the papers she'd written. And I can't find any of her stuff on *IMeMine*." She blew her nose. "Some of her poems were there — poems she wrote for me."

"I see," I said. "Do you suppose any of her profs might know where her stuff went?"

"You'd have to ask Professor Gerrity," the girl snuffled.

Lux. Lux and luck. Just what I needed.

"Hana, shut up!" the brunette hissed.

"It would be a comfort to her parents if they had some ... you know ... mementoes of what she was working on before she ... um ... you know," I said.

"Was murdered?" The brunette again, who stood with arms folded, a skeptical expression on her face.

"Jazz!" The girl called Hana looked frightened, and a couple of the others in the group were looking over their shoulders to see if anyone was close enough to have overheard.

"Well it's true, isn't it?" she said. "And you're no friend of the family. You were snooping around Rosie's just now. You made a Fone call to Alfi's landlady." She squared her shoulders and looked at me defiantly. She was a tall girl, nearly as tall as I am, and her dark, angry eyes were nearly level with mine as she stepped forward to confront me. "You've already talked to all of us, anyway. So why are you hanging around the campus now? Spying? Well, go ahead. Listen in all you want. I'm not afraid of the Darmes."

"You aren't?" I said. "Cazzo crap on a cracker, I am. So, what do you think happened? The Darmes claim Alfreda was pushed off a building. And that it was an accident."

"Why don't you just ask your Darmes buddies? Or read the file? Why are you bothering with us? We told you. We don't know anything."

I shrugged. "I'm not Darmes, I'm a cop. A city cop. Darmes don't talk to the likes of me. And I don't believe their story anyway. I'd like to know what really happened."

"I don't know what happened," the brunette said. "But I will tell you this — Claire had nothing to do with it. Leave her alone."

At the word "cop" several of the group shifted uneasily and began gathering their belongings, preparing to put distance between themselves and authority.

"Claire who?" I asked, but one by one the girls stood up and began moving away. I didn't try to stop them. My visit to Rosie's had shaken loose far more than I'd dared hope for. I had names now.

"Well, thanks anyway," I said as they scurried off.

The brown-haired girl glared at me and then broke into a trot to catch up with her friends.

I pulled out my Fone, leaned against the tree and brought up the university's WirePage. There was only one Gerrity on the Faculty List. A.E. Gerrity, Department of History.

No one challenged me as I entered the central foyer around which the university administration offices were clustered. There was an information desk in the middle of the cavernous hall, staffed by a bored looking guard who ignored me. She was too busy filing her nails. I ignored her in turn and went to look at the directory on the wall.

There it was. Department of History. Anthropology, Archeology, Ancient, Middle, Modern and, right down at the bottom, Men's Studies, A.E. Gerrity, Rm. 299, McClung Building. That was at the other side of the campus. With a sigh, I headed for the door. It was a long walk, but not long enough to warrant going back to retrieve my bike from the stand in front of Rosie's.

"Excuse me, can I help you?" It was the guard, who had finally taken notice of a stranger in the hall.

"No," I said. "Thanks anyway." I flashed my badge. I was supposed to get a visitor's pass, but the last thing I wanted at that point was an official record of my visit.

The guard looked confused. "Oh ... um ... okay."

If I had been head of university security, I would have fired this woman on the spot for not taking a closer look at the badge, but as the laxity served my purpose, I let it go and continued walking through the door.

It took me quite a long time to find Gerrity's office. The McClung Building was one of the oldest structures at the university, having stood for more than two centuries. It had been remodeled numerous times over the years, never very successfully, or, it appeared, with much thought given to the aesthetics of the result. The corridors were dark, with exposed pipes and heating ducts running across the ceilings, and the far end of the building had been divided and subdivided until it was a warren of small rooms and offices. The fact that Gerrity had been assigned an office there was an indication of her stature at the school. That is to say, not very high. Men's Studies. As if anyone needed to know anything about such fabled creatures. Dragons and unicorns and men. The memory of their existence was dim. Obviously, they must have been around at some point, and the study of their habits was something that might be vaguely interesting to a certain sort of person, but not terribly important in the everyday order of things.

I finally found Room 299, having been for a time confused by my assumption that it must be on the second floor. It was on the third, tucked into a corner, and in spite of the obvious decay of the building itself, was nicely painted and boasted windows that looked out over the paved walkways that led to the adjacent building. The office was big enough only for a battered desk, four filing cabinets and two straight-backed visitors chairs placed under the window.

Professor Gerrity was not in, but there was a student waiting for her, so I claimed the other unoccupied chair. "Do you know if the professor will be long?" I asked.

The student sighed. "You never know with Gerrity. I had an appointment for ten minutes ago."

"Do you take Men's Studies?"

"I'm supposed to be writing my thesis right now. But I want to change the focus," the girl said. "That's why I'm meeting Gerrity. She'll try and talk me out of it."

"Any particular reason?" I asked.

"Why I'm changing, or why she'll try to talk me out of it?"

I shrugged. "Either."

"She offered me a position as a research assistant next year. But I don't think I can handle the field work."

Field work? In Men's Studies? I wondered what kind of field work there could be, with no concrete examples of anything to study.

"Did you have an appointment?" the girl asked.

"No, I just want to ask her a couple of questions." I looked at the student closely. "About a girl that was killed."

The student paled. "I don't know anything about that."

"Did you know Alfreda?"

"Who are you?"

"Are you Claire?" I guessed.

The girl stood up and began to back away. "How did you know that? Who are you?"

"Just someone who's looking for a few answers."

"Are you Darmes? Here to check up on me? I haven't said anything to anybody. You made it clear what would happen to me if I did."

"Now just wait a minute…"

"I didn't have anything to do with what happened, you know that. She wasn't anywhere near the oriole camp that day. But everybody thinks she died on a field trip, and everybody thinks it was me who pushed her and now everybody hates me. You've already ruined my life, so why can't you just go away and leave me alone!" She turned and ran through the door, her appointment forgotten.

Poor girl. She was obviously taking the blame for what had happened, and she wasn't taking it well. And what was the oriole camp?

Five minutes later the tardy Professor Gerrity arrived, panting from exertion and checking her watch. She was small and round with flyaway hair and a flustered manner, one of those women who seemed to fall into a room. She dumped the overstuffed tote bag she carried onto her desk and then looked at me in confusion. "Oh, hello. I was expecting to see one of my students now."

"I'm Carson MacHenry." I held out my hand. "I have a friend whose daughter is coming to the university next year and was thinking about taking Men's Studies. She asked me to check it out for her." The friend of the family ploy hadn't worked very well with the girls on the lawn, but it was better than anything else I could come up with.

"Of course, of course," Gerrity said. "I'd be happy to speak with you, but I do have another appointment now."

"With Claire? She was here, but she had to leave. She said she'll probably check in with you later."

The professor looked troubled, but after a moment's hesitation she went to the wall of filing cabinets and pulled open one of the drawers.

"I can provide you with a reading list, if you like. There's also a first-year course outline I can give you." She rummaged through the files until she found what she was looking for. I waited while she flipped through several folders, until she finally extracted two sheets of paper, each with a long list printed on them.

"*Contrasting Bonobo and Chimpanzee Social Organizations*; *Religion's Role in the Entrenchment of Male Domi-*

nance; The History of the Testosterone Wars," I said, reading down the list. *"Male Reference Group Identity Dependence.* Wow, this sounds pretty deep."

"It's not as bad as all that," Gerrity said. "In fact, it's pretty interesting stuff. It's all available on UniWire, so she shouldn't have any difficulty finding the texts."

I nodded. "I'll tell my friend's daughter to hit the list. I assume it's all theoretical stuff — I mean, there couldn't be any field work or anything, right?"

Gerrity's eyes narrowed slightly at this question, but she recovered quickly. "Of course not," she said. "How could there be?"

"I heard something about a girl who died. Somebody said they thought it had something to do with a field trip. But maybe it was some other course. I'm not too clear on the details."

"I'm not sure what you're talking about," the professor said. "I had a student who died recently, but it was nothing to do with the university."

Oh really? That's not what the Darmes claimed. You'd think that if they were trying to cover something up, they'd try to keep the story a little straighter.

"Oh well," I said, "I'm sure it's nothing to worry about. Thank you so much for the information."

"What's the girl's name? I'll keep an eye out for her."

I hadn't expected to have to come up with a name. "Alfreda," I said quickly. It was the first name to pop into my head. I watched Gerrity's eyes widen in surprise. "Alfreda Carson," I added hastily, and waved my goodbye before I put my foot into it any further.

I wandered around the maze of corridors for ten minutes before I finally located an exit that spilled me out into a green area in front of the sciences building. The space was full of demonstrators who carried placards and chanted as they marched up and down. *Repent Now* some of the signs said. *God is Coming.*

Sakers. I was surprised to see so many of them in the city center, but I supposed they'd crawled out of their hidey-holes because of the election, and the publicity given to the proposed GeneShare Treaty. *Forsake the Instruments of the Devil*, I read. *Forsake Your Evil Ways*. They were obviously opposed to the treaty, but all their demonstrations ever really seemed to do was to make life inconvenient for everybody else. Sakers have zero political clout. I wondered why they bothered, except that part of their creed seems to be to shout out their beliefs. Loudly.

Squared off against the sakers was another group of women with signs that proclaimed an opposite point of view. *Ratify GeneShare Now* and *We Want Healthy Babies* were two of the messages they were sending, along with the far more direct *Down with PM Singh*. The two groups were shouting at each other, and in a couple of instances, pushing and waving their placards in each other's faces.

Unless I was prepared for another very long walk, I would have to make my way through the mob in order to reach my bike.

I knew from past experience that the women on both sides were perfectly prepared to shove and yell at anyone who dared venture into the middle of the demonstration. Anyone, that is, who wasn't police. I pulled my Fone from my pocket, flashed up my badge and held it up over my head. The police insignia was easily seen from my position on the top step of the doorway and I waved the device back and forth as if I was shooting video with it. The demonstrators parted in front of me and covered their faces with their arms. Dirty pool, I supposed, but what was the point of being a cop if you couldn't use it to your advantage once in a while?

I was soon across the lawn. I retrieved my bike and wheeled onto Jessup Boulevard and down to Chan Road where I knew there was a great hamburger joint. I was starving.

CHAPTER 4

I waited until I got home that evening and had started the makings of a pot of tea before I routed my Fone into the wall Vu and entered the name "Cedar Lake."

The official municipal WirePage popped up. It didn't look like much of a town if the vid was anything to go by. There was a disease research facility a few miles out of town that probably provided some local employment, but other than that, the chief industry seemed to be cottage tourism. According to the map, the surrounding area was dotted with a handful of small lakes and there were numerous ads for family resorts and trailer parks, campgrounds and cottages. A quick cross-reference to the town's taxpayers' database took me to Longwell, A.K. and Lucas, F.P. at 22 Lakeside Lane.

I clicked on the map and zoomed out. I figured it would be about a two-hour ride from the city, but it did appear that the town had train service, no doubt because of the research center. That was good. It would save me trying to come up with a plausible excuse for requisitioning a police vehicle. I had the next day off work. Maybe I'd take a ride north. I had nothing else to do with my free time anyway. Not with Georgie gone.

I wandered into the kitchen and poured myself a cup of tea. I briefly wondered about ice cream, but when I opened the freezer compartment of my fridge I realized that there was only a spoonful left in the carton, and it had crystallized beyond redemption. I grabbed a handful of soda crackers and took them, along with my tea, back to the living room.

"She wasn't anywhere near the oriole camp that day," the girl, Claire, had said. "Everybody thinks she died on a field trip."

I keyed in "oriole camp." There were no hits for the phrase itself, only a huge amount of information regarding a songbird of the species *Icterus galbula*, its range, its habitat, color pattern, behavior, and related species, and far, far down the list, a couple of references to Oriole Avenue, which, at one time, had been part of a main thoroughfare through the western outskirts of the city. It was all Decayed Area now, and when I accessed a map, I realized that Oriole was far enough out that, in all probability, it didn't even exist anymore. If there was a camp anywhere near it, it would no doubt be populated by sakers or scavengers. I tagged the map and turned to the reading list that Professor Gerrity had suggested for my fictitious friend's daughter.

The first title was an overview of the causes and major events of what is now termed the Testosterone Wars. Like most people, my historical knowledge is sketchy in the extreme. I could remember only the broadest outline of what I had learned about this in high school history class, but some of the details began to come back to me as I scanned through the text.

The withering of the Y chromosome in modern humankind had been a continuing trend, I read, but its complete extinction had been almost entirely caused by modern medicine. The early twenty-first century had been plagued by outbreaks of various infections, influenzas, and other communicable diseases, hastened in their transmission by frequent travel and global commerce. The biggie, though, was a virulent H1 virus popularly dubbed Mighty Mite, that jumped from rodents to humans via a bug that is so small as to be nearly invisible to the naked eye. At first the disease didn't appear to be any different than the others that swept periodically across the face of the earth. A bunch of people got really sick. A bunch of them died. Scientists worked feverishly until they found a vaccine for it. Governments bought billions of dollars' worth of the stuff, jabbed whole populations, and some pharmaceutical company somewhere made a fortune.

Everyone was assured that Mighty Mite had been wrestled to the ground. And in fact, the mojo vaccine worked like a charm as far as the disease was concerned, but it carried a kick that no one had been prepared for: it attacked the reproductive system of human males and rendered them incapable of fathering male children. It didn't take the scientists long to figure out what the problem was and discontinue the massive vaccination program, but they hadn't realized that Mighty Mite had saved the real stinger for last — the vaccine did some kind of wacky symbiotic tango with the virus and, instead of making a lot of people sick, the merry little mite had a new mission. It began spreading the vaccine along with replicas of the virus. It took a few generations, and a lot of political upheaval, but eventually women inherited the earth.

Many of the other sites on Gerrity's list were scientific papers explaining the chemistry of what happened. I skipped through these quickly. They were highly technical and I couldn't follow much of it.

There were more detailed history sites on the list as well, and they all more or less repeated what I'd learned in school. As fewer and fewer males were born, the remaining men consolidated their power until eventually the women more or less got fed up with it and took over, and that's how things ended up the way they are today. That's the handy-dandy encapsulated version of the story, anyway.

The history links were followed by a number of references to papers on modern reproductive theory and the disasters that followed the cloning experiments.

I read on until my eyes burned and my head ached, but it all just seemed to be more of the same. Just as I reached the end of my pot of tea, I wondered if Jo Hines had found out anything more about Alfreda Longwell's case from the medical point of view. Then I remembered that I had no way to contact the doctor outside of working hours. She hadn't left me the number for her personal message pod.

— «» —

I had not often been out of the city. Unless you were into camping and wilderness hiking of the sort touted by the Cedar Lake WirePage, there wasn't much point in leaving the familiar jumble of buildings and shops. Whenever Georgie and I had gone somewhere on vacation, it had been to another city, where we had fallen easily into the comfortable streetscape of the downtown centers.

The train I boarded the next day sped through the city outskirts and into the unfamiliar landscape of abandoned buildings and empty roads. The Decayed Area. The DK — crumbling mountains of disintegrating concrete, asphalt and steel that were slowly being turned into bushland.

According to the history books, these structures were once the monuments of industry, emblems of progress, the tools of financial kingdoms and commercial empires that serviced and exploited the teeming mass of humanity that clamored for its endless output. The concrete had grown like a malignant tumor, engulfing once-fertile fields and sylvan wilderness, until, like a cancer, it had threatened the very existence of its host. Only the most aggressive of treatments had halted its spread. Half of humankind had been eradicated and now the tumor no longer threatened. In fact, it was receding, small portions of it taken away every year for use in city projects, its raw materials scavenged, the rest gently succumbing to a natural, weedy reclamation.

The tallest structures had become a mass of grapevine and creeper, their crumbling foundations sprouting stubborn weed maples and sumac. Here and there roadways and parking lots had been colonized by ash and cedar, or by groves of locust trees and lilac that had escaped from gardens and parks and spread into small forests.

As a police officer, I occasionally got sent out to the DK. There are small enclaves of people living here and there in the ruins. A lot of them are a little wacky — wild-eyed creatures who resist all attempts to get them into shelters or hospitals or hostels. Short of forcibly dragging them to somewhere safe and warm, there is little the authorities can do about the odd-balls and there's not even any point in doing that. They just run right back again. Occasionally one of them goes haywire and starts setting fires or jumping out in front of vehicles or something equally unsettling, and that's when the City Police will be called out to corral them. Technically, the DK is part of our jurisdiction. In practice, we mostly ignore it.

Many of them are scavengers, who scrape out a living by harvesting the detritus of a previous time. Copper wire and pipes, aluminum of any kind, steel rebar when they can get at it. Any kind of metal will bring a few dollars, I'm told. Plastic. Bricks. Lumber ripped from what once were walls. All the stuff that can be used to good purpose again. These groups are not above the occasional banditry, and there have been a few mugging incidents, leading city dwellers to believe that the DK is lawless, dangerous, and worth avoiding if at all possible. The residents of the DK are just as happy that they believe this, because then they get left alone.

A lot of the sakers live there as well, in small insular communities. They keep to themselves mostly, except when they travel to the city core to march up and down with their signs. Sometimes different sects of sakers get involved in shouting matches at these marches, each proclaiming that the other is subverting the truth. The one tenet they seem to hold in common is the belief that the end of the world is imminent, and that all of the ills of modern society are God's punishment for our sins. It's in the definition of these ills and sins that they differ. That, and which deity must be appealed to. Most of the time, we just ignore them and let them shout at each other. We interfere only when they start pushing and shoving, or if they block traffic for too long.

All of the denizens of the DK are there by choice, I suppose. All any of them has to do is come into the city center and they will be found a place with good food and running water. Social do-gooder groups make a lot of noise about "cleaning up" the DK, and "doing something" for the people who live there. The people who live there refuse to have anything to do with these groups. I can't say I blame them, but the price of their independence is high.

Before long, the train left the jumble of concrete and asphalt behind and sped through the agricultural zone that feeds the city. Dwellings once covered this land, if the old maps can be believed. Hundreds of square kilometers filled with homes for families and their inordinate number of cars. The people who lived here were so far removed from the city center that they required two or three or four cars just to function, apparently, and everyone spent hours of their day in their vehicles trying to get to their jobs. These tracts of houses have long since been cleared away, the land reclaimed for farming, the roads empty, the sky clear and blue.

I watched out the window as little white farmhouses and red barns slid by, the spaces between them given over to neatly fenced fields of crops or grazing cattle and sheep. Eventually even this vestige of civilization was left behind and then there was nothing to see but trees.

Bored by the monotony of green and brown, I opened my Fone and flipped through more of the Men's Studies reading list that Professor Gerrity had provided. I'd already skimmed through all the papers concerned with Mighty Mite and the Testosterone Wars, but there was one whole section on ancient history, a topic that I was not even remotely familiar with.

Many of the papers detailed the social history of various cultures, specifically those in which male humans claimed dominance over females — which was basically all of them, as far as I could tell. There was a concise table of contents at the beginning. Buddhism, Christianity, Confucianism, Hinduism, Islam. It appeared that nearly every religion from the beginning of time had held a grudge against the female gender.

Women were subservient to men and, in some cases, were even regarded as property. They were expected to do as their masters bade them. The men, on the other hand, were uncertain in their mastery, for there were untold numbers of proscriptions to enforce. At various times women were forbidden to show their breasts, their hair, their ankles, their legs and in some cases, not an inch of their skin. A glimpse of any of these tantalizing bits would, according to religious dogma, throw the men into fits of maniacal lust, and they would therefore not be able to control their actions. This was an ever-present temptation and entirely the woman's fault, for no other reason than the fact that she was a woman. As a result, she could not go to school, get a job, hold property, handle money, or, in some societies, leave the house unless in the company of a male relative, who was, presumably, immune to her alluring ways.

None of this made any sense to me. If men were so unreliable as to go off the deep end whenever they saw a stray tress or two, wouldn't it make more sense to lock *them* up and just let the women get on with their lives? Otherwise, it would be like having a dog that bites and insisting that the people on your street stay inside so they won't get bitten.

The next section of recommended history texts detailed some of the outrages perpetrated against a woman if she didn't toe the line, and often even if she did. At various points in time, she could be beaten, gagged, impregnated against her will, robbed of her property, denied access to her children, sequestered, sentenced to hard labor, starved, walled-up, exiled, ridiculed at a whim, or accused of witchcraft, tortured and burned at the stake.

I remembered a little bit of this history from high school, although it hadn't ever been spelled out in quite such gruesome detail. It had been a joke to us, so ludicrous that we'd snickered about it behind the teacher's back. What a bunch of idiots, we'd said. What were they thinking? And why did women put up with it? We'd have kicked their butts to Barnard's Star and back.

There was no coffee on the train, but I'd bought a bottle of juice from the snacks trolley just as we'd left the city limits. Now I realized that it had made its way all too quickly through my system. I looked for a washroom sign. It was at the far end of the car. I made my way along the aisle, bracing myself against the movement of the train, which had not been apparent while I remained seated, but became evident as soon as I stood up. I had not really been paying any attention to the other passengers when I boarded, and the high seat backs had prevented me from seeing them once I sat down. Now, as I made my way down the aisle, I had the advantage of looking at them as I passed.

They were obvious commuters, most of them with their heads down, studying their Fones. Here and there I saw women who wore uniforms. They must be security guards at the research facility north of Cedar Lake. There wasn't much else around Cedar Lake that would require a contingent of guards.

One of the reasons that you can always tell a cop is by the way they look at you. They automatically take note of details. They judge. They assess. They're always on the lookout for trouble. It's sort of bred into the bone, at least in the ones who are good at their jobs, so I was astounded that not a single one of these guards looked up at me as I passed. Like the other commuters, they sat with their eyes glued to their Fone screens, or gazed out the window, or in a couple of cases, were fast asleep. I knew guards weren't police, but I would have expected at least one of them to notice that there was an out-of-the-ordinary person on the train, someone who wasn't a regular feature of the morning commute.

Just at the back of the car there was an older woman with a small child. Grandma on her way home after taking the little darling to the city. When the train pulled into the Cedar Lake stop, they were the only two people besides myself to get off. The others carried on up the line. I was right. The cars were full of commuters on their way to work. I was surprised by the number of them. I'd assumed, in my ignorance, that the research center to the north of the town consisted of a half-dozen lab-coated scientists clustered around a few test tubes and a Bunsen burner.

The village of Cedar Lake itself was tiny, and it didn't take me long to find Lakeside Lane. The road curled off from the downtown area, which was only a few hundred feet long. There were no sidewalks on the lane, just wide gravel shoulders, but it didn't really matter, since there was virtually no traffic. The houses I passed were all wooden one story buildings, that looked as though they had been constructed as cottages originally, and added to and winterized over the years. They were built into the hillside and screened by the trees that gave the lake its name. On the opposite side of the road the hill sloped sharply down to the water, the shore a jumble of stones and driftwood. It would be a pretty nice place to live if you were into the quiet life.

It took only a few minutes to reach number twenty-two. I had not really decided how I was going to approach Alfreda

Longwell's parents, so I walked past the house a little way and stood looking out over the lake, as if I were a tourist scouting the best places to picnic.

Should I pretend to be a university prof come to express my condolences? It felt wrong, to lie to these people who had just lost a child. But if the Darmes had locked the parents down as fast as they had everyone and everything else connected with Alfreda Longwell, I stood little chance of getting them to open up. I might have to pose as something that would improve my odds of extracting useful information.

I still hadn't decided what I was going to do by the time I walked back to the house and knocked on the door. I'd play it by ear.

"It's open." A voice from somewhere inside. Obviously Cedar Lake was the kind of place where you didn't worry about strangers wandering in. Maybe that changed during the tourist season. Maybe not.

"Hello?" I opened the door and poked my head in.

A woman emerged from what appeared to be the kitchen area. Her face was lined, her hair grey and untidy. "Oh, hello. Can I help you?" Another woman, the other parent presumably, was sitting in the living room, in a reclining chair that faced the door. At the sound of the first woman's voice, she stood. She too looked haggard and ill-kempt. I could hear that the Vu was on, but the sound was turned so low, I couldn't make out what program was playing.

I decided then and there that I'd play it as straight as I could. "Hello," I said. "My name is Carson MacHenry. I'm with Capital City Police. I'd like to ask you some questions about your daughter."

The woman in the living room sat down again, a wary look on her face.

"We talked to the Darmes already," the first woman said.

"I'm not a Darme. I'm with City Police."

"We were told not to say anything."

I smiled slightly, a conspiratorial look to allay the fears of these two anxious women. "I can understand the Darmes not wanting you to talk about it with the neighbors or anything. After all, we're still investigating. But I'm the City Police officer who has been assigned to the case. I'm just following up on a few things I had questions about, that's all. Things the Darmes may not have asked you about the first time. I'll let my superior know you talked to me, and that you're being careful not to talk to anyone else." An encouraging nod, a glance between the two, and I could see that they began to relax, even to look eager. Damn the Darmes, I thought, sewing the case up so tight that there was no opportunity for these women to access the comfort of friends and neighbors, the people who would express their sympathies with memories of the girl, small stories of when she was a child and reminders of her accomplishments as a young woman. No wonder they looked haggard.

The first woman stepped forward, her hand out. "I'm Alicia," she said. "And this is Fredricka. Would you like a cup of tea?"

Alicia and Fredricka. Alfreda. The name made sense now.

Alicia beckoned me to follow her to the kitchen where there was already a pot of tea on the table, then she bustled around and produced not only an extra mug, but a slice of blueberry pie. It was still warm, fresh from the oven. Country food. I approved. If it wasn't for the fact that I would have to live in the country, I could move to somewhere like Cedar Lake, where real food was served up unapologetically.

Fredericka shuffled in from the living room to join us, grunting as she lowered herself into the chair opposite me.

"Have you always lived here?" I asked, between mouthfuls of pie.

"Oh my goodness, no," Alicia replied. "We lived in the city until we were lucky enough to have Alfi. Then we moved here. We thought it was a nicer place for a child to grow up in, you see." She sighed. "It was lovely when she was a little girl. The lake right at our doorstep and all sorts of things to do outside. But as soon as she became a teenager all she could talk about was going to the city."

"Too much time on the Wire," Fredericka muttered. It was the first time she had spoken since I'd walked in the door.

"Yes, probably," Alicia agreed. "You try to give your child the best of everything. It's hard to know what's right and what's wrong."

"She was studying history, is that right? Men's Studies?" I asked. "It seems kind of an odd subject to me. I understand history is important, but it doesn't seem that there's much of a career path there."

"Too many old texts," Fredericka muttered.

Alicia sighed again. "She was always interested in the olden days, reading all these old stories, pretending she lived back then. Even when she was a little girl and played dress-up with her friends, they'd be all decked out in floor-length gowns and capes and hats with feathers, and they'd all be princesses or beautiful orphans or something, and there would always be a Prince Charming who would come along and sweep them off their feet. Fairy tale stuff, you know. But she had this idealistic notion about how romantic it all was. I tried to tell her about all the wars and the fighting and the terrible state the planet was in."

"A lot of little girls do that," I said. "It's like pretending there are gnomes in the garden, or trolls under the bridge."

"But with Alfi it wasn't all just pretend. As she grew older she became genuinely interested in history. She was always reading history books and that's what her best marks were always in, so it stood to reason that she would take a history-related degree."

"I wanted her to go into engineering," Fredericka said. "There are always jobs for technicians."

"Yes, well..." Alicia laughed apologetically. "Once Alfi made up her mind to do something, there was no stopping her, that's what she did. I thought all along that she was going to be a teacher, because, really, what else can you do with a history degree?"

I allowed that there wasn't much.

"Three years ago she came home for Christmas and all she could talk about was the Men's Studies course and how great her professor was and how she was going to go on and get a Master's. And then an M.A. wasn't enough, she wanted her Ph.D. And we thought, 'well, that's fine,' because then if she ended up teaching it would be at the university level. I kind of liked the idea of having a professor in the family."

Fredericka snorted.

"And then something changed?" I asked.

"No. Nothing changed. If anything, she was even more excited about what she was doing. And then last summer when she was here, she said that there might be a great opportunity for her through the university." Alicia hesitated for a moment, her brow knit. "I never did find out what kind of job she was talking about. I mean, what could there be?"

"It wasn't a teaching position?"

"No. Some kind of research. But she wouldn't tell me any more."

"It certainly sounds odd, doesn't it?" I said, but I didn't place much importance on what Alfreda had said to her mother. It was almost certainly some sort of theoretical sociology deal, no more than a hop, skip and a jump away from a clerical position, and, to tell the truth, I wasn't all that interested in Alfreda's career path. There were other questions I needed to ask and I took a long sip of tea while I thought about how to ask them diplomatically.

I started with, "Do you have a recent photograph of Alfi? I couldn't seem to locate one from the university."

Alicia walked into the living room and returned with a framed picture of her daughter in cap and gown. A graduation picture. It showed a fine-featured young woman with curly blonde hair and an enormous grin. It was a sharp contrast to the battered face I'd seen on Jo Hines's autopsy table.

"Pretty girl," I commented and Alicia nodded her head in agreement. I scanned the photo into my Fone and handed the picture back. She didn't put it down, but held it in her hand, looking at it instead of me as I asked, "Was Alfreda — Alfi — popular? With the other girls?"

"Oh, my, yes," Alicia said. "She was pretty and outgoing. There was a constant stream of girls in and out of the house all the time. Sleepovers, swimming parties, skating parties." She looked at Fredericka and chuckled a little. "It made us feel young, to have them around all the time, didn't it Fred?"

Fred didn't say anything, but nodded her head in slow agreement, lost in memory.

"It's been a lot quieter since she's been gone, that's for sure," Alicia continued. "Of course, we were looking forward to a grandchild someday…" Her voice trailed off as she was reminded once again that there would be no grandchild now.

"Did she date at all, when she was a teenager?"

Alicia came back to the present. "There were one or two girls who were special, I guess, but nothing ever lasted for more than a few months. She'd get a crush, like all girls do, but then she'd seem to get over it and go back to hanging around with a crowd."

"These special girls — are any of them still here?" The easiest way to get a handle on Alfreda Longwell's sexual practices would be to find an old girlfriend. Most parents had no idea what their kids got up to.

Alicia's brow furrowed as she thought about this, but it was Fredericka who supplied a name.

"Lisa down at The Market."

"But Alfi only saw her for a little while," Alicia said. "She wasn't part of the gang, if you know what I mean. She was always … I don't know, I don't mean to be unkind, but she was always sort of … *tough*.

Lux. Lux and luck. A tough ex-girlfriend. Just what I needed. "Any others?"

"Yes, of course," Alicia said, "but none of them are here anymore. Off to uni in the city, just like Alfi."

I took out my Fone and switched it on again. "Could you just give me their names?" I asked. "Chances are we won't need to talk to them, but I'd better get the names just in case."

She looked a little worried by this. "I'm not sure we should be giving you any names. They don't have anything to do with what happened to Alfi. That was a student she met in the city."

I put the Fone back in my pocket.

"I'm sure you're right," I said. "There's no point in bandying names around if we don't have to." I stood up. "Thank you for the pie, and for talking with me. I'm so sorry that it had to be for such a tragic reason."

"Do you know when we might be able to bring her home?" Fredericka asked. "It was only supposed to be a couple of days, but we haven't heard anything yet. We need to make arrangements."

I was stunned. The Darmes had made it sound as though the body was being released to the family right away. I had assumed that she had been brought back to Cedar Lake already, the funeral held, the body buried.

"I'm sorry, I don't know," I said, "but I'll check into it when I get back to the city. I'm sure it won't be long now." Was Alfreda Longwell still lying at the morgue, or had her dead body been swept under a carpet in the same way her life had been? I needed to talk to Jo Hines.

"Thank you for your trouble," Alicia said, with a wistful tone in her voice. "It was kind of nice to talk about her. We haven't been able to, you see."

Freakin' Darmes.

—— «» ——

The Market wasn't hard to find. The useful part of the main street of Cedar Lake consisted of a post office, bank, library, hardware store, and a grocery store. The rest of it was a jumble of little hole-in–the-wall souvenir shops, fly-by-night art galleries and here-today-gone-tomorrow clothing shops, pizzerias and hair salons.

This was the slow season for camping, so there were only one or two people in the aisles at The Market, and only one check-out open.

"Hi. I'm looking for Lisa," I said to the cashier. "Is she by any chance working today?"

"She's on her break. Probably out back. Just go through the double doors." She waved toward the back of the store.

I made my way down the aisle and through a set of swinging doors. Opposite these was a big, open loading door. Sure enough, there was a girl standing by the dumpster, smoking a cigarette.

"Hi. I'm Carson MacHenry."

She shrugged.

I flashed my Fone badge at her. "Could I ask you a few questions?"

She shrugged again. That wasn't the usual reaction to a badge, unless you'd had previous experience with police flashing badges at you and knew it doesn't mean a heck of a lot. Alicia Longwell had characterized Lisa as "tough," and I thought it was probably a fair description. The girl looked tough — brittle, dirty blonde hair, too much makeup, a slouching posture that telegraphed a barely-hidden insolence.

"I'd like to ask you a few questions about Alfreda Lucas Longwell."

"Haven't spoken to her in months." She took a deep drag on the remains of her cigarette and stubbed it out on the ground.

There was no protest that she had already talked to the Darmes, or that she had been told not to talk about Alfi. Apparently, no one else had thought to track down the home town girls to see what they had to say.

"You went out with her for a while?"

"For, like, a couple of months maybe," Lisa said. "When I was seventeen."

"That's all? How come?"

Another shrug. "Her parents didn't like me. I think she took up with me just to piss them off."

"She was a rebel then?"

Lisa threw her head back and laughed, and just for a moment I could see that she must have been quite pretty when she was seventeen and hadn't yet been knocked around by life. "Alfi? No way. She was a baby." She lit another smoke. Apparently breaks were long here in Cedar Lake. I fished a crumpled pack out of my pocket and lit up. Sympathy smoking, I told myself. Something in common with the interviewee. Who was I kidding? I was dying for one.

"I was just some little tantrum Alfi was having," Lisa went on. "And then she got over it. After that it was all about clothes and what she was going to study at uni. I was sort of dropped by the wayside."

"I see," I said, although I didn't. None of this sounded like a description of a girl who was into kinky sex. "So there was no question that you were going to go off to the city together, or anything like that?"

Lisa shook her head. "I think I already knew I was going to be stuck in Cedar Lake for the rest of my life."

"No uni for you?"

"Don't have the brains. I knew that by the time I was ten. Besides, my mom's not well. She needs me to stick around." She narrowed her eyes at me defensively. "I don't plan to work here for the rest of my life, you know. I'm trying to take some courses. Maybe get a job at the plant. I have a friend who says I might be able to get on as a lab assistant if I can pass the exam."

I felt an unexpected sympathy for this tough-looking girl. There was no shifting of blame for her circumstances, no apology. Just the bald statement that she wasn't smart enough to do much better, but she'd try anyway. And she'd look after an ailing parent while she did it. That was a rough row to hoe.

But there was no point in pussy-footing around with the Lisa's of this world, either. They'd seen too much. I knew she wouldn't be shocked by anything I asked her, so I went straight to the point.

"Do you think there's any possibility that Alfi was into some kind of weird shit?"

She laughed again. "You mean, like sex? You've gotta be kidding me. Not unless she changed a lot from when I knew her."

"No rough stuff?"

"Not a chance." Lisa flicked her cigarette into the alley and walked toward the double doors. "She was a big time romantic. She loved greeting cards with kittens and puppies on them." And then she disappeared into the store.

I stood by the dumpster and finished my cigarette, while I tried to figure out how to connect what I had learned about Alfi Longwell with the battered corpse I'd seen lying in the morgue. The two just weren't meshing.

CHAPTER 5

The morning after my trip to Cedar Lake, I walked into Division and was greeted by leers and not a few gibes.

"Going out for lunch today?" Detective Diva asked.

"Wish I could afford to eat where you do," Detective Lum said.

"She can't," Diva said. "But she's probably not paying anyway, right?"

"From what I hear, you don't exactly eat anyway, when you're there."

"No, it's more like a nibble. In preparation for more nibbling later."

It just got silly after that, with everybody smacking their lips at me every time they walked by.

The police community is a small one. News gets around fast and there are eyes everywhere. There's always a lot of speculation about who's dating who, who would like to date who, and who just broke up with who. Even if you aren't particularly interested, you can't help but overhear the gossip. I knew, for example, that Detective Lum was suspicious that her partner was seeing someone else on the side, but couldn't prove it; that our Division Clerk Zuri Rodriguez and her partner had just applied to the Parent Program; that Detective Simard had a girlfriend who worked at City Hall; and that the despicable Detective Diva Davis was a cruiser who wasn't really important enough to attract any bijou girls, which didn't, nonetheless, prevent her from trying. There was even conjecture about Inspector Trent now and again, although the general consensus was that she must be a solitaire — one of those women who seem happy to go it alone. No one knew much about her personal life.

The severe tailored suit jackets, which had given her the nickname "Boss Tweed," her fussiness and her standoffish manner only tended to confirm that opinion. Certainly none of us could imagine living with her.

All the blather had gone right up my nose during the rocky break-up with Georgie, but I found I really didn't mind the current gossip at all — my standing in the status sweepstakes would definitely shoot up out of the basement if everyone thought I was dating someone like Jo Norris Hines. The problem was that if everybody in Division already knew all about it, chances were that the Darmes did too. On one hand, romance could make a pretty good cover. On the other, the Darmes might not be so quick to buy the story. It could be attracting more attention than it was worth.

I tried to block out the jokes and set about clearing away the paperwork for a number of yawner cases that hadn't been filed yet, but my mind was mostly occupied with what I'd found out so far about the Longwell case.

From what the old girlfriend in Cedar Lake had said, it didn't sound at all like Alfi Longwell was rough trade, nor did her parents' descriptions of her lead me to believe anything of the sort.

However, the most useful tool in police work is dogged persistence, and now that I had a picture of the girl I'd cruise the bars, just to make sure that she hadn't been leading some sort of secret S&M double life. I would have to wait until that evening to do it, though. In the meantime, I'd practice a knowing smile every time Davis made another stupid remark about me and Jo Hines. To tell the truth, I kind of liked it.

— «» —

There is every kind of bar you could ever want in this city. There are juice bars, wine bars, coffee bars, tea bars, gossip bars, bars for cops, bars for accountants, bars for crooks, bars for the serious drinker, bars for lonely hearts who just want somebody to talk to — but the vast majority of bars exist so people can find sex. Some of them are upscale bars for the bijou girls who will hang around all evening looking for someone rich to attach themselves to. Some of them are down and dirty — the beverage is just an excuse to find someone anonymous to go home with for a night. Some are for finding a soul mate in. But in most bars, no matter what drinks they serve, it all boils down to someone looking for someone to have sex with.

Most bars try to hide this fact behind low lighting and soft music, hard glass and flashing lights, or something that falls somewhere in between, but in a tiny subset of bars the terms of the exchange are made crystal clear: I'll cater to your particular sexual fantasy if you cater to mine. It was this last category of bar that I needed to visit.

I went to *Velvet Glove* first. The owner is a woman named Sarong. I knew it wasn't her real name — none of the people in these kinds of bars ever use their real names — but I had no idea why she chose an impractical and generally uncomfortable southeast Asian garment as a *nom de sexe*. Sarong and I had a pretty good professional relationship. She'd given me useful tips on a couple of other cases I'd been on. In exchange, I wouldn't bust her on the many infractions I've seen at her club, unless they were really blatant. There were so many rules and regulations on the books that it was possible to bust almost anybody for almost anything, but generally speaking, I ignored the piddling stuff unless it suited my purposes. Sarong had remained grateful, and occasionally helpful.

She greeted me at the door. "Detective MacHenry," she purred. "How nice to see you again. I hope you brought your handcuffs."

"Nah, I left them on my girlfriend."

She laughed, then took me by the arm and steered me toward the tiny office to one side of the foyer, away from the main floor where her clientele sported chains, leather bustiers, dog collars and, in one case, a giant dildo. Sarong would cooperate, but she didn't like to be seen doing it.

"What can I do for you?" she said when she had firmly closed the door.

I pulled out my Fone and brought up the picture of Alfi Longwell I'd gotten from her parents. "Ever seen this girl?"

She took the Fone and studied the image carefully, then shook her head.

"No."

"Not even if you mentally add a lot of make-up, or a wig, or some weird get-up that would make her look like some sort of sex-starved alien from outer space?"

Sarong handed the Fone back. "No, not even then. Trust me, she's not the type. I can tell just by looking at the picture."

That was more or less what the girl in Cedar Lake had said. I wondered how they could tell so fast. It must be like when two dogs sniff each other's butts or something.

I snapped the Fone shut. "Hearing any strange stories?" I asked.

"Like what?"

"Like somebody who gets carried away?"

She frowned at me. "You know there are too many safety protocols."

"And I know that most of them are ignored."

"We've had a hundred and fifty-two accident-free days in a row."

"Only because the accidents were minor and you didn't report them," I said. "But I'm not talking about here, necessarily. You hearing any rumors? Anybody scared?"

She looked alarmed. "What are you saying? Has something happened I should know about?"

I shrugged. "I don't know what I'm saying. I don't know for sure what's going on. But you might want to tighten things up a little until I find out, okay?"

"Don't worry. The last thing I need is trouble."

"Just keep your eyes peeled. Thanks Sarong."

She walked me to the door and saw me safely out to the street.

It was the same at the other places. Sarong was always my best informant, but the owners of the other bars of that ilk could always be persuaded to impart at least a few nuggets of information, if pressed. No one recognized Alfi's face. And there didn't seem to be any whispers about sessions getting out of hand, or any reports of particularly sadistic sadomasochism. It was pretty clear that Alfreda Longwell had not been part of the scene.

That was too bad — it would have been an easy explanation for what had happened to her, and, to tell the truth, I was a little surprised that the Darmes hadn't used it. But if Alfi's murder wasn't S&M gone awry, then someone had criminally assaulted her. Beat her to death. But who would she ever have run across that would do that to her? She was a student. Who could she have met at university who would be so dangerous? Unless it was someone not connected with the school, or someone from Cedar Lake. I wasn't naïve enough to believe that small towns didn't spawn their share of crooks and wackos. But even if Alfi had somehow got herself mixed up in a feud or stumbled across some shady business deal, why would the Darmes lie about it? Murder would have been the last, final nail in some criminal's coffin, and they wouldn't have hesitated to use it for all its worth.

Was it a case of Alfi being in the wrong place at the wrong time? Did somebody go berserk and take it out on the first person she ran across? It happened, from time to time, but not often. And not with such brutality. Whoever had done this was a seriously disturbed human being.

And if it was anything other than a random act of violence, I'd have to find out who Alfi Lucas Longwell had been hanging out with prior to her death. The girl I'd run into at Professor Gerrity's office, Claire, was probably too spooked to talk to me. The girl with the long brown hair, who claimed that Claire had had nothing to do with it, might be a better bet. And then, of course, there was Gerrity herself. Or better yet, her files.

Having to fly under the Darmes's radar was a definite handicap. Under normal circumstances, I could just get a subpoena, march into the university and look at whatever I wanted to. This case was anything but normal. It would have to be a midnight raid.

— «» —

When I unlocked my door that night, I was hit all over again by the empty feeling of the apartment. On a normal day, it was no big deal to go home to nobody. But whenever my mind was occupied with something else, I'd forget. I'd expect, just for a split second, to catch a waft of the strawberry shampoo Georgie always used, or to hear the music that she always had playing in the background.

It had been a warm and welcoming place when she was there, the walls hung with bright posters, the sofa littered with cushions and afghans. I'd often arrive home to the smell of coffee and something kept warm in the oven, or if I was working a really late shift, there would be a note for me on the fridge. No urgent message or instructions. Just a scribble to say, "Glad you're back safe."

Most of all there would be laughter. Sometimes, if I made it home at a decent hour, the apartment would be full of friends, Georgie's friends mostly, and then there would be wine and good food and great conversation. I didn't often take part in the talk that spiraled and zigzagged and looped. I would hang back in the kitchen, elbows on the counter, and just listen as opinion was proffered, agreed with, shot down, ignored or laughed at, witty rejoinders or serious consideration given in return.

The laughter would continue long after the friends left. Georgie, flushed and happy from the evening, would repeat the sillier statements and laugh again at the funnier remarks as we tumbled into bed.

No Georgie anymore. No friends. No laughter. But with any luck there might be something in the fridge. Half a bag of curd and three butter tarts. I debated for a moment, weighing sugar versus salt. Salt won. I'd have a glass of wine, too. It would send me to sleep.

There was still a bottle of merlot in the wine rack. The trouble with wine is that it doesn't come in single-sized servings, and it goes to waste if you only have one glass. The trouble with everything is that it doesn't come single-sized. I didn't bother with a wine glass, just poured it into the plastic cup that sat beside the sink, grabbed the curd and took it into the living room.

I flipped on the wall Vu. My viewing choices were a silly movie about three country girls who moved to the city, a comedy show I'd already seen, and the news magazine.

I hadn't been paying a lot of attention to the election. I intended to vote, of course, but I figured if I just dropped into the dialogue in the last day or so I'd be able to make at least a mildly informed decision.

Most of the coverage concerned Prime Minister Miller Singh and the stalled trade talks with the South Central Zone. The proposed GeneShare Treaty had once again been taken off the table, at the insistence of Prime Minister Singh, who was quoted in a sound bite as saying, "We have an obligation to protect our resources for future generations."

SoCen was prepared to make an issue of it this time around, and as a result they were hogging (my interpretation) the cocoa and coffee that formed a significant part of their exports. And a significant portion of everybody's daily buzz, especially, in my case, the coffee. The South Central Zoners were currently making do with reduced supplies of wheat, beef and reclaimed lumber. No contest in my book. I'd be perfectly willing to give up my daily ration of two-by-fours in exchange for an espresso.

The opposition party, led by Kirsty Chin Littlecrow, hadn't been expected to unseat Singh's government until this latest breakdown in talks. Now she was making a real run for it, according to the polls, and all projections were that it was too close to call. It was amazing how testy people got when you took their fixes away from them.

The wine did its work and I fell asleep on the couch with the Vu still on, but I was jangled awake again when my Fone buzzed. I grabbed it and checked the screen. One a.m. Jo Norris Hines.

"Hi there. Did I wake you up?" a voice purred.

"No, of course not," I lied.

There was a tinkling laugh. "So, are you in your jammies? Or did you forget to put them on tonight?"

This was Jo Norris Hines? And then my befuddled brain finally clicked into gear. The Darmes must be listening in.

"What are you doing tomorrow?" Hines asked. "Want to have lunch? And then maybe I'll give you something you really, really want."

I changed the tone of my voice. "You got it, sweetcakes. Are you sure we need the lunch part first? Maybe we should just skip to what I really, really want."

Another throaty laugh. "Oh no, you don't get away with that. You'll have to buy me lunch first. Meet me at Billie's on Landon Street at one o'clock."

"Okay. See you then."

"Byeee."

There could only be one reason Hines had called — and only one reason she would want to have lunch with me — she wanted to find out if I'd made any progress on the Longwell case. And the Darmes must be watching her very closely, judging by the silly exchange we'd just had. I'd almost blown it. If I'd asked who was calling, or hung up, the whole ruse would have fallen apart, but I did wonder how many of these inane conversations I would be expected to participate in.

I'd never been into Fone sex. Georgie had tried once, when we'd first started dating. She'd been away at a conference and had called late at night. In response to the question of what I was wearing, I had pointed out that it was one o'clock in the morning and I was in my flannelette pajamas, what did she expect? The conversation had ground to a halt in rapid order.

Still, as a subterfuge, it wasn't a bad idea, and it would confirm the speculation about Hines and me that was floating around the station. It might be useful later, if the shit hit the fan. Not only was it an immediate excuse, it could be a future justification.

CHAPTER 6

I was early. On purpose. I liked to size a place up when I didn't know it well. The restaurant was long and alley-like with booths marching down both walls. This wasn't one of Hines's trendy lunch places with a lot of brass and glass and bijou ass. This was standard greasy spoon, the sort of place where I fit right in, and I intended to confirm that by ordering the meat loaf special. I chose a seat at the back and surveyed the rest of the clientele while I waited for the doctor. I could see no one out of the ordinary. Three teenage girls camped out by the front window, giggling and laughing and making their pot of tea last as long as they dared before they had to either order another one or leave. A woman in a nurse's uniform sat a couple of booths down. Obviously on her way to work, or just coming off shift. A tough-looking older woman with a vacant expression sat in the booth across from her. There was no one in the place who looked too well dressed or too assured to be patronizing such a dump.

I almost didn't recognize Hines when she walked in the door. She wore a pair of torn jeans and a scuffed leather jacket, her dark hair was swinging loose, and big sunglasses masked most of her face. She strode down the aisle and slid into the seat across from me.

"Wow, you've changed your look."

"You haven't."

I shrugged. "This way I won't be embarrassed if I run into someone I know."

"I'm hoping I don't."

Hines was unsmiling and her voice was tense.

"Trouble?"

She removed her sunglasses and leaned forward across the table so that she could speak in a low voice. "I think both my official and personal communications are being monitored."

"Oh. That explains your Fone call last night."

"If we're being watched we need to have an excuse to meet. That was the only one I could think of."

"Oh," I said. "Should I have made some gesture of affection or something when you came in? You know, given you a hug or something?"

"Of course not," Hines said. "We don't need to make it too obvious." She grimaced, and then glared at me. "Sweetcakes?"

"I was asleep when you called. It was the best I could do on short notice."

"Well, don't do it again."

"What do you want me to call you? Honeybunch? Angel face? Lambey-pie? The Darmes will expect to hear something of the sort."

"On second thought, sweetcakes will do just fine."

"Snookums? Schmoopsie-poopsie?"

"Stop!" Hines held her hands over her ears, but she was smiling. I wondered if she knew how much her smiles lit up her face. They reached all the way to her eyes and made them sparkle. Oh crap.

"*Cara mia?*" I ventured, wanting to hold on to the moment.

"Watch it. You're edging perilously close to sophistication with that one."

"Oh okay. I'll back off then." Get a grip, MacHenry, I told myself. Just forget about it right now.

She turned serious again. "I can't even find Alfreda Longwell's medical records. They've been wiped."

"That doesn't surprise me at all. Information on this case has been sewn up in a burlap bag and thrown into the river with a cement block attached. The Darmes have shut this one down. They'll want to make sure it stays down, you know."

"Shh."

The waiter was plodding in our direction. Hines studied the menu that was printed on the plastic placemat, wrinkling her nose at the choices. "Greek salad, please, and a glass of water."

"Meat loaf," I said. "Extra gravy please, and lots of coffee."

"Give me a break," the waiter said. Okay, so they didn't have any coffee. But she didn't suggest an alternative, either, before she disappeared through a set of swinging doors at the back of the restaurant.

Hines leaned forward again. "Have you found out anything?"

"I went north to see her parents. Did you know that the Darmes haven't released the body yet?"

"What? That can't be right. They took it away the day of the postmortem. That evening in fact."

"Well it certainly hasn't arrived in Cedar Lake."

"Cedar Lake? Is that where she's from?" Her forehead wrinkled in thought for a moment. "Isn't there a disease control center in Cedar Lake?"

"Yes, just north of the town. Why?"

"No reason," she said. "I just knew that I'd heard the name somewhere. How are her parents taking it?"

"About the way you'd expect if you lost a child. It would help if they could go ahead with the funeral. I also had a snoop around the university. One of Alfreda's friends is suspicious about what happened to her, but I don't think she knows what to do about it. I also cruised the usual bondage haunts, but there really isn't any indication that the girl was into anything kinky."

Hines nodded. "I'm not surprised. That just didn't fit. So where do we go from here?"

"I go back to basics. If it was a random killing by somebody with juice, and the girl just happened to be in the wrong place at the wrong time, then I'll need to track her movements — figure out who she was hanging out with, where she went, who she might have met — and hope I can make a connection to her murder. I figure the place to start is with her prof, see if anything shakes loose there. If not, then I'll have to try to rattle some of her friends enough to get them talking."

I decided not to tell Hines that shaking something loose from Professor Gerrity might well entail breaking into her office. If I got in and out without difficulty, she'd never know about it. On the other hand, if I got caught, she wouldn't be implicated.

"What was the girl majoring in anyway?" she asked.

"She was post-grad. Working on a Ph.D. In Men's Studies."

"Men's Studies? Basically history, then."

"Yeah, I would have thought so, but then an odd thing happened. I went to talk to her prof and ran into another student. Claire somebody. She said she was there to talk to Gerrity because she wanted to get out of whatever she was doing. She said she couldn't handle the field work."

"Field work? What kind of field work could there be in Men's Studies?"

"I know," I said. "That's what I thought. I mean, it's not like there are even any monuments to visit or anything."

"She didn't say anything more?"

"No. She was really upset. She said everybody thinks she was the student who pushed Alfreda off the building, but that Alfreda was nowhere near 'the oriole camp,' whatever that is."

"Oriole camp?" Hines shook her head. "Means nothing to me."

"Me either. Mind you, she was kind of yelling at me when she said it, and then she got so freaked out she ran off. The Darmes must have been leaning on her pretty hard. And the student who's suspicious claimed that Claire had nothing to do with Alfreda's death."

"Have any charges been laid?"

"Not that I can find. And that's weird all by itself. Even if Alfreda's death was an accident, I would have thought they'd haul somebody in. There should have been any number of people questioned, maybe even an official inquiry. But that would have resulted in too much publicity, I'm guessing."

The waiter appeared with our meals. She plunked the plates down in front of us and walked away without asking if we wanted anything else. My plate held a gigantic slab of meat loaf slathered with thick gray-brown gravy and surrounded by a mound of mashed potatoes and a few mushy peas. It was perfect. Hines wrinkled her nose at it and then began picking at her salad as though she was looking for bugs hidden in the lettuce leaves. I shoveled a forkful of mashed potato onto my fork, mixed it with a chunk of meat loaf and jammed the whole thing into my mouth. Just then I happened to glance up at Hines, who was watching me with a pained expression on her face. Okay, so it wasn't the most elegant of cuisines, but the food was darned good. Besides, I didn't pick the place. She did.

"So what are we left with here?" Hines gave up on her lunch and leaned against the back of the booth.

"Since I can't connect Alfreda to the S&M scene, I think we have to work on the assumption that it was a random killing. Somebody lost it and she was in the way. But I can't think of any case in my experience that shows a similar level of savagery, and I can't go into the records. It would be like waving a red flag at the Darmes."

"Is that something I could do?" Hines said. "There might be something in the medical archives."

"Can you access them without drawing too much attention to yourself?"

"I suppose."

"It would be good if you could stay away from digital collections. They're too easy to trace."

"I'll try one of my old profs. I seem to recall that she had an extensive collection of books. Case studies, outdated treatments, stuff like that."

"She'll let you look at them?"

"She'll be delighted that anyone is interested. And she's retired now, so she's not on any university rosters." She idly reached forward and picked up a piece of lettuce, took a small bite out of it, then deposited what was left of it on her plate.

"Perfect," I said. Chances were the Darmes would never think of that. As tight as they'd tried to shut Alfreda Longwell's case down, I'd discovered some tantalizing loose ends. The link on the website, the old girlfriend in Cedar

Lake, a retired uni prof. And most of all, too many people who knew about the death. It was funny how, when you told somebody not to talk about something, they nearly always let something out of the bag. Either they tried too hard to stay away from the secret, or they were desperate to set the record straight. Professor Gerrity had given herself away by the look on her face when I'd said the name "Alfreda." The girl, Claire, had let slip the information about the "oriole camp."

I sopped up the last of the gravy on my plate with a roll while I thought about what I should do next. The only reference I had been able to find to "oriole" that wasn't about birds was to Oriole Avenue. If the oriole camp turned out to be on Oriole Avenue, I supposed it was possible that one of the ragtag residents of the DK had gone crazy and killed the Longwell girl. Except that the other student, Claire, said that Alfi hadn't been anywhere near the camp. Even if I could find it, it might well turn out to be another dead end, but like I said, dogged persistence is my best thing. I was pulling a late shift the next day. I would have time to do a little snooping before I went to work.

"There is something else you can do for me," I said to Hines.

"Sure. What is it?"

"There's an old Oriole Avenue in the DK. I want to go check it out."

"Out in the DK? Do you really think there might be a connection?"

"I don't know. It's a long shot at best. And I'm going to have to leave my Fone behind."

Every Fone has a leash — a locator device that can track its location, and by extension, the location of its owner. It's a useful tool in law enforcement. But it's also a useful tool for keeping track of cops themselves. Division monitored our leashes at all times. If there was ever a question about where a particular cop was at a particular time, the evidence of her whereabouts had been recorded in the logs, and could be used to bolster her testimony in court. It was also a safety net. If an officer got into trouble, division would know where she was. It's a good idea. It just got in the way sometimes. I'd long since gotten my friend Ricky to show me how to turn it off for those occasions when I was working a hunch and didn't want to be tracked. Inspector Trent had a conniption every time I did it. I could fob her off with some mumbled excuse about hitting the wrong button, but I had a feeling that if the Darmes were watching as closely as Hines thought they were, a gap in my leash record might be just the sort of thing that would attract their attention. Better to let Division think I was home asleep. But it would leave me vulnerable out in the DK.

Hines looked alarmed at what I was proposing to do. I wanted to think that she was worried about my safety, but I knew that she probably just didn't want to have to do another hurried postmortem with the Darmes peering over her shoulder.

"So, what do you need me to do?" she asked.

"If I don't check in with you by tomorrow night at eight, hit the panic button. Call Trent and fill her in on what we've been doing. She'll be pissed off, but at least she'll send somebody to look for me."

She nodded. "Got it."

"So how do I get a hold of you?" I asked.

She grabbed my Fone and punched in some numbers. "That's my private pod. Call up and say something sexy to me."

"That's quite an invitation," I teased.

"It'll give somebody a thrill." She balled up her napkin and threw it onto her barely-touched salad. "But if we're going to keep meeting, we need to find a better restaurant. And if we're supposed to be dating, you'd better start calling me Jo."

CHAPTER 7

Oriole Avenue was somewhere in the jumble of reinforced concrete and wilderness to the west of the city, but street signs began to disappear as soon as I rode into the fringes that occupied the ill-defined zone between the civilized part of the city and the DK. As I rode further, the pavement began to deteriorate as well, weeds and clumps of grass poking up through the asphalt, huge cracks and potholes catching the wheels of my bike and threatening to send me flying. I'd reached a hit and miss neighborhood — some of the buildings occupied, others fallen into disrepair, still others collapsed into the ground.

I pulled over to check the locater on the burner Fone I'd bought especially for the occasion. It showed my current position and directed a northerly course along a road that looped around and merged with Oriole Avenue.

It was a cheap machine and the maps were out of date. The route it showed was, in reality, blocked by slabs of cement and twisted steel girders. A building had partially fallen in and the debris had never been cleared away. That was the thing about the DK. Buildings were always falling down, or being torn down by scavengers, or washed away by storms. Landmarks didn't stay marked. Features faded. Maps were mere guidelines.

My bike was a hindrance, too heavy to drag through the mess in front of me. Even if I left it behind, I wasn't sure I could find my way through the rubble on foot. The part of the building that still stood looked fragile, as if one good burst of wind could finish the demolition. I could break a leg scrambling over it, or be hit on the head by falling chunks of cement. The scree could shift under my weight and pin me.

It would be a long way to a hospital, even if I was lucky and someone found me.

I headed further west, hoping to find some way around the obstacle, but every time I tried to turn north again, there was another collapsed building or a tangle of underbrush, weed trees and stone that blocked my path. Frustrated, I decided to go east instead, back toward the city. When it appeared that I had reached a relatively undamaged area, I would veer north, and try to work my way back to the other side of the collapsed buildings.

I rode along for a half hour or so, then judged that I had traveled far enough to have cleared the wrecked zone. North along a street that fringed the city limits, then west again. I stopped and checked the locator again. If its map could be believed, and I had no reason to believe that it could, I should be standing at the foot of Oriole Avenue. At one time, it had stretched for ten kilometers or so, until it became lost in a tangle of roundabouts and ramps, and emerged on the other side with a different name. Now the pavement had disintegrated almost entirely into gravel and weeds, the shoulders crowded with sumac and briar. I rode as far as I could, swerving to miss the worst of the ruts, but, after a couple of kilometers, I had to give up and walk. It would take a heavy-duty vehicle to get down this road with any ease. Here and there I could see the evidence that this had occurred — tire tracks, a record of someone's passing imprinted in mud and frozen until spring. Some of the brush along the sides of the road had branches snapped off. Here and there saplings had been uprooted. Somebody had driven down Oriole Avenue, and not too awfully long ago by the look of it.

It was hard work pushing the bike and, in spite of the chill of the wind, I started to sweat. I had stopped to unzip my jacket when suddenly I heard the scrabble of loose rock off to my left, and caught movement out of the corner of my eye. It sounded too large for a rat. A raccoon maybe, or a coyote? The DK was overrun with wildlife, although to my eye there appeared to be little for them to eat there. Anything that liked rats would probably do well, I figured.

I sincerely hoped that whatever had made the noise wasn't a bear. There had been a couple of reports of bears prowling the far reaches, but no one had taken those tales seriously. Still, it paid to be cautious.

I pushed my bike in the direction I thought I'd heard the noise come from. I bulled my way through the scrubby growth toward a gigantic pillar that still thrust upward toward the sky. A chimney, perhaps, or an elevator shaft. As I rounded the debris at the base of the pillar, I saw a small alleyway, a tunnel really, that seemed to lead deep into a jumble of shattered structures.

I stopped for a moment just to take stock, aware of my vulnerable position. It was standard procedure for a police officer to take a buddy or two or twenty with her when she went into the DK, and someone at the station was always designated to track their locations until they all returned safely. I was alone, nobody knew where I was and my police Fone was sitting on my kitchen counter. Taking chances was not the money play, but I knew that if I didn't confirm that the noise had been made by an animal of some sort, I would get that creepy feeling that somebody was watching me and I'd spend the rest of the day looking over my shoulder.

I snapped open the cover on my WhamGun and loosened it from the holster, then nosed my bike through the gap in the concrete. I pushed the bike through first, but I had to put it on its side in order to clear both the ledge of cement at the bottom of the opening and the overhang at the top. Then I squeezed myself through, all too aware of how helpless I was in such a crouched position.

There was a little more room on the other side of the gap. At least I could stand upright, although my shoulders and the handlebars of my bike bumped against the sides of the passageway. The alley was open to the sky for the first ten meters or so, then concrete closed over my head, forming another tunnel. I felt vaguely claustrophobic, but shook it off. I could see light ahead.

The passage widened abruptly and spilled out into a clearing. Quite a large clearing. It had once been a parking lot, maybe; if so, the asphalt had been grubbed up and carried away, exposing the rich soil underneath it. Now, tidy furrows marked the surface where once there had been lane markers. Fruit trees grew in the place of light posts. The clearing was ringed by a ragged skyline of ruined buildings, almost entirely enclosed by them, some of the debris a couple of stories high, others three or four, punctuated at intervals by pillars like the one I had passed. The gardens would be well-protected from the wind, and the mass of the surrounding ruins would radiate the heat they soaked up from the sun. It was a well-chosen site for a permanent encampment.

Across from where I stood were giant slabs of intact concrete that had fallen crazily against each other, forming a warren of caves and cubbyholes, their entrances draped in old canvas. There was not a soul in sight, although I could smell a fire smoldering and there were bits and pieces of faded clothing hanging from a makeshift line. I could feel the eyes that were hiding in the ruined buildings, watching. It wasn't an animal that had sent gravel skittering, but one of the ragtag citizens of the DK. It remained to be seen which variety I had stumbled across.

"Hello? Is anybody here?" No answer, but I heard more scrabbling off to my right.

"Hello? I just want to talk to you. I mean you no harm."

Silence. I leaned my bike against the tunnel wall and walked out to the center of the clearing. I waited. Let them know I wasn't going anywhere until they crawled out of their hidey-holes.

"Throw down your weapon." The voice that floated out from behind a flapping piece of canvas was deep, and spoke with authority. An old woman, I guessed. Probably the leader of whatever scruffy little group this was.

"No."

"Then go away."

"No. I just want to talk to you." I took another step forward, my body tensed to make a grab for my gun.

"Why should I consort with the agents of Satan?" the voice asked. Just my luck. Sakers.

"Because I know where to find you now," I shouted back. "I can always come back with reinforcements, you know."

The canvas was pushed aside and the woman stepped out. Her appearance matched her voice. Sometimes it's difficult to tell the age of these women who live so rough, but if I had to guess, I'd have put this one at somewhere just over a hundred and two. Her hair was a straggly gray mass of braids that hung lankly down the sides of her weathered face, and she walked with a peculiar gait that incorporated both a limp and a shuffle. She stumbled to the center of the clearing. "Forsake the ways of Satan, for the Lord will judge and He will find you wanting."

I had to choose my next words carefully. You never know what will set the sakers off. "The Lord isn't judging today. I am."

The woman shook her head and hobbled over until she was standing no more than a foot away from me. "You are not a Darme."

I've never been happy with people getting too far into my space, but stepping back right then would have been a show of weakness, so I held my ground.

"No, I'm not a Darme. I'm City Police."

"And what does the city want with us? We bother no one here."

"I want to know if there was a girl found near here. Not one of your" — I hesitated, unsure of what to call this scrofulous collection of humanity — "community. A girl from the university. Did you hear about any sort of altercation? Where somebody got pushed off a building?"

The old woman shrugged. "What do I know about uni girls?"

"It wasn't you who found her, then?"

"Nobody found a girl."

"What about some of the other groups out here. Did you hear anything from them?"

Another shrug. "Nobody found a girl." And with that she turned and hobbled back to her canvas awning.

The DK is hard to navigate and impossible for a cityite like myself to know well, but I found it difficult to believe that the old woman would know nothing about anything that happened near the camp. This was her territory. The group had been watching me approach. They had seen me coming. They'd had time to hide. It was possible that they had not seen a couple of students or heard an argument, but if this was where Alfreda Longwell had died, the sakers would most certainly be aware of the commotion that a group of Darmes would make collecting a dead body. The student, Claire, claimed that Alfi hadn't been anywhere near the oriole camp. Even if I was in the right place and this was the camp she'd been talking about, it was clear that the old woman either didn't know anything about it or wasn't prepared to tell me if she did.

It had been a long shot anyway.

I walked back to my bike and wheeled it around into the narrow tunnel that had led me into the clearing. Just as the walls closed in around me, I turned and looked back. A small child, no more than three or four years old, darted into the middle of the clearing and stopped, peering over at me, her thumb in her mouth. There was a shout, and, to my astonishment, a heavily pregnant woman waddled out and scooped her up.

I emerged, dusty, on the other side of the passage and nearly dropped my bike when a voice to my right hissed, "What do you want?"

I turned in the direction the sound had come from, but my eyes were slow to adjust to the bright sunlight after being in the shadowy tunnel, and it took me a few moments to locate the source of the noise. Even so, I'd have missed seeing the figure entirely if it hadn't moved. It was a raggedy, gray wraith of a woman who blended almost perfectly into the muddle of broken rock she perched on.

"Who are you? What do you want here?"

"Who wants to know?" I asked.

"Never you mind who wants to know, you wants to know, she wants to know."

She climbed down off the rock and scampered towards me. She stopped five feet away — out of WhamGun range — and peered at me.

"You forsake?"

"No, I'm not a saker. I'm a cop."

"Ooooo…" She backed up a step or two, then peered at me again. "Cops have badges. You have badges?"

I didn't, of course. It was on my Fone, lying on the kitchen counter back at my apartment. But since when did anybody who lived in the DK ask to see a badge?

"I have a WhamGun," I said, patting my pocket. "That's even better."

"Who has a wham, you has a wham, she has a wham." She twirled around in a circle while she chanted.

Something wasn't right with this creature, and it wasn't the same kind of not right that you usually found in the DK.

"You know anything about kidnappers?"

She stopped twirling and looked at me again.

"The napping of kids? No napping kids here."

"There's been another kid snatched. In the city. You know anything about that?"

"No kids, no kids, no kids here."

There was one just on the other side of the mass of concrete behind her, but I didn't point this out.

"If you hear anything, you let the police or somebody know, okay?"

"Okay, okay, okay." She nodded her head up and down as she said this, then she leapt back up onto the rock and disappeared.

Something wasn't right. But I didn't know what.

Just to be sure that I'd covered all my bases, I decided to head a little further down Oriole Avenue. I nosed around the remains of a few side streets, but many of them were blocked. I didn't see anything else that I would categorize as a camp, but it was hard to tell. The saker camp had been well-camouflaged. I'd found it only by accident. Nor did I see any more vehicle tracks frozen in the mud, or broken branches either. In fact, there were whole sections of the road that had been almost completely taken over by bushes and small trees, with just a narrow strip of pavement leading through them.

I was just thinking that it was time to turn back when I came to where the street ended. It wasn't the end of the street in the usual sense — it was where the street, quite literally, came to an end. The cracked, grass-invaded pavement fell away abruptly over the edge of a gulley. The avenue had originally been constructed along the edge of a ravine, but the foundations had long since been eroded by wind, rain and snow, and had fallen in a heap down the bank. I could see the scar stretching away into the distance until it met what had once been the cloverleaf. Oriole Avenue truly came to an end where I stood.

I stepped cautiously along the crumbling edges of the gulley. I didn't know if the collapse was recent or not, or how stable the rim of it would be, but it seemed to hold, and when I peered over the side, I could see a stand of sumac and, here and there, an opportunistic elder sapling straining toward the sunlight.

I poked along the edge in both directions, but there was no sign of any recent disturbance. No tire tracks. No crushed grass. No muddy footprints. No indication that anyone had driven up, or climbed down the bank or even looked over the side.

The old saker woman had responded to my questions in a very strange way when I'd asked if someone in her group had found the dead girl.

"Nobody found a girl," she'd said.

There was no girl to find. Not here.

There was no evidence anywhere along Oriole Avenue of the massive disturbance that attended the investigation of a crime scene. There would have been many ruts left by many vehicles, not just the single set I had noticed earlier. Brush would have been slashed in order to look for evidence. Grass would have been trampled under many feet.

It looked like this was a dead end in more ways than one.

I turned my bike around and headed north again for a bit, until I once again reached the point where Oriole became something else and swooped south. Then I headed back toward the city as fast as I could go.

As soon as I had left the DK well and truly behind, I stopped at the first bar I came to. I was thirsty, dirty and puzzled. There were only two other people there besides the bartender, and one of these hurriedly downed her drink and slid out the back door as soon as I entered. Let her go; whatever she was hiding, I had more important things to worry about.

I ordered a beer — it was that kind of place — and chugged it down, just to get the dust out of my throat. Then I asked for another. I'd noticed an ashtray on one of the tables, so I fished a crumpled pack of black-market cigarettes out of my pocket. Two left. I lit one of them up. Rules were laxer out here in the boonies.

The unexpected indulgence of smoking indoors kicked my mind into high speculation mode. I went round and round the details, both of what I'd seen and what I hadn't. No crime scene. The Darmes hadn't indicated any specific location in the papers I'd signed. It was only Claire's chance remark that had sent me along Oriole Avenue in the first place. Maybe I had it wrong and the oriole camp had nothing to do with Oriole Avenue. Maybe the oriole camp had been given its name by someone with a particular liking for songbirds.

The discovery of a group of sakers with a kid was, however, astonishing. The one common thread in all of their holy roller rantings was the insistence that all of modern society's ills were punishments from God, and that the only route to salvation was through a return to the natural order of things. As a body, they rejected the trappings of modern technology, including, and especially, artificial fertilization techniques. Nor would they ever have been accepted into the Parent Program, living as they did in squalor on the edge of civilization.

This should have made them a self-limited phenomenon, except that as soon as one bunch of them died off there always seemed to be others to take their place — but this happened by recruitment, not by natural increase.

I supposed it was possible that the saker child I had seen had been kidnapped. In spite of what I had said to the woman who had accosted me outside the camp, I doubted that there was any connection with the Tanaka Tyler case. The kid wasn't the right age, for starters, but there were still unsolved kidnappings on the books. Not nearly as many as there used to be, of course. The snatching of someone else's child had been an epidemic forty or fifty years ago, until the registry had been established to track every pregnancy, every birth and every result of every insemination. Desperate, middle-aged couples still tried kidnapping now and then, but they were invariably tripped up by the paperwork. A trip to the hospital, a place at a daycare, an inoculation at a public health clinic — any one of a million routine events of childhood could prompt a search of the registry, and anything that didn't match was reported to the police.

Those cases that remained were the very devil to crack. Parents who were wealthy or influential enough to buy private tutors and doctors could get away with walking off with somebody's precious bundle and never returning it. A little jiggery-pokery with their birth certificates and the children could maintain their new and, to them, real identities for the rest of their lives.

The saker group I'd seen appeared to have few resources of any kind. They had been one of the hardscrabble cults that drift around the DK, convinced that whatever deity it is that they worship wants them to live that way. On the other hand, I supposed, sakers seldom visit hospitals or doctors and wouldn't see the need to send a child to school, what with the end of the world coming and all. In such a cloistered setting, perhaps they would be able to hide a kid they had snatched.

Except that anyone who saw her would be suspicious. Sakers are unmistakable, with their peculiar braided hairstyles and the fluttering ribbons they sew to their long dresses. A saker with a baby in tow would raise all kinds of alarms. It would be hard for them to walk down any street unremarked. Kidnapping seemed unlikely, but I was at a loss to come up with any other explanation.

I wondered if I should report them, but there were two good reasons not to. One — I might want to talk to them again, and if they were raided I'd never get the chance. And two — nothing in this case was fitting together very neatly, and I was loath to throw away any informational advantage I had, however remote or seemingly unrelated. In all probability, the saker group had nothing whatsoever to do with Alfreda

Longwell's death, but I'd reserve judgment on that until I figured out what did.

I was even more puzzled by the woman who had confronted me outside the clearing. She had been even dirtier and more bedraggled than the old woman saker, but it had all been recent dirt, if you know what I mean. Truly homeless people have layers and layers, built up over years of non-bathing and sleeping in the open. Nor had the woman's crazy speech been quite the right kind of crazy. Too studied. Too obvious. You know, you can always tell a cop — and I was pretty damn sure that's who I had been talking to. Undercover. Doing a pretty good job of blending in. But not quite right.

Again, I wasn't really sure that it had anything to do with the Longwell case. For all I knew, she was working the Tanaka Tyler kidnapping. After all, it was a Darmes case essentially, with City Police called in only as liaison. Maybe she was following a lead. If that was the case, I would just have to hope that my presence in the DK wouldn't end up being reported to Trent.

What I really wanted just then was a coffee. That and a second smoke, but I knew how unlikely it was that a place so far out would have access to coffee. Besides, the bartender was regarding me with a distinctly sour expression on her face and by the time I reached the city center, it would be just about time to report for duty. I drained my glass and threw an extra credit on the counter before I went on my way, less thirsty than I had been but every bit as puzzled and slightly woozy. I hoped the effects of the alcohol would wear off before I got to work.

CHAPTER 8

It looked like my best shot to find out what was going on was to get a look inside Professor Gerrity's office. If I could figure out what Alfi Longwell had been working on and who she had been in contact with, that might lead me in a direction that would produce some answers, something that I was sorely lacking at the moment. I knew it would do no good to approach Gerrity directly. Even if, under normal circumstances, she was the kind of person who was inclined to cooperate with police, she would have been cautioned by the Darmes not to talk to anyone, and that included me.

And then there was the brown-haired girl who had been in Rosie's — what was her name? Jess? No — Jazz was what one of the others had called her. She had quite openly called Alfi's death a murder, but I didn't know if she had hard facts to back up her accusation, or if the claim of murder was just her interpretation of what had happened. She appeared to have been correct about Claire — as far as I could tell, the girl had had nothing to do with the death — but how had Jazz known that? I needed to talk to her. But I would have to find her first.

It turned out that whatever I wanted to do would have to wait for a few days — there was a sudden rash of break and enters in a cluster of residential complexes near the downtown core, and I was sent to investigate, along with one of the junior detectives, Susan Somebody Nguyen. I didn't like having partners — they got in the way and I didn't like having to explain what I was doing every time I worked on a hunch. I supposed it was inevitable, though, that sooner or later I'd be saddled with a junior. There were too many of them to go around just then.

Nguyen had been with Division for only a few months,
but already had a reputation as a by-the-book, fill-out-the-
paperwork kind of cop. I didn't. I flew by the seat of my
pants most of the time. On the other hand, Nguyen was one
of the few juniors who didn't appear to be awed by Detective
Davis, a big plus in my book. I recalled that she had also had
the courtesy to step out of my way when I'd been trying to
get to my desk.

I also knew that the case would involve wearing out a lot
of shoe leather and covering a lot of ground. Methodical was
good for that kind of investigation. I'd have to see how useful
she could make herself. If the answer was not at all, then I
figured I at least had somebody to send on runs for regular
caffeine hits.

The fact that the robberies were clustered geographically,
and the stolen property consisted of electronics, jewelry
and a small number of credits indicated a single culprit
who needed money. The security surveillance cameras at
the buildings had all been conveniently not working when
the crimes were committed, and there had been no sign of
smashed windows or forced locks. The security codes had
been hacked. A single culprit who was not only a good
programmer, but also knew exactly what to do with the
things she had taken.

The credits would be spent in short order, and the jewelry
had probably been sold for the value of the metal, melted
down and sent to a recycle center, but we might be able to
nail her on the Vus. We would simply cover all the second
hand shops and the known fences until the goods began to
turn up. With any luck at all, we'd eventually intercept the
thief in the process of a transaction and look for evidence
that serial numbers had been altered or removed. Once that
happened, it would be a simple matter to persuade one of
the fences to turn. It was smarter for them to plead ignorance
and pay a fine than it was to bluff it out and risk being closed
down.

But that meant that a great deal of my working time over
the next few days was going to be spent standing around
in junk shops with Nguyen. I wouldn't dare leave her to

investigate on her own while I went off and did something else. Although she was apparently attentive to detail, I guessed that she didn't have much imagination. She wouldn't know how to read an individual, or recognize the intuitive leap that tells you when somebody is up to something. She would accept everything at face value, and either miss the thief, or harass everyone who went into the shop, tipping the owner to the fact that the police had staked the place out. Cops like Susan Nguyen, who played by the numbers, were seldom great detectives. That was probably why she had been assigned to the case in the first place.

There were several junk stores and pawn shops in the immediate area of the residences that had been burgled. We'd try those first. On the buying end of their transactions, these places catered to lower-income workers who needed a boost to get them through to payday, students who had run through their allowances before the end of the month, and people who were moving and found it easier to sell their stuff than to load it up and take it to their new digs. On the selling end, their customers were mostly middle-income people who wanted to upgrade their Fones or Vus but couldn't afford brand new ones, or high rollers who were slumming in search of antiques. It wasn't hard to tell the difference between the two ends.

We went to *Angel's* first. I had caught Angel out on a few minor infractions in the past. Angel knew who I was and could guess why I would be in the store, so I sent Nguyen in, with instructions to browse through the merchandise and go to the electronics section only after she had looked at everything else, and to do it as casually as possible, as if it were an accident that she had noticed them at all. She was to take careful note of what was displayed, to see if it matched the general description of the things that had been stolen. I hoped she would be able to manage this small piece of deception.

I waited at a nearby coffee shop, which had, alas, no coffee, where I sat and mumbled over the puzzle that was the Longwell case. I wondered if the Darmes had destroyed the girl's academic work as effectively as they had destroyed her identity. If so, I could only hope that the professor had squirreled copies away somewhere. It might be the only thing that would lead me to where Alfreda had been and what she had been doing on the night of her murder. I figured that profs were likely packrats. After all, they spend years researching their subjects. I found it hard to imagine that a prof would stand idly by and see any kind of research thrown away.

I needed to get into the professor's office. I needed to look at the student records.

I was drumming my fingers on the table, lost in thought, when I looked up and realized that Nguyen was walking toward me.

"Almost nothing in the way of Fones or Vus or anything," she reported, as she slid into the chair across from me.

I wasn't surprised. If Angel had indeed taken the stolen goods, she was smart enough to wait a good long while before she offered them for sale. She would, however, have to do so eventually in order to recoup the expense. That was all right. If the goods didn't turn up right away, I was willing to make a return visit.

We moved on to the next store, *Reuse,* an enterprise that had opened only a short time previously, and one where the proprietor was unlikely to know me by sight. This time I went in, but the store was so new that it had had little time to collect much in the way of inventory. If the stolen items had been brought here, I decided, the owner would probably have put them out right away. A single glance around the shelves and the display cases was enough to confirm that there was nothing of interest.

Previously Enjoyed was the next stop. Again, I sent Nguyen in. The shop wasn't high on the priority list. I had never caught the owner out on anything — as far as I could tell, the business was strictly on the up and up — but it was only a couple of blocks away from *Reuse* and it made sense to check when we were so close.

There was no convenient coffee shop or restaurant nearby, so I sat on a bench and idly played with my Fone while I waited, just so I wouldn't appear to be too obviously watching the street. It was the middle of the morning. The sidewalk was crowded with the usual number of joggers, window-shoppers and women pushing strollers. And then, out of the corner of my eye, I saw someone at the corner who looked like she was trying not to be seen. The figure walked with her head down, looking neither to the left nor the right, her hands shoved deep in her pockets. Then she stopped and peered along the shop fronts, checking the street numbers. She was young. Her clothes were good. Her hair was nicely cut and her sunglasses were expensive. And then she removed the glasses to get a better look at the grimy numbers pasted above the doors, and I realized that I knew the face from somewhere. It only took a few moments for recognition to click in. She was one of the group of girls I had spoken with on the university lawn. The one who had been crying over lost poems on *IMeMine*. Hana.

I lowered my gaze to the Fone so that my hair would fall forward and hide my face, my eyes sliding sideways so I could keep an eye on the girl. After a few moment's hesitation, she found the address she was looking for and went in the door. *Previously Enjoyed.*

I cursed myself for sending Nguyen into the store. In all probability the girl had something she would like to pawn or sell, and if that something happened to be a Fone or a Vu, Nguyen was just as likely to accost her on the spot. If it was a Fone, I desperately wanted to have a look at it before anyone else did. This girl had known Alfi Longwell, was a close friend, a girlfriend who was profoundly upset at her death. Her Fone might well hold some clue buried in the cache of files and text messages.

I debated whether or not I should just barge into the store, but I was too afraid of scaring the girl off. I'd just have to hope that Nguyen would show some discretion.

Lux. Lux and luck. Just what I needed. The girl had no sooner gone in than Nguyen came out and sauntered over to where I was sitting.

"There's some stuff there, but most of it's old," she said. "Doesn't match the description at all. A young kid came in just as I was leaving. She's selling a Fone. I waited until she unwrapped it. I got a good look at it, but it's not any of the brands we're looking for, so I left."

"Good work."

"So ... on to the next place?" she said, when I made no move to leave the bench.

"Yeah, in a minute. There's something I want to check out."

She shrugged and sat down.

The last thing I wanted was to have to explain to Nguyen why I was so interested in a student Fone. I needed to get her out of the way so I could go back into the store. I decided to pull rank.

"Can you go back to that coffee shop we were at? I'm hungry. I need a croissant or something. And a cup of tea." It was mid-morning break time. With any luck, the shop would be full of junior assistants who had been sent out to get pastries for their bosses. There should be enough of a line-up at the counter to hold Nguyen up for a few minutes at least.

She rolled her eyes. "You were just there a half-hour ago."

"I wasn't hungry then. I am now." I handed her a credit. "Get something for yourself as well. It's on me."

She could scarcely refuse. I was the senior officer. But she made her annoyance known by wrinkling her small, freckled nose and stomping off.

The transaction at *Previously Enjoyed* must have taken place quickly, with not much haggling, because Nguyen had been gone for only a minute or two when the girl came out of the store. I waited until she was just out of sight and walked into the shop.

"Can I help you?" the clerk asked.

"I'm looking for a good used Fone," I said.

I glanced over the assortment of wares that were displayed in a large glass case next to the pay counter. Nguyen was right. Most of it was obsolete.

"Wow, you've got some real antiques here," I said.

"You were looking for something a little more current?" The clerk hesitated for a moment, then she went on. "I've got something that just came in. I haven't even really filled in the paperwork on it yet, but you can have a look if you like." And she pulled a top-of-the-line Zakio off the shelf behind her.

"Oh, that's perfect," I said. "How much?"

The clerk looked puzzled. "Don't you want to try it out?"

I shrugged. "It works, doesn't it?"

"Well, of course. I just tested it. It's good, but it didn't have any programming loaded in. I threw a game on just to make sure, so you could try it if you wanted to."

"No, no, that's fine. How much?"

It was more than I'd hoped, but less than I had been afraid of. "Okay," I said. I checked my pockets. I didn't have enough credits on me to make the purchase, so I pulled out my bankcard and held my breath while the clerk processed the payment.

It went through without difficulty, although I was sure my balance was taking a beating. It would have been just too stupid to have missed out on the Fone for lack of a few credits.

"It will take a few minutes for me to get it ready for you. I need to do a buy order and then a sell order, otherwise my books won't be straight. Do you mind waiting?"

I consulted my watch. Nguyen would be returning at any moment. "I tell you what," I said, "take your time. I'll drop back at the end of the day and pick it up then."

And by the time Nguyen came back with a stale croissant and a disgusting cup of green tea, I was again sitting innocently on the bench.

— «» —

We staked out two or three more shops that I knew specialized in the sort of gear we were looking for, but there was no sign that the thief had transacted business at any of them. I wasn't worried. It was early days yet. It would all turn up eventually, and if we had no results from the shops, we could always spend a few days haunting the street-side markets. The open-air bazaars were set up primarily for farmers bringing their goods into the city to sell directly to customers, but there were always a number of stalls set aside for the purveyors of crafts, artwork, used clothing and miscellaneous household items. Occasionally home electronics would turn up at these, the vendors invariably claiming that they were personally-owned items that they just wanted to get rid of. Most of the time that was the case, but sometimes a fence would rent a market stall and use it to move product that was a little too hot for the junk shops. Buyers at markets don't usually check for serial numbers.

It had been a long day, and my feet hurt. I was relieved when the shift finally ended. I was in a lather to go pick up the Fone I'd bought. I'd retrieve it, go home, have a shower and a makeshift meal from whatever lurked in my fridge. Then I'd have a crack at whatever files were there. I hoped that they might have something to do with Alfi Longwell, and that they weren't just the usual meet-you-at-Rosie's, did-you-get-the-last-assignment stuff.

We checked back in at Division, and I was headed for the door when, to my surprise, Nguyen said, "Hey, wanna go get a beer?"

I hesitated. I found Nguyen's company uninspiring, if not downright tedious, but I didn't want to antagonize her either. We would be working together for a while, and it was important to keep the wheels oiled and the machine running smoothly, or so Inspector Trent was always telling us. But I had only just enough time to get back to the store before it closed.

"Gee, I'd really like to," I said, "but I'm bagged."

Nguyen's face fell, and I wondered if the offer had been a gesture to cement a working relationship, or if there was something else behind it.

"Listen, let's plan on it for tomorrow night, okay? You can pick the place."

She smiled then and nodded. I groaned inwardly as I walked out of the station. The last thing I needed was some sort of complication with a fellow worker. I'd seen too many offices poisoned by it.

I arrived at the store with five minutes to spare. The clerk had my purchase all wrapped up and waiting to go, and seemed relieved that I'd made it before closing time. She flipped the sign over to "Closed" as she saw me out the door. I wasn't the only one anxious to go home, apparently.

When I reached my apartment, I kicked off my boots and went into the kitchen where my evening plans immediately fell apart. I'd forgotten that there was nothing in my fridge. I slammed the door shut, rattling the pots and pans that lived on top of it for lack of any better place to put them.

Food and beverage had been Georgie's department, and I had not ever developed any sort of provisioning routine. I rummaged through the cupboards, but there was nothing there, either, other than a can of sardines and a small bottle of scotch that Georgie had bought for a special occasion. Scotch is hard to come by — not many people drink it — and I hesitated about opening it just to have a lonely drink at the end of the day. Besides, it would probably knock me out. I debated for a few moments, then tucked it back into the cupboard, ordered some Thai from the curry shop across the street and jumped into the shower.

I resisted booting up the Fone until the food arrived and I knew I would be uninterrupted for the rest of the evening.

I set the device on the kitchen table, took a bite of mee krab and pressed the power button. Nothing.

I wondered if it had a defunct battery. The clerk at *Previously Enjoyed* said she had tested it before she bought it, but maybe she'd simply plugged it in. I rummaged in the kitchen drawer until I found a cord that would fit, shoved the respective ends into the pad and the wall socket and tried again.

The Fone whirred a little as the screen lit up. When it finally loaded, none of the usual icons were there. Only the game the clerk had installed and an odd, octagonal shape with a round hole in the middle. Fortunately, I knew exactly what the octagon represented. I had one just like it on my own Fone. The symbol denoted a program that encrypts files and saves them on the device itself, rather than on the Wire.

Most cops have something similar. It saves a great deal of trouble down the road. Any files that go onto the Wire are subject to the will of the courts and can be called into evidence at a trial. Only when a cop is certain that information from an investigation is either untroublesome or carved in stone will she load it into the official program. Conjectures, hunches, working theories and the names of informants are stored in the encrypted files. Anyone who uses the program denies its existence, of course, and the individual access codes are a closely-guarded secret.

This device had gone one step further. Not only did it have the capability to encrypt files and keep them off a server, it didn't have any connectivity to the Wire at all. But why dump the Fone and leave the unusual and suspicious program in place? Most people have no use for a Fone that isn't connected to pages or messaging. In fact, it's extremely difficult to buy one that isn't. I was lucky that I had moved so fast. The shop owner must not have looked at the machine carefully before she bought it, otherwise the resale price would have been prohibitive. Cops aren't the only people who want protected files.

I clicked on the icon, but, as I expected, a window came up asking for an access code. I knew that there was no point in trying to guess what the correct combination might be. After three wrong guesses, the program would shut down.

I wasn't worried by this; in fact, I was encouraged. It meant that the program was intact, and even if all of the files it contained had been wiped, it should still be possible to retrieve at least some of them. Amateurs always assumed that deleted files were just that — deleted. But if there was anything at all on the screen, there should still be some remnants of history left somewhere, some clue that would tell me who the Fone had belonged to, and maybe some indication of what the files contained. Even a filename could be informative. Many a criminal had been tripped up on this fact, not realizing that her Fone left a trail a mile wide for those who knew how to read it.

The bigger question was where a university student had obtained a program like this, and, even more importantly, why? Unconnected Fones weren't the sort of thing you bought just so you could keep your messages away from the prying eyes of parents, or disguise the fact that you spent your entire allowance keeping your girlfriend happy. You didn't just walk into the local Fone store and pick one up on the off-chance that it might prove useful.

I stared at the Fone screen while I finished my dinner, but the icon didn't even blink in return. I would need some help with this. There was, of course, a resident techno-guru at the station. Fernandez was generally uncurious about the content of any Fones she was asked to work her magic on, but I was beginning to experience a rapidly escalating sense of paranoia about the Longwell case, and I was unwilling to take the chance that Fernie's eyes were really as un-prying as they seemed. No, this called for a visit to Ricky.

— «» —

I tried not to seem too impatient as Nguyen and I slogged through the next long, tiring and unproductive day. Again we staked out the most likely resell shops, but there seemed to be little traffic of any sort, never mind the buying or selling of the kind of merchandise we were looking for. At noon we grabbed a couple of stale sandwiches from a hole in the wall vendor, then went to cruise the market stalls, but there were only a couple of Vus set out for sale. Otherwise just the usual mounds of fruit and vegetables and jumbles of odds and ends.

At the end of the day, we checked in at Division and I was about to leave, but stopped when I realized that Nguyen was looking at me expectantly. It was only then that I remembered about the getting a beer offer that had been made the previous day. I sighed inwardly. I'd already spent the entire day with Susan Nguyen. The last thing I wanted to do was sit around and make more small talk. I could tell, though, that a second refusal would result in an extremely difficult partnership dynamic. And after all, it was the sort of kumbaya-tic bullshit that the inspector encouraged in the ranks.

"Drink?" I said, and then suffered the humiliation of having to walk past the curious stares from everyone else in the office as Nguyen swaggered along, shoulder-high, beside me.

We went to a trendy bar that I would never have gone to on my own. The canned music hammered me with a wall of sound as we entered, and Nguyen headed straight for a small table with stool-like chairs pulled up to it. I hate chairs like that. I can never get comfortable. I much prefer a booth with a bench that I can sprawl across.

There were a number of other cops already there, young ones who liked loud beats and fruity mixed drinks, and I realized that Nguyen had chosen the bar for maximum exposure. This was apparently not about a friendly drink with a workmate, or even, spare me the embarrassment, a romantic overture. This was about an ambitious young officer scoring points by being seen with the notoriously anti-social division maverick Carson MacHenry. There was more to Susan Nguyen than I had realized.

One beer, that's it and I'm out of here, I decided. But the first beer slid down my throat in a couple of gulps, so I ordered another one. I'd sleep that night.

"Hey, Mac! How's it going?" It was Detective Bloody Garin Diva Davis, approaching the table with a twenty-something blonde in tow. Nguyen wasn't the only one out to score points. "Don't often see you here. I didn't think you were ever this social."

I shrugged. "We've had a long day. We thought a beer would go down good."

"Ah yes." The detective smirked. "The break and enter case. Exciting stuff."

"So how's your work going?" I asked, even though I already knew the answer. Turn your nose up all you like at B&E, Davis, but at the end of the day, I'll solve my case.

"The Tanaka Tyler kidnapping? It's a beaut. Nothing's turned up anywhere. It's like the kid just vanished into thin air."

I had a brain wave. "Have you tried poking around out in the DK?"

"Out with the kooks? Nah, I don't think so. They aren't into kids out there — after all, the apocalypse is coming, why would you bother with a kid just to have it snuffed out by the wrath of God?" The detective chuckled. "Besides, they're all so wacko they'd never get organized enough to do anything more than a snatch and run, and we'd have tracked them down in no time. This seems to be a lot more sophisticated than that. We can't even pick up any video on it."

One of the most useful tools the police have is video surveillance. There are cameras covering nearly every public area, and some private ones as well, although that isn't something that is known by the general public.

I shrugged. "I heard a rumor down in the marketplace."

I had Diva's attention now. "What sort of rumor?"

"Just that pickings are getting a little slim out there. People are wondering if it's tapped out. Maybe the scavengers have turned their attention to more lucrative enterprises."

"I haven't heard anything like that."

"Well," I said, "I don't usually hang out in places like this. You hear more when you're a little closer to the bottom."

"Now that's the truth." She laughed and put her arm around the blonde. "I couldn't take Marcie anywhere you go."

"I can't take anybody where I go."

"Especially not to the DK, eh?" I could see that she was turning the notion of scavenger involvement over in her mind. It would suit my purposes just fine if she decided to follow it up. Davis was a talker — she liked to yak about the ins and outs of every case she worked on, in order to impress the junior officers who hung on her every word. I didn't really think the scavengers had anything to do with the Longwell case, but if Davis shook loose any tidbit of information that might help me, I would hear about it right away. Besides, the notion of Davis stumbling around in derelict factories and collapsed office buildings amused me, and if there was any justice at all, she'd run into a saker or two just for good measure.

"Ah well, good luck with the case," I said. "If you decide to follow up on the rumor, I'd look in the east end. I heard it's been pretty well mined." I had no real expectation that Davis would pay attention to anything I said, but if she did, her first inclination would be to conclude that I was lying and in all probability that would send her galloping off into the west end. Davis was like that — kind of linear. North and south wouldn't occur to her as options.

"Yeah, well don't wear out too much shoe leather on your case," Davis said with a smirk, and pulled her date across the room to join the crowd sitting in the front window.

I finished my beer, made my excuses and left, and by the time I got home I was so tired that all I wanted to do was fall asleep on the couch. Which I did. For about an hour. I woke up with a start and was suddenly wide awake, the beer fuzziness worn off. That happened sometimes when I drank. I only got temporary oblivion.

I clicked the Vu on but there wasn't much to watch except talk shows and re-runs of old sitcoms. I needed to find something to occupy my mind until I grew sleepy again. For lack of any better options, I flipped open my Fone and scrolled down the Men's Studies reading list. The only two sites I hadn't at least scanned were *Male Reference Group Identity Dependence* and *Contrasting Bonobo and Chimpanzee Social Organizations*. The first sounded awfully technical. I knew that it would be full of jargon that I wasn't familiar with and that it would take far too much concentration to try to pick up the meaning from the context. I'd read about monkeys instead.

Bonobos, I learned, are chimpanzee-like creatures who live mainly on the other side of an African river from real chimpanzees. Both species are our two closest living relatives, sharing ninety-nine percent of the human genome. I nearly closed the Fone again at that point, fearing another technical catchword morass, but what followed proved to be surprisingly absorbing.

According to the paper, Bonobos live in tightly-knit, female-dominant groups that limit aggression mostly by having a lot of sex. Females, in particular, form alliances amongst themselves against males, giving them social dominance as a group. Female to female bonding is of paramount importance and conflict tends to be resolved through sexual encounter in an anything-goes kind of way. They also don't fight with the neighbors, preferring instead to screw the brains out of anybody they meet.

Chimpanzees, on the other hand, form male-dominant, aggressive societies that can engage in violent, sometimes lethal, interactions with other chimpanzee groups. There is a clear alpha male who monopolizes and guards females in estrus (I had to stop reading and look up the meaning of the word "estrus" on my FoneWord app, but that was the only term that gave me a problem). Chimps are territorial and routinely patrol their boundaries to prevent incursions, but generally practice avoidance of neighboring troops, which is a good thing, because whenever two groups do meet, all hell breaks loose. Sometimes they go so far as to eat the babies of their rivals.

Of course, that's the Carson MacHenry abridged version of the paper. The real thing was couched in far more formal language and had lots of studies cited and observations noted, but when I finished reading I couldn't help but reflect that the paper could just as easily have been describing the human world before and after Mighty Mite.

I must have dozed off again, because I was jarred awake when my Fone buzzed. I looked at the ID. Didn't Hines ever go to bed?

"MacHenry."

"Hi, it's Jo," purred a voice, "Are you free for lunch tomorrow?"

"Sure, where would you like to go?"

She named a spot away from the city core. "Around one?"

"Should work for me," I said, and then, after I had hung up, I realized that the next day was a working day, and I would have to get Nguyen out of the way before I could make my lunch date.

— «» —

We drifted around the marketplace for most of the morning. Noon came and went, and Nguyen suggested we buy some cold cuts and bread at one of the stalls.

"We could have a picnic in the park," she said brightly.

"Let's wait a bit," I said. "I'm not that hungry and if the thief is a kid, she might plan to do her business on lunch break."

Nguyen shrugged. At quarter to one, I said, "If this was going to happen today, it would have happened by now. I've got a little bit of personal business to take care of. Why don't you grab some lunch and then cruise through the shops we checked the other day. You know the drill — just don't be too obvious. I'll meet you at Murphy's Grill around three."

For such a perky little thing, she sure could get pouty sometimes, and her annoyance showed on her face, but as I was her superior officer there was little she could do but obey. I strode off down the street and left her standing there. I turned the corner and doubled back, checking my watch. I would just make my one o'clock appointment.

Hines was already there when I slid into the chair opposite her.

"Hi. What's up?"

She gestured toward the waiter who was approaching with menus. The conversation would wait until we had ordered.

Judging by the menu, the restaurant catered to lunch goers in the mid-range price category. There were a wide variety of salads offered, but some hearty sandwich platters as well. There were also some decent draught beers listed, but I resisted the temptation to sample one of them, even though falling asleep might be my only defense against another afternoon of trudging the streets with Nguyen. And I'd have given up all the draught beers in the world for one decent cup of coffee.

Hines ordered a wine spritzer with her salad. I wondered how she managed to put in a full day's work with so few calories in her. I would never make it back to the station on such light fare. On the other hand, it made her a cheap date. Except that she was paying anyway, I reminded myself.

As soon as the waiter had taken our orders, Hines leaned forward. "I've been doing some reading. And some asking. I don't know if what I've found out will help much with the ... case that is of mutual interest to us, but it's quite fascinating stuff."

Case of mutual interest? Obviously, she was loath to mention the name Alfi Longwell in such a public place. The Darmes must be leaning in pretty hard to warrant such caution.

I glanced around the room, but everyone seemed to be deep in their own conversations. "Go on."

"I could find only a few cases where the victim had been so brutalized. And none of them demonstrated the same kind of repeated sexual assault."

"How many is a few?" I asked.

"Exactly five over the last fifty years. But that's not the most interesting point."

She glanced around to make sure no one was listening, then leaned forward and spoke in a low voice.

"Three of them involved relationships that had fallen apart. The other two were cases where the victim had been the object of unrequited infatuation. The murderer had worshipped the victim from afar for a period of time, and when an approach was finally made and the victim didn't respond in the anticipated way — well, the murderer lost it."

"You know, if you want people to notice that you're having a conversation you don't want overheard, the best way to attract attention is to do what you just did."

Hines blushed furiously. "I'm not very practiced in deception."

"I noticed." I wanted to stay silent, so I could watch her continue to blush, just because she did it so prettily, but that would have been unkind. "So what you're telling me is that our … um … case of mutual interest might have been done in by someone she knew. That it might be a case of love gone wonky?"

"Based on what I could find, yes. Five cases isn't exactly a big enough sample group to draw conclusions from, but, honestly, that's all I could find."

Unrequited love turned violent? Alfreda's uni friend Hana had certainly been upset by her death. She'd cried over lost poems. "She wrote them for me," she'd wailed that day on the lawn. The others had been unhappy as well, but I would be too if one of my friends had suddenly died. The other friend — Jazz — had called it murder. Did she say that because she knew for sure that's what it was? Because she had committed it? That didn't make any sense. She wouldn't have said anything at all if that were the case. She'd have agreed with the Darmes's version of the story. And then there was the girl in Cedar Lake. Lisa-at-The-Market. She'd had a relationship with Alfi Longwell. And she'd been more or less dumped. She was a lot tougher than the pampered uni girls, or at least she seemed to be. Had she been nursing a grudge all these years and finally decided to take her revenge? A spurned romantic overture could explain what had happened, but it wouldn't explain why the death was covered up so quickly.

"I think the question we should be asking ourselves is why the Darmes are involved," I said. "If we work on the assumption that Alfi was killed by someone she knew, then I need to take a good hard look at her friends. If one of them has connections, it would explain why everything was shoved under the rug."

"Someone from the university, do you think?"

"Maybe. Or someone from her home town. Or someone her parents know. It's a bit of a fishing expedition, but if you cross-reference enough records, sooner or later something should match up." Unless it didn't. My best hope, I realized, was to retrieve whatever files were still on the Fone that Hana had taken to the second-hand shop. With any luck, there would be something there that would narrow the search.

We stopped talking as the waiter walked over and dumped our drinks on the table. Hines swirled her wine around in the glass and smelled it before she took a small sip.

"You didn't find anything of interest in the DK I take it?" I had called her that night from the office, but her instructions had been to say something sexy, just to let her know that I was home safe. Calls from the office were monitored, but I didn't care. I figured the salacious message I left would only provide more fodder for the gossip-mongers.

"No, not really," I said. "I found a sakertown on Oriole Avenue, but I don't see how it could be the 'oriole camp' the girl was referring to, and they didn't seem to know anything about an accident. The avenue itself is a bit of a bust — most of it has fallen into a gully. I did see one thing that was strange, though. The sakers had a kid. Maybe three years old or so. And one of the saker women was pregnant. Due to pop any day, I'd say."

"Really?" Hines said. "That's weird."

"I know. I wouldn't think sakers would be accepted into the Parent Program. Not these sakers anyway. Their settlement was pretty primitive."

"Maybe the mothers are recent converts and brought their baggage with them. It happens sometimes. Somebody gets religious and it breaks up the relationship. They go their separate ways."

"Would a saker convert be allowed to take a child?"

"I don't know," Hines said. "I don't think turning saker would necessarily be an argument against custody. But if I were the other parent, and knew that my daughter was living in the DK, I think I'd be going to court."

"I know," I said. "It's hard enough to get a kid even if you're normal." I knew all about it. I'd gone through the selection process. With Georgie. Before everything fell apart.

"It has to be something like that," Hines said. "The sakers don't even believe in assisted reproduction. Or maybe both parents saw the light. In that case, there wouldn't be anybody to object."

"It did occur to me that the child I'd seen had been kidnapped, but it seems improbable. It's just not their style."

"Weird," Hines said, "But I'm not sure where you're going with this. Do you think it has something to do with the murder?"

"I don't know. All I know is that it's very odd, and whenever I find odd things in a case, I pay attention. It's sort of like doing an autopsy. You want to take special note of the things that shouldn't be there. Like finding a surgical sponge where an appendix should be."

"Cute," she said.

"So what do you know about Men's Studies?"

"Not a damn thing. Why?"

"I don't know. But since we've drawn a blank with everything else, that seems like a good place to go next. That and checking out all the friends."

The waiter arrived with our meals. Hines fiddled with her salad dressing for a few moments before finally spooning a little onto a piece of lettuce and taking one tentative bite.

Somebody should introduce this woman to the mouth-
and soul-satisfying benefits of poutine, I thought. It might
put some roses in her cheeks. Then I realized how fussily
protective that sounded. Georgie had always accused me
of mother-henning her. I was going to have to knock it off.
Hines wasn't Georgie, and I had no say in what she ate. Or in
anything else she did for that matter.

"You think the case might have something to do with what
she was studying?" Hines asked between tiny mouthfuls.

"Again, I don't know. But there are a couple of things I'd
sure like to have a look at." For some reason I was reluctant
to tell her about the Fone I'd scooped. I didn't know for sure
if there was anything on it that would have anything to do
with Alfreda Longwell, and I hadn't had a chance to take it to
Ricky for decryption. Leave things on a need to know basis,
I decided, just in case the Darmes really were listening as
hard as Hines thought they were. "I'll let you know if I find
anything. Oh, and by the way…"

"Yes?"

"Even though you're not practiced in deception, as you
put it, your misdirection is working nicely. Apparently it's
all over Division that you and I are in love."

I was rewarded with another blush.

CHAPTER 9

Ricky Vanek Chan is one of those strange birds who is probably a genius, and could probably be making huge amounts of money somewhere, if only she didn't have such a warped sense of the ridiculous. Right out of university, she had been scooped up by a major security outfit that had contracts with the government, and they had assigned her to a position in the department that tested the integrity of the systems the company designed.

Ricky reasoned that the best way to defend against hacker attacks was to hack the system and then point out how it was done. She wasn't content, however, to demonstrate her expertise with a mock-up, in-house version of the program she was testing. Instead, she successfully accessed the Gendarmes Corps' deep six files and paralyzed their network by looping a mildly obscene, home-produced version of the popular kidvid *Ginny Gones: The Gentle Gendarme*. Then she offered to write a program that would keep it from ever happening again.

Her company briefly considered moving her from programming to sales, but, in the end, the Darmes and the government insisted that she be fired. Now she runs a private consulting firm that specializes in tracking people on behalf of other people. Executives dogging expense accounts, girlfriends who are seeing someone on the sly, kids who are into some shit their parents don't like. Ricky can hack into anything.

I'd used her on any number of cases. At one point, I even suggested to Inspector Trent that Ricky be put on the payroll in order to clear up the backlog of cold cases, but, even after all these years, the taint of *Ginny Gones* was still following her around and Trent nixed the idea. Besides, money doesn't work with Ricky. It's the thrill of cracking codes that gets her off.

I'd spent another fruitless afternoon working the B&E case with Nguyen. She'd been in a foul mood. I was late for our rendezvous at Murphy's Grill and she'd been sitting and fuming at a table just inside the door. She'd communicated in monosyllables all afternoon. The upside of her annoyance was that she made no mention of socializing after work. We'd gone back to Division, signed out and gone our separate ways. I went straight from the office to Ricky's.

I climbed the two sets of worn stairs that led to her network central, located conveniently over a deli.

"It saves time," Ricky claims. "They'll send stuff up so I don't have to leave the console." I don't think she leaves her apartment for months at a time.

I waved into the security camera she'd installed on the stair landing, just so she would know I was on my way up. Like she hadn't already spotted me from the public camera on the corner. As I reached her door, it swung open — a remote-control feature that was a new addition since the last time I'd been there.

She didn't even look around as I entered. She sat like a spider at the center of a cyberweb of multiple Vus, watching, listening, ready to pounce. I just didn't know why — she never used any of the information she gathered for any kind of personal benefit, other than to satisfy the requirements of her clientele.

"Yo, Rick," I said, by way of greeting.

She still didn't look up from the screen she was hunkered over. "Leave it on the table."

"How do you know why I'm here?"

"Saw you buy a Fone at a second-hand shop. Figured it's something you'd like me to look at."

Ricky has eyes everywhere.

I finally located the table under a pile of cardboard boxes, empty take-out cartons and dirty clothing. Just as Ricky herself never leaves the one-room apartment, neither, apparently, does anything else. The narrow bed in the corner served as a shelf for a couple of old Vus, a rat's nest of cables, three boxes of cereal and a pair of winter boots that sat triumphantly on the pillow. The small section of kitchen counter along one wall was an archaeological testament to the number of take-out teas Ricky ordered, but never quite drank up entirely. The whole place smelled of old curry and sour milk.

In order to make room for the Fone, I grabbed a discarded pizza box and, for lack of anywhere else to put it, threw it into the kitchen sink. It was the only place in the room that remained uncluttered. Ricky never cooks, or eats from anything that isn't cardboard.

"So what's it all about?" she asked. "Does it have something to do with the case the Darmes shut down so fast?"

"How do you know about that?"

She swung around then and looked at me. She wore big, thick glasses that reflected the light, so it was hard to read her expression.

"I caught some whispers — they're just whispers, though. They were hard to pick up, so I figure it's gotta be big."

"As big as I've ever seen. If I get caught, my ass is grass."

She giggled. "Cool. I haven't had anything interesting to do for a long time. You still at the same address?"

She knew perfectly well that I was.

"I'll call you when I'm done. Do me a favor?"

"Sure." I had a pretty good idea what she wanted me to do.

Her brow wrinkled, and just for a second she sounded lost and bewildered.

"Could you go buy me some toilet paper?"

— «» —

One of the things you soon learned about Ricky was that she couldn't be rushed. There was no point in checking in to see how she was getting along. If she could do the job, she'd let you know when it was done. If she couldn't, she'd let you know after she tried everything she could think of. The latter hasn't happened very often.

After I left the Fone with her, I went to the groceteria on the corner and bought five packages of double-roll. I took it back to her apartment, shoved it in the door and left. Then, instead of worrying about the encrypted files, I turned my attention to getting into Professor Gerrity's office without being tracked. The electronic part of it was easy — if worse came to worse, I could use a burner again, but I figured a badge might not be a bad thing to have if I got caught snooping around where I wasn't supposed to be.

It was my physical presence that was going to be harder to disguise. Like I said, it's hard not to get marked as a cop, wherever you go. It's like people have a sixth sense about it or something. I stewed about what I was going to do until I realized the opportunity had been lying right under my nose.

Everywhere we'd gone during the last few days, we'd seen posters — in store windows, on lampposts, tacked to bulletin boards, plastered on fences — but it wasn't until we stopped for lunch the next day, and happened to overhear a newsfeed, that I finally recognized a completely obvious opportunity.

There was a big do coming up at the uni, a gala fundraiser with a special performance by *Aurora!,* a singer who was hugely popular with the kids and had attended the school before embarking on her musical career. I'd heard a little of her stuff — whiney she-done-me-wrong laments with synthesized beats that got on my nerves after only a couple of songs. Her biggest talent seemed to be that she could sing and do aerobics at the same time, only she called it dancing.

I decided that my best shot to get in unnoticed would be to pretend I was outside security, hired in for the occasion. The university often contracted off-duty cops for special events, especially if there was going to be a celebrity of some kind in attendance. Major celeb, major security I figured. It shouldn't be too hard to blend in when there were so many strangers on campus anyway.

I did a cursory background check on *Aurora!* just because I could, and I noted that she had not actually graduated from the university — she had just taken a few courses once upon a time. But the uni was anxious to raise funds for a new concert hall and was prepared to overlook the fact that no diploma had been awarded.

I had a look at my schedule. I was off on the Saturday night of the concert. As long as no one checked with Trent — and even if they did, there was no reason that I shouldn't be at the gala. I toyed with the idea of officially signing on for the security detail — it would make my presence bona fide and my position unassailable — except that it might seem suspicious if the Darmes were watching as closely as Jo Hines thought they were. Better to go in, look like I belonged, get what I was after, then disappear.

If only I knew what I was after. It wasn't going to be a quick hit. I'd need time to sift through the professor's filing cabinets a little, look at student records, try to narrow down what Alfi Longwell's activities had been in the weeks leading up to her death.

On Saturday afternoon, I brushed down my coat, shined my black service shoes, ironed a white blouse and combed my hair before heading off to the university. When I had a look in the mirror, I wondered if I should make the effort more often. I looked almost presentable.

When I reached the university, I threaded my bike through the masses of kids milling around in the street. The parking area was filling up steadily. I found a spot at the far end, well away from the entrance. I parked my bike, plugged it into the recharger and locked it, then walked purposefully through the crowd, glancing here and there, trying to look official.

There were groups of girls sitting in huddles in sleeping bags, others perched along the wall, more on the steps, all of them hoping to get a glimpse of their idol when she arrived. They looked away when I passed. I was marked already. Good. I'd fit right in.

I saw that both City Police and private security firms had been hired to bolster the uni's own squad. Over the next half-hour they straggled in, parking their bikes and heading for the main administration building. I waited until the influx started to slow, then joined a group of latecomers as they went through the front door. I recognized a couple of young newer constables from Police Services, and nodded a hello. That was good too. No one was apt to get too nosy if I was seen talking to other cops. And then, over on the other side of the room, I saw Susan Nguyen. She waved at me and started to make her way over to where I stood. That was not good.

The university's head of security called for attention and outlined the plan for the evening — standard crowd control, patrolling of the periphery, making sure that there were no bottlenecks where people could be trampled, and that no one would try to crash the concert — and then she divided the force into groups designated for each task. I elbowed a couple of people out of the way to make sure that I was assigned to patrol. Then we all lined up and were handed our ID tags. It was as simple as that.

Nguyen followed me into the patrol line-up, and was at my heels as we broke off to our assigned positions. Cazzo crap on a cracker.

"Mind if I tag along?" she said. "This is my first time working a real security detail."

"Sure," I said, and shrugged. I minded very much. I'd have to find a way to goose-chase her. As we walked along the east wall of the administration building the noise level from out front rose, then erupted into a roar. The talent had arrived.

"Do you think we'll get a chance to see *Aurora!*?" Nguyen asked.

"No," I said. "Our job isn't to watch the talent, it's to watch the crowd."

"Oh," Nguyen said and her face fell. Just what every celebrity needs, I thought, a star-struck security guard anxious to have a little of the glamor rub off. But Nguyen's awe did present me with a way to get rid of her.

"I'll tell you what, though," I said. "Let's just check around the back of the building, and then if you want to go and see if you can get close enough for a glimpse, I should be able to manage without you for a while."

"Really? Wow, that would be great." Her face lit up, and for a moment I almost felt guilty about raising her hopes.

We poked around here and there, checking the contents of a couple of trash bins just to make it look like we were working. When we reached the rear of the McClung building, I turned to Nguyen. "Why don't you go on? There's not much going on here."

"Great," she said, and she was off like a shot. As much as she was getting her jollies from hanging out with the infamous Detective MacHenry, I was obviously no competition for a real live glam star. She didn't even think to ask where she could find me later.

The McClung building is so old and has been renovated so many times that its rear wall is a hodgepodge of doors leading nowhere and windows that illuminate nothing. Most of these openings have been bricked up, but there were several that were merely boarded-over, the result of the most recent renovations, I expect. Nothing made permanent until it was evident that the renovation had been prudent.

Gerrity's office had been on the third floor at the end of the building. And right below it, at ground level, was a doorway covered with plywood and nailed shut. The bottom right-hand corner of the plywood had warped a little and pulled away from the door frame it was nailed to. A combination of damp and the fact that the wood had been green to begin with, I figured. The wood underneath was grey and rotten-looking.

Like most public places, the campus grounds are covered by security cam, but here, at the rear of the complex, the coverage had been skimped. There were cameras mounted at intervals along the back wall, and several more on light standards, more or less sweeping most of the grassy lawn, but I realized that none of them was trained specifically on the doorway in question, and that if I slid along close to the wall, none of them would pick me up.

I ambled across the lawn beside the building, so I would look like just another security guard making the rounds. Then, just at the point where I judged there was a blind spot, I took a step to the side and flattened myself against the brick wall.

I glanced around to make sure there were no eyewitnesses to my peculiar behavior. There was no one nearby. Everyone had been drawn to the front entrance by the tumult there. I slithered along, keeping as close to the wall as I could, until I reached the doorway with the wonky piece of plywood.

I'd brought a small crowbar with me, and now I slipped it out of my pocket and slid it under the section of wood that bubbled away from the frame. Lux and luck — instead of the corner coming away in a chunk, the entire sheet lifted. Another sharp tug and the nails popped out of the rotten wood underneath, leaving just enough space for me to slip through as long as I didn't mind a few scratches from the pointy ends of the nails. The board snapped back into place as soon as I was through — from the outside, someone would have to look closely to tell that it had been tampered with.

There was only blackness inside. I groped for my flashlight and discovered that I was standing in a cleaner's closet, the sour smell of disinfectant and floor polish making my nose tingle. The great thing about broom closets, though, is that they are seldom locked at night when the cleaning staff need easy access to mops and pails. Slowly, I turned the handle and opened the door a crack. There was no one in sight. The janitorial staff had probably, like Nguyen, migrated toward the front of the building in the hope of catching a glimpse of someone so famous. I ran down the hall and up two sets of stairs to the third floor.

The thing about offices, though, is that they, unlike closets, *are* locked at night, but like I said, the building is old, and no one had ever replaced the ancient lock on Gerrity's door. A quick look both ways to make sure the coast was clear, a moment's jimmying, and I was in.

I swept the office with my flashlight, taking care to keep the beam away from the windows. I checked the desk. It had only one drawer, which was unlocked and held nothing more interesting than pens and staplers. I moved to the wall of filing cabinets. I reasoned that the files the professor used the most would be in the cabinet closest to the desk. Course outlines, stuff like that, and this was the cabinet that she had retrieved the reading list from. There was a chance, of course, that the Darmes had scoured the files clean of any relevant material, or that none of the information I was looking for existed anywhere but on the uniWire, but Gerrity really struck me as a paper back-up, don't-take-a-chance-of losing-it kind of person. Otherwise, why would she have so many filing cabinets?

The student records were in the left-hand cabinet, second drawer from the top. No Alfreda Lucas Longwell. No Longwells at all. But the Darmes had left the other grad students' records. There was only one Claire. Claire Comeau Sullivan. I fired up my Fone and scanned her files. I flipped through the rest of the drawer looking for anyone named Jazz or even Jasmine. Nothing. No Hanas either. Alfi hadn't picked her friends from among her classmates.

I selected a couple of other records at random and scanned them. I would have liked to check out every student in the course, but there wasn't time. Nguyen would be looking for me as soon as she realized that there wasn't a hope of getting close to her idol.

I opened the top drawer of the second cabinet and riffled through the neatly printed labels at the top of each file. These seemed to be mostly historical explorations of the status of women in pre-Mighty Mite civilizations. *Witch hunts in 15th, 16th and 17th Century Europe*, *Malleus Maleficarum*, *The Rise of the Taliban in Muslim Society*, *Male Sexual Self-Schemas* and *The Objectification of Women in 20th Century Cinema*. And on and on, spilling over into the cabinet beside it. The study of men seemed to consist, in large part, of a litany of the awful things they had done to women. Not helpful to the issue at hand.

The last filing cabinet was a puzzle. First of all, it was locked, unlike the others. I popped it without difficulty and opened the middle drawer. *Experiments With Stem Cell Reproduction*, *The Decline and Fall of the Y Chromosome*, *Agamogenesis*, a whole section on the failure of cloning.

I knew about cloning. You still sometimes see the poor souls on the street being pushed along in wheelchairs. They are lovingly attended by their caregivers, of course, but it's hard not to feel sorry for them. They'd grown old before their time, and they haven't had much of a life to begin with, given the limitations imposed by their profound disabilities and morbid diseases. Cloning had proved to be a complete cul de sac, in terms of solving the world's reproductive crisis.

There had been problems every time it was attempted on a large scale. The scientists would scuttle back to their labs, only to emerge a year or two later and once again announce that the problems had been solved. Each time the results were more catastrophic than before. Professor Gerrity had a whole raft of files that detailed just how catastrophic it had been, but most of the papers appeared to be highly technical, and I didn't understand much of the little bit I read. I still don't know what "agamogenesis" is.

I checked the clock on my Fone. I figured I had time to look in one more drawer. I opted for the top one of the locked cabinet. Gerrity didn't strike me as the sort of person who was into any unnecessary physical exertion. She'd put the files she needed to access on a regular basis in either the top or the middle drawers. That way she wouldn't have to bend down to get them.

These files appeared to be family trees of some sort, two alphanumerics at the top of the page, then descending and expanding and changing as the graph worked its way down, individuals marked by a cross or an arrow, here and there a circle around one of them. I flipped through the pages, but there was no indication of why a particular result had been singled out.

Not much help in terms of what I was after, but I quickly scanned a couple of the pages anyway and then closed the drawer. There wasn't much I could do about the jimmied lock on the cabinet — I'd pretty much destroyed it. I'd just have to hope that the professor would figure she'd broken it herself somehow.

I opened the office door a crack and peeked out. All clear. I turned the lock and closed the door gently behind me, then made a beeline down the stairs to the first-floor closet. I'd just slipped out through the gap in the plywood, when I heard someone call my name.

"That was awesome," Nguyen said. She was beaming. "I was no more than ten feet away from her!"

"No problems then?"

Nguyen looked puzzled. "No. There was nothing unusual going on."

"Okay, that's good. Because we may have a problem here." I grabbed the edge of the plywood barrier I had just popped through. "This is loose. I don't know if it's big enough for someone to get through or not. It looks like there's just a closet on the other side, but I don't know what's beyond that."

"Should we report it?" Nguyen's face was a wrinkle of concern. I couldn't believe she had to ask me that.

"I doubt it's anything, but we'd better let the uniguards know. At the very least they can send someone to nail it shut again. Why don't you go and report it? I'll make sure everything is secure here." The last thing I wanted was any official interaction with security. Besides, sending Nguyen would put a shine on her day.

She beamed. She was like a puppy dog, really; a little pat on the head was enough to make her happy. She disappeared around the corner of the building at a run. I waited until she was out of sight, then I walked toward a guard who was coming around the other side of the building.

"Hey, did you know about the loose board over there?" I asked.

She followed me over to the gap.

"You'd better stay here. I'll go report it," I said. And then I walked off the campus, removed my ID tag and spent the rest of the evening in a coffee shop where I had a clear view of the administration building. As soon as it looked like everyone was clearing out, I walked over to the parking lot and retrieved my bike, lost in the rush of others doing the same thing.

CHAPTER 10

The next day Trent hauled me into her office as soon as I arrived at work.

"There was a break-in at the university last night," she said without preamble.

"Really?" I said. "Was anything taken?"

"Apparently not. But the files in one of the professor's offices were riffled. Locks broken, that sort of thing."

"Someone looking for information?" I ventured. "A student, maybe, wanting to see what a prof wrote about her? Change a grade?" I shrugged. "That sort of thing is hard to track down."

Trent poured herself a cup of tea, blew on it and took a sip before she spoke.

"The leash puts you at the university last night."

"Yes. There was a concert. I'm a big *Aurora!* fan."

"Really." She didn't look at all convinced.

"Yeah. I have all her recordings."

"Detective Nguyen says you signed up as off-duty police security, but there's no record of you on the uniguard list."

Crap. I did my best to look puzzled. "I'm afraid Susan is mistaken. I was there, yes, and I saw her, but I wasn't there in an official capacity. She must have just assumed that I was."

"I see," Trent said, and stirred another packet of sugar into her tea. "And yet Detective Nguyen says it was you who spotted a loose piece of plywood covering an old entrance to the McClung building."

Oh, Susan, Susan, Susan. I offered you the opportunity to take all the credit for discovering the break-in and you were too stupid to take advantage of it.

"Well, yes, I saw it," I said. "I was walking around the building when I noticed it. Then I ran into Nguyen and pointed it out. She immediately notified the uniguards, as is standard practice." I stopped for a moment and let my eyes grow wide. "You don't think that's how the intruders gained access to the building?"

Trent glared at me. Okay, so that was pushing it. I quickly continued before she could comment.

"Detective Nguyen certainly showed great presence of mind, then, to realize that a loose piece of plywood constituted a security breach. That was good work on her part. She should be commended."

"And she will be," Trent said. She took another sip of tea, then set the cup down and fixed me with a very direct gaze. "I'm taking you off the break and enter case you've been working on. Detective Nguyen has shown herself more than capable of a solo investigation."

I mentally groaned. I could see what was coming. I'd be heading up the investigation into every crappy ass Tiresome Task for the next six months. Why couldn't Nguyen be like every other detective in the division and jump at an opportunity to take all the credit at the expense of someone else who'd done the work? Then I nearly fell off my chair at what Trent said next.

"I'd like you, instead, to investigate the university break-in. It is, as you said, the sort of case that is difficult to track down, but I'm sure some diligent digging on your part will allow us to, at the very least, assure the university that no information of value was compromised. You can send whatever details you find directly to my pod."

I was speechless. Trent knew damn well I wasn't an *Aurora!* fan and had some other reason for being at the university the previous night. And if she'd been checking the leash records, she knew I'd gone to Cedar Lake to talk to Alfreda Longwell's parents as well. She'd warned me not to ask questions about the autopsy, yet she'd just given me carte blanche to go snooping for Longwell's school records. But she didn't want anything I found entered into the official log. What the hell was going on?

"That's all." She glared at me again. "For now anyway."

I rose to go, but just as I reached the door, she said, "Oh, and Mac?"

I turned, waiting for the other shoe to drop, but when it came, it was more like a cozy old slipper.

"Some of the information in this particular professor's files are rather sensitive. It would be best if you didn't mention your assignment to anyone else. I'll put you down on the roster as being on Accident Investigation. Use whatever resources you need, but be discreet." Her mouth twitched a little at one corner. "If that's possible, of course."

I passed Nguyen's desk on the way back to my own. She glanced up, her face shining and expectant, as if medals were in order for our work the previous evening.

I slouched down into my chair, and made a great show of shuffling papers around, but my mind was in overdrive.

I'd loaded everything I'd scanned at Gerrity's office the night before into my Vu as soon as I'd arrived home, but the results had been disappointing. The student records were perfectly straightforward. The files I'd chosen at random belonged to a couple of undergrads who were taking Men's Studies as a gimme course, and, in all probability, they were happy enough with the Cs they'd earned from Gerrity. In contrast, Claire Comeau Sullivan was a stellar student in the process of writing a doctoral dissertation on *Methodological Perspectives on the Psychobiology of Play,* whatever that was. Her data was extracted from something called *Project BW.* The rest of the files I'd scanned were just as unrevealing. Everything was either highly technical, or historical, psychological and sociological in nature.

Trent knew perfectly well that it had been me who had broken into Gerrity's office. I may have been picked up by a security cam after all, or maybe she just put two and two together. Whatever the reason, she'd seized on the break-in as an excuse for me to go back and have a really good look around.

But why? And when I thought about it, I really couldn't figure out why she had assigned me to the autopsy sign-off in the first place. Why not send a junior detective who wasn't doing anything anyway, other than listen to Detective Diva blow hot air? Someone like Nguyen, who didn't have either the imagination or the experience to realize that something was screwy. It didn't occur to me at the time to question why it needed a senior detective to do nothing more than salute and say "Yes, Ma'am." I had been happy just to get out of the office.

Trent wanted the Longwell murder investigated, that much was clear, but she was going about it in a very strange way. Except that the Darmes were involved. And the Darmes wanted it hushed up. Rule-bound, proper-chain-of-command Boss Tweed would never directly buck the system. But, for the life of me, I couldn't see what motivation she had to buck it at all, never mind in such an oblique fashion. And until I could figure that out, I had no intention of sending details of the investigation straight to her private message pod.

Whatever was going on, I realized that I wasn't going to get any answers by stewing at my desk. I rose and grabbed my coat. Nguyen looked up.

"Should we go check those shops again?" she asked. She apparently didn't know yet that she was to be in sole charge of the B&E investigation.

"I'm off the case," I said. "I'm on Accident."

"Oh." Her face fell. "How come?"

"In trouble with the boss."

"It doesn't have anything to do with last night, does it?" she asked anxiously.

I shrugged and walked away. Let her figure it out herself. And when she did, she would owe me one.

— «» —

I marched up to the information desk at the university and flashed my badge. It was a different woman on the desk this time, and she nodded, then punched numbers into her Fone. Five minutes later, a uniguard appeared.

She held out her hand. "I'm Marika Kruger Sengal," she said. "How can I help you?"

"I'm here to investigate last night's break-in," I said. "Have you ascertained whether or not anything's been taken?"

"Professor Gerrity doesn't think so. At first I thought it was just a case of someone trying to get into the building for a closer look at the pop star who was performing here. But with the office being broken into, it sounds more like somebody was looking for something specific that had nothing to do with the concert."

"Show me the entry point."

We walked over to the McClung building. I had to remind myself to pretend not to know which particular boarded-up door we were looking for.

"Here we go."

I stood back and made a great show of studying the board carefully. After three or four minutes, during which time Sengal impatiently shifted her weight from foot to foot, I said, "Someone's taken a crowbar to this." I pulled the loose end away. "You can see where the nail heads have ripped out of the wood."

She looked unimpressed. She'd already figured all this out, and now some hotshot cop was telling her what she already knew.

"Where does this lead?"

"Into a janitor's room. Normally those are locked, but sometimes the custodial staff leaves them open when they're working. It saves time not to have to lock and unlock all the time, and there aren't usually any people in this part of the uni at night."

"Hmm," I said. "Sloppy."

"I agree. They've been told to stop the practice."

I walked first one way, then the other, stopping every now and then to look at the ground, the building, the surroundings, the security cameras and, at one point, even the sky, while Sengal leaned against the wall of the building.

"Okay, now show me the inside."

There was a back entrance to the McClung building that led in a fairly direct fashion to Gerrity's office, so we didn't have to wind through the claustrophobic corridors that snaked from the main door.

Gerrity wasn't there. I noted that the old lock on her door had already been replaced with a shiny new deadbolt.

Sengal selected a key from the jangling ring at her belt and opened it.

I stopped at the threshold. "How many people have keys to this office?"

"The professor. The janitorial staff on this floor. The guards all have masters."

"Hmm," I said.

Sengal looked alarmed. "We haven't had any reports of keys gone missing."

"So maybe it was someone on staff."

She hadn't considered this. Uniguards were really good at making sure nobody scribbled graffiti on the walls, and that parking regulations were observed. Beyond that, they didn't have much experience with security breaches. It didn't seem to have occurred to her that someone could simply pop the lock on a door.

"What does Professor Gerrity teach?" I asked.

"Something in the history department."

"Not exactly a hotbed of state secrets then?"

She shrugged.

"What's in the filing cabinets?" I slid open the top drawer of the cabinet nearest the desk and began looking through them.

Sengal looked alarmed. "Shouldn't you wait for Professor Gerrity?"

"No," I said, but just then Gerrity stumbled through the door and dumped a pile of papers on the desk. "What's going on?" she asked. "Who are you?"

I didn't know whether or not she would remember me, or if she would connect my face with "Alfreda who was thinking of taking Men's Studies." It would be much, much better if she couldn't place me, but if she did, I'd stick to my story. After all, cops have friends too. Sometimes.

"I'm Detective Carson MacHenry from City Police," I said. "I've been assigned to investigate the break-in."

She hesitated, just for a moment, her brow wrinkling with puzzlement, then it cleared. "I see," she said. "Were you looking for anything in particular?"

"No. I was just looking. Can you tell me, please, whether or not you've noticed anything missing?"

"I'm not sure. I mean, nothing obvious, but I don't keep track of every scrap of paper in the office. It did seem as if some files were misplaced, though."

"Which ones?"

"The student records. They weren't in strict alphabetical order — although I sometimes mix those up all by myself." She laughed a little. "Absent-minded, you know."

"Anything else?"

Her eyes wandered over to the far cabinet, the one with all the genetic stuff. The one that had been locked.

"Maybe in that one as well," she said, pointing.

"But you don't know for sure?"

"No."

I heaved my best impression of an exasperated sigh. "In that case, the first thing to do is to inventory the contents. Then maybe we can tell if anything's been taken."

"Is that really necessary?" Gerrity said. "I mean, it was just somebody breaking into the office. Most likely a student. Why would the police go to all this trouble over a minor break-in?"

"We take every crime seriously," I said with a straight face. "We will leave no stone unturned until we find the culprit."

"Oh, very well," she said. "As long as you don't need me here the whole time. I have classes, you know. Research." She was practically wringing her hands, she was so anxious.

"I don't think your presence is necessary. I can document the ... um ... documents, and then I'll simply present you with a list. But," and here I turned to Sengal, "I'll need a key."

"I'll get you one," Sengal said, "as long as you're willing to sign for it."

"No problem."

And with that all sorted out, I knew I could rummage to my heart's content.

— ‹› —

Nuygen blushed as soon as she saw me walk back into the office at the end of the day. Word had gotten around, apparently, that I'd been called on the carpet, and apparently Nuygen felt personally responsible. She made a studied effort to avoid my eye, busying herself with entering data into her Fone.

I really wanted to sit at my desk as the office emptied out for the night, review what I'd discovered at the university, and think about what it all meant. Nguyen owed me — and I intended to collect — but, in fact, I couldn't have engineered things any better if I'd tried. Besides, if I needed to call in the favor, I'd rather have it proffered willingly.

I walked over to her desk. "Wanna get a drink?"

She looked up, confused. "Um, well ... sure," she said. "I wasn't sure you'd want to."

I shrugged. "I get to pick the bar though."

I waited while she signed out. I didn't bother. I was pretty sure Trent wouldn't make a fuss if my timesheets weren't kept in apple pie order. Besides, as far as I was concerned, I was still working.

I took her to one of my usual haunts — no chrome, no brass, no flashing lights. Just good beer, rib-sticking food and comfortable booth seating. Nguyen slid into the bench across from me and grabbed the menu, burying her nose in the list of everything that came with chips.

"It's not your fault, you know."

"It feels like it is," she said, without looking up. "And I still don't know what I did."

"It's a long story," I said, "and you're probably better off without the details. You should learn how to take advantage of your opportunities though."

She finally looked at me. "But I didn't do anything but run off to find a uniguard. You were the one who noticed the gap in the plywood."

"I know. But I deliberately disappeared so you could take the credit."

She shook her head. "That wouldn't have been fair. I don't work that way."

"I appreciate that," I said. "That's an admirable quality, even if it didn't turn out quite the way you thought it would. But in any event, I just want you to know that you didn't do me any harm and there are no hard feelings here."

She must have thought I'd invited her out to rip into her. Now that she realized this wasn't the case, I thought she was going to cry, something I was desperate to forestall. I wasn't good with emotional stuff.

"Listen Nguyen — Susan — there is something you could do for me."

"Anything," she said. That's how relieved she was.

"It would be really cool if I could count on you to watch my back."

"Well, of course." She sat up straighter. "Of course I will."

"I can't give you any details, but if I holler, I'd like to think you'd come running." A request like that, even from a fellow police officer, should have set every alarm bell in her head ringing.

Instead, she said, "Absolutely. You know I will."

"Thank you. Enough said. Now let's get some food and drink into us."

Nguyen opted for a beer and a burger, but I settled for a plate of poutine and a glass of water and scarfed it all down in short order. Nguyen was so busy talking, she took forever to get through her food. Now that I was her friend, her *partner* as she dared to put it a couple of times, she wanted to tell me her life story — her parents, her school, her hobbies, why she'd wanted to go into police work in the first place. As she spoke, her face became animated with enthusiasm, and she waved her hands around a lot to emphasize what she was saying. The info I'd scanned into my Fone that afternoon was burning a hole in my pocket and, after a while, I wondered if I should have pretended to be angry with her, rather than try and make her an accomplice. I certainly would have gotten out of the restaurant faster. Finally, the meal wound down and we found ourselves standing out on the sidewalk in front of the restaurant.

"See you tomorrow," I said, and immediately began walking away. I was prepared to be civil. I certainly wasn't prepared to have it go any further than that.

As soon as I got home, I started transferring the files I'd copied. I had taken all of the student files. There were only about forty of them. Men's Studies apparently wasn't one of the most popular courses, and, judging from the marks awarded, the students seemed to be evenly split between those who were genuinely interested in the subject and those who had taken the course because they thought it would be easy, or because nothing else would fit into their schedules.

There were a couple of students working on their Master's Degrees, but Claire was the only doctoral candidate. Except for Alfreda Longwell, of course. And that was according to her parents, who I supposed should know, but I could find no trace of it in the records. I wondered how Gerrity managed to hang on to her funding when so few students were interested in her subject.

When Gerrity failed to return to her office in the afternoon, I had started sampling the other cabinets, picking and scanning files at random. I flipped through what I had gathered. A lot of history, as far as I could tell. Witch burnings. Virgin sacrifices. A lot about the position of women in the various churches, which seemed to be that they didn't have one, other than as brood mares or bakers of pies. The equal rights movements of the twentieth and twenty-first centuries. Mighty Mite and the wars that followed.

One title caught my eye — "The Role of 'Uncle Thomasinas' in the Entrenchment of Male Dominance in Post Mighty Mite World Governments." I skimmed through the document. According to the author, as the number of men dwindled in the wake of the Mighty Mite epidemic they made a desperate attempt to consolidate power, aided and abetted by females who bolstered their authority and coat-tailed on their power. Ah — the bijou girls of a past time, basking in the reflected glory of whoever was important, clambering over whoever got in their way in their scramble to rub elbows, or some other body part, with the rich and the influential. The "Uncle Thomasina" label was in reference to some obscure nineteenth century work of literature, apparently. Something to do with slavery, I gathered. Interesting, but not particularly germane to the case.

I had taken only a few things from the locked cabinet, the one with all the genetic stuff, since I figured I wouldn't understand any of it anyway, but I picked up my Fone and entered "Genetics" in the hope that there might be something on the Wire that would help me get my head around it. *Human Reproduction for Morons* or something like that.

After scrolling through a number of sites that discussed cloning and current methods of insemination, I found one that shed at least a little light on the complicated diagrams I'd found. Light, but no revelatory lux lightbulb.

"XX" was the female. "XY" was male. Put the two together and you make a baby. Okay, that much I already knew. The female always contributed an X, but the male's donation could be either X or Y, the gender of the offspring determined by which one was passed along. Hence the problem with the Mighty Mite vaccine — no more viable little Y worms and you get only girls.

I found a chart that demonstrated the genetic transmission of color blindness, tracking the trait through multiple generations. It was a lot simpler than the material I had lifted from Gerrity's locked cabinet, clear enough to show the general pattern of how it worked. The entries that had been highlighted in Gerrity's studies must carry a particular trait, but there was no indication of what that might be. Or what any of it might be, in the absence of any explanatory notes.

I was a little puzzled. The subject seemed highly specialized, belonging more properly in the science department, not in the history department, especially not in an arcane sub-section of it. On the other hand, the course was called "Men's Studies," and I supposed if you were going to study men, you needed to understand what had happened to them. But if the files were merely a diagrammatic representation of the effects of Mighty Mite, why keep them in a locked cabinet?

I turned to my Vu again and went through everything I'd taken that day until I started to get bleary-eyed. I hadn't done that much reading since my university exams. Maybe, I thought, I should go back to school and take Men's Studies. I'd be way ahead of the game, since I was already familiar with most of the material.

I was about to pack it in for the night, when, at the tail-end of a study on twenty-first century pay disparities, I found a single, obviously misfiled paper on the scientific theory of "Hormone Wash" — some chemical *presto chango* that would turn a female fetus into a male one, if the right cocktail was applied at the right time. I read through the paper as best I could — there was so much of it that was beyond me — but at the end it was clear that it was being presented as speculation only, a tantalizing theory that apparently had no hope of ever reaching anything as practical as a clinical trial. I scrolled back up to the introduction. The paper dated from forty years ago. I couldn't find anything more on the subject, but then I had sampled only a few of the files in the cabinets. Intriguing idea, if I understood it correctly, and then I realized that I really didn't understand it at all, any more than I could follow the dizzying downward spiral of alphanumerics that wove in and out of the chromosomal family trees.

I needed some help with this. I picked up my Fone and then hesitated before I punched in the number. The student records had been disappointing in terms of providing me with any indication of where to take the investigation next. The material in the middle cabinets was quite literally ancient history. No clues there. No red flags. No sudden hunches that would lead me off in a different direction. I wasn't sure that anything else I'd found would be any more relevant. I only knew that I didn't know whether it was or not. And that the cabinet had been locked. And that Inspector Trent had, for some reason, wanted me to have a good look at whatever was in there.

I called the number Jo Hines had given me.

"Hi there." Her voice was husky.

"Did I wake you?" It was close to one a.m., but I didn't want to take the chance of missing her if I waited until morning to call.

"Well, yeah," she said, "but that's okay."

"Can you come over?"

"Now?"

"Oh, well, I guess not," I said. "It is kind of late, isn't it? Tomorrow? I'd really like to see you."

"Mmmm, I'd like to see you too." She was getting into the swing of things for the sake of listening ears. "But you know what? I'm tired of being indoors. I'm inside all the time. Why don't we go to the park? We could have a picnic."

It would be freezing. I'd have to dig out my heavy gloves and some sort of headgear that featured earflaps. Not exactly the alluring picture I wanted to present for a date with Jo Norris Hines, but I could understand her caution.

"Listen, have you got a portable Vu you could bring? I got some great pictures from last weekend. You're going to want to take a real good look at them."

"Oh my," she said. "Pictures? I hope they're not dirty."

And we spent the next five minutes in a very silly conversation that featured a number of juicy anatomical references. I hoped the Darme who was listening got a kick out of it.

CHAPTER 11

We'd arranged to meet at the fountain in the middle of Belo Park. It was a good choice for a tryst. It's a popular place in the summertime, with little wading pools set all around the fountain, the spray gently blowing onto the kids who paddle under the watchful eyes of their parents. There are paths that lead under the shade of the big maple trees along the river, a bowling green, tennis and badminton courts, and numerous benches for those who like to sit and watch the birds, or read, or just bask in the warmth of the sun.

Nearly as many people use the park in the deep of winter, when the city plows a section of the frozen river for ice skaters. Then the fountain area is surrounded by kiosks that offer hot chocolate and bear claws, extra mittens and skate sharpening.

In the late fall, though, when the bitter winds had started to blow but there was no snow to play in, it was mostly deserted, the leaves lying in heaps waiting for the city to take them away, the trees slowly revealing their skeletal winter forms. There were still occasional joggers and walkers along the paths, but the fountain was silent, the benches empty.

We found a sheltered corner at the edge of the park and hunkered down on a bench that had been shoved up against a stone retaining wall. It offered at least a modicum of protection from the wind. It was the first time I'd sat beside Jo Hines. There had always been a gurney or a table between us. I could smell the scent of her shampoo every time she moved her head.

I filled her in on the pertinent details of the great office break-in caper, and the subsequent, puzzling assignment by Trent.

"How odd. It's almost as though she's cleared the way for you."

"I know. If I didn't know better, I'd think she wanted me to figure out what really happened to the Longwell girl."

"Do you think that's possible? That she would do that?"

"I don't know. I'd have figured that she'd never buck a Darme order, but unless it's just some strange coincidence, that's the only conclusion I can come to. It sure is a useful development. Or it will be if you can make sense of some of the stuff I found."

I transferred a sample of the genetic mumbo jumbo onto her Vu. "It's way too complicated to try to read on a Fone screen. There's a bunch of other stuff, as well, but there's no need for you to go through it all. Mostly student files and history papers. But I don't get these."

She quickly scrolled through a few of them.

"These are gene charts."

"Yeah, I figured that much out. Each one seems to be tracing a particular genetic trait, but I'm not sure what. Is there any way you can tell?"

"Hmm ... not really. It's a fairly complex transmission. It could be any one of a number of syndromes. It looks to me as though the first page is missing. That's where you'd expect to find a legend, or at the very least a title, with an indication of what they're charting."

"Like a legend on a map, explaining what the symbols represent?"

"Yes, exactly," she said. "Otherwise it makes no sense." She peered at the Vu again. "There is a number on the top of the pages. I expect it's the study number. If you can find some sort of master list, you should be able to correlate the numbers and find out the particulars."

"Okay. Maybe I just missed it. I haven't had time to go through everything." That was good. It would give me something specific to look for, instead of randomly selecting files and hoping to find a smoking gun.

"I can tell you one thing about them — they're old. They pre-date Mighty Mite."

"How do you know?"

"There are male offspring. See?" She pointed to a line halfway down the Vu screen. "The circle with an arrow indicates a male, and he's the son of the individuals denoted in the line above."

I peered at the screen. I hadn't realized that before. Just more historical crap, then, like all the papers in the middle cabinets. So much for Gerrity's files pointing me in the right direction.

"Okay, I've got one other file to show you. I can't make anything of it at all." I fed the paper on hormone wash theory into her Vu. "What do you make of this?"

"Hmm." Her eyes were darting rapidly back and forth across the page.

"What do you think?"

"Shush, this is complicated."

I shushed. The sun peeked out from behind a cloud and I leaned back on the bench and closed my eyes. And then Hines moved and I caught her smell again. I opened my eyes and turned my head slightly so I could watch her read. Sitting on the bench like she was, immersed in what she was reading, she reminded me even more strongly of Georgie. The profile, the set of her mouth, the way her brows furrowed as she concentrated. But Hines was the polished version, a diamond that had been cut perfectly. The rough edges had been sanded down, the color enhanced. Hines was burnished to a brilliance that Georgie had never attained. I closed my eyes again. *You're a fool. Give it up, give it up, give it up.*

I'd hauled my old winter coat out of the closet for this meeting in the park, and as the wind picked up and started to blow into our corner, I shoved my hands in the pockets. I hadn't cleaned them out before I'd put the coat away the winter before and now I found the usual junk that takes up residence in my pockets — pieces of paper with important reminders written on them, old Kleenexes, both unused and otherwise, a couple of small denomination credits, receipts, one mitten, and, way down in the corner of the left-hand pocket, a mini chocolate bar. I drew it out. It was a little squished, but I was pretty sure it was no more than a few

months old. Besides, chocolate doesn't go bad, does it? I
began peeling back the wrapper.

At the rustle of the paper, Hines looked up from her Vu.

"Oooh, you have chocolate?"

"Only a little."

"Are you sharing?"

"I'll give you half if you tell me what that paper means."

"Okay." She held out her hand.

"Say pretty please." I waggled it a little, but didn't move
it any closer to her outstretched hand.

"No." She made a quick grab for it.

Her sudden movement took me off guard. I pulled the
chocolate bar out of her reach, lost my balance and fell back
across the seat of the bench.

"Give it to me!"

She was practically on top of me as she strained to reach
the chocolate. We were both laughing and neither of us
noticed the approach of a jogger.

"Oh, hi."

Oh, shit. It was Nguyen. I sat up.

"Oh, hi Susan. Jo Norris Hines, this is Susan..." Oh cazzo,
I'd forgotten what Nguyen's full name was.

"It's Susan. Susan Ife Nguyen." She glared at me, but
nodded at Hines.

"Pleased to meet you," Hines said.

"I work with Mac," Nguyen said. She was polite, but stiff-
mannered, and I could see that Hines was puzzled by her
coldness.

"Oh," Hines said. "We're ... um ... friends. Mac and I."

"I can see that," Nguyen said. "Well, I'm off. See you at
work, Mac." She jogged away.

"Well, that was silly," Hines commented as soon as
Nguyen was out of earshot.

"And awkward."

"Problem?"

"No, not really. She's just got a ... bit of a crush." Just like
I do, I thought. And it's just about as pathetic. Before Hines
could make any comment on the folly of workplace romances,
I broke the chocolate bar in two and offered her the tiny piece.

She popped the morsel into her mouth and closed her eyes as she let it slowly dissolve. Only when it was completely gone did she turn her attention back to the paper.

"Well, it was an interesting bit of reading," she said, when she finally finished. "An intriguing theory."

"Had you ever heard of it?"

"Nope. Of course it dates from forty years ago. If it had been a valid approach, I'm sure everyone would have jumped on it. It would solve so many problems."

"You mean in terms of making babies more available?"

"Probably in terms of ensuring the continuation of the human race." Her face was serious now, the chocolate-inspired delight wiped away. "Have you ever heard of something called the Founder Effect?"

"Not really."

She sighed. "Okay — brief history lesson. After the human male died out, most fertilization was accomplished in a fairly straight-forward way using raw material that had been banked previously."

"Was there a lot of it?"

"Yes. Years ago, when it became apparent that the effects of Mighty Mite were unlikely to be overcome, there was a concerted effort to collect gametes from the small pool that still existed, including those from recently deceased individuals who had been unwilling to cooperate."

"Dead bodies?" For some reason, I was mildly shocked by this.

"I know. It sounds macabre, doesn't it? But it ensured our continuation. For a time, anyway. The problem is, in terms of a gene pool, it was pretty limited. There are problems."

"This Founder Effect thing?" I guessed.

"Yes." She paused for a moment. "This is a really simplified explanation, okay?"

"Simple is good," I said. "I don't have any background in this stuff."

"Any genes that are present in the donor, that pre-dispose to anomalies or disease, can get passed along to the offspring. Depending on the abnormality, it might not be a problem unless the mother carries the same gene. Even then, it might be a problem for only some of the offspring."

"But don't they screen for that stuff?" When Georgie had applied to the Parent Program, it had been an endless round of physical and psychological testing.

"Yes, they do. That's why it's so difficult to get approved. You have to be careful, you see, because a problem arises when the kids grow up and want kids. You can't go back to the same paternal donor line, because the chances of triggering an abnormality are so much higher — it's … well, I don't know the exact odds because it's not my field, but it's certainly much, much higher."

"And with each passing generation, the problem gets worse, because you've got a smaller and smaller pool of useable material to choose from," I said. Just like the schematic I'd found that charted the transmission of color blindness. The more you use the same old mixture, the better the chance of having it go sour.

"Yes, that's it exactly," Hines said. "It severely limits the number of children that can safely be made, and researchers have been looking for some way around that for years."

"But isn't that why the SoCens are so anxious to get a GeneShare Treaty? New blood and all that?"

"GeneShare would solve the problem for a while, but ultimately you would run into the same difficulties again. Worldwide, it's just too small a pool. Besides, a treaty would be far more advantageous to them than it would to us. They have a relatively small amount of banked material. But even with their new material, we'd eventually run into the same problems again."

"So we're faced with the ultimate choice of extinction, or a world full of gimps? Is that what you're saying?" It seemed like a Hobson's choice to me.

"Well, 'gimps' is pretty ungenerous."

"I'm not a generous person."

"I noticed," Hines said. "I had to wrestle you to the ground to get a piece of chocolate."

"No, you wrestled me to the bench."

"Same thing," she snorted. "Anyway, extinction isn't really in the cards. They're having a lot of success with some kinds of gene therapy, to eliminate some of the most straightforward of the problems, but they've been successful with only a limited number of congenital disorders. It's incredibly expensive, and it can't be done on a large scale. So, no, we won't die out, but neither can we reproduce ourselves at a replacement level."

I was stunned. Like most people, I went about my business and didn't pay much attention to anything that didn't immediately affect me. The thought that we might just dwindle away until we resembled little more than one of the tribes that live in the DK was sobering in the extreme.

"So the human population will just keep getting smaller and smaller, unless somebody comes up with something," Hines went on. "There are some geneticists who believe that eventually we'll evolve a completely different mode of reproduction, one that doesn't require a Y chromosome, but until that happens — say about a million years from now — we've got a problem."

"So why haven't I heard about this before?"

Hines rolled her eyes. "It's hardly a state secret. Anybody with any sense could figure it out in about five seconds."

Well, that was depressing since I hadn't exactly figured it out at all.

"Anyway," she went on, "I don't understand what all this has to do with our murdered girl."

"Neither do I," I admitted. "But I can't begin to figure things out until I know what it is I'm dealing with. I'm not even sure what I should be looking for in Gerrity's office. There may not be anything there to find."

"That's been the problem with this case all along," Hines said. "Everywhere you look, there's nothing to find."

"I found chocolate," I said.

Hines looked at me, puzzled at the change of subject until I held up the other half of the mini-bar.

"You want?" I wafted it under her nose.

"What do I have to do to get it?"

"I wouldn't be that mean," I said. "You more than kept your part of the bargain. Here."

I'd have given her all of the chocolate in the world just to keep her sitting beside me a little longer.

CHAPTER 12

The meeting in the park put me into a blue funk all evening. It reminded me all over again of why Georgie left, and, for the millionth time, I wondered if I'd been too stiff-necked, if I should have done whatever she asked.

She'd wanted a baby so badly. It must have been hard for her, going off to work every day and looking after other people's kids. She hadn't ever wanted to do anything but work with little ones — she'd told me that many times — and her enthusiasm for it was unflagging. When she came home from the Child Center every evening she would be full of the little milestones that each of her charges had reached, a first word, a first step.

It wasn't surprising when she began putting on the pressure for us to have one of our own. I didn't mind the idea of a daughter. Georgie would make a wonderful mother. I would muddle along in her wake, like I always did.

The initial application process for the Parent Program was intimidating in the extreme — an endless series of psychological testing, designed to measure how well we would do as parents, how prepared we were for the commitment. I was sure all along that I would blow it somehow.

I must have given at least some right answers though, because we got the okay for Georgie to go ahead with the physical testing. She had been over the moon the day we got the notification, hardly able to stop herself from crowing the news out to whoever we passed in the street.

That night, in bed, we talked about names. What would flow nicely with MacHenry Berri? I vetoed any of the flower names that were so popular, like Lily or Rico or Lan, or the most popular of all, Hyacinth, a name bestowed in honor of Hyacinth Belo Bree, the famous hero of the Testosterone Wars, who had been the leading figure in bringing down the last male stronghold at The Seige of Monte Castra.

Not very many people know this, but it's the ridiculous first name I've been saddled with. A mania for naming children after famous historical figures had swept NowZo right around the time I was born. As a result, I'd gone to school with any number of Hyacinths, as well as a few Belos and Brees; either, in my opinion, would have been a preferable choice.

I'd shelved the name when I was fourteen and refused to answer to anything but my middle name, Carson. Georgie called me Carsey sometimes and that was okay. Then, when I joined the police force, everyone just started calling me Mac and that was fine too.

Georgie hated her name as well. "Georgina is so old-fashioned," she said. "All those old names that get shortened to Jack and Sam and Billy are off the table, as far as I'm concerned. Besides, have you ever noticed that all the biggest women have these delicate flower names, while all the frail little things have really direct names like Ed?"

Or Jo. Such a tiny, ethereal woman. And just as tough as nails, so maybe her parents' choice hadn't been that far off base. I'd bowed to Georgie's insistence, however, that those names be excluded from the list of potentials. We spent hours discussing what should be included instead.

The psychological testing proved to be a walk in the park in comparison to the physical testing that Georgie went through. There were many days off work — for both of us — Georgie for the tests and me to hold her hand. When the verdict came, it was devastating. A baby was just not in the cards for Georgie, they said, something to do with a malformed uterus. Not impossible, but improbable, and there was too much at stake to take a chance on anything that wasn't a sure bet.

I should have seen it coming, I suppose. It was, after all, the next logical step in the baby quest, but for some reason I was completely unprepared for it. A few days of mourning, and suddenly the subject was out there in the open.

"I don't know, Georgie," I said. "I'm not sure I'm ready. There's too much going on at work."

"It's only nine months," she pointed out. "All you have to do is carry it. I'll look after her."

It was a lot more than nine months. There would be testing for me too. Then the procedure itself, and the gestation time, the recovery time, the necessary time off work until everyone was sure that the child was thriving and could safely join a baby program. Not to mention the nitty gritty physical stuff, like morning sickness and the delivery and lactation.

"Well, so what?" Georgie said. "Women do it all the time. Besides, you'll probably make more on maternity allowance than you do with the police."

That was a low blow. As the director of a Child Center, Georgie made heaps more money than I did, but she'd never made an issue of the fact that she covered the lion's share of our household bills. I should have realized then how desperate she was.

"I don't know, Georgie..." I was finding it hard to put my objections into words. How to explain that, unlike most women, I had no overwhelming desire to experience the apparently soul-affirming process of producing a new human life. I found the prospect of being an incubator unappetizing. I'd gone along with the whole baby idea just to make Georgie happy, and on the assumption that it would be her, not me, who would do the actual producing. I didn't mind at all being a parent who would rock and walk and cuddle and play, even change diapers from time to time, but I was completely unprepared for the discomforts of actual maternity.

My profound reluctance turned into stubborn resistance. Things changed. The apartment was no longer a place of music and laughter. Georgie fell into what I realize in retrospect was deep depression. We stopped talking. I started avoiding the apartment, working longer and longer hours, volunteering for cases no one else wanted, just so I wouldn't have to go home.

She left about a year later. She was very generous and left me both the apartment and all of the things in it. Things we'd collected over the years. Things we'd bought together.

She wasn't long finding someone new. I heard through the grapevine that they have a little girl now. Believe it or not, they called her Rose. Would've been over my dead body. Or my live one, I guess.

My rather maudlin reverie was interrupted by a call. Ricky.

"I've cracked it, but I don't know what it is," said the voice on the Fone. No preamble. No introduction. Just a bald statement of fact. That was Ricky. "You wanna come over?"

I squinted at the time icon. Eleven already, and I had to work in the morning.

"Sure," I said. I had a feeling I wasn't going to be getting much sleep that night anyway.

There was a slurry of snow blanketing the deserted streets, and my wheels skidded and slipped on the greasy pavement. I chained my bike to the lamppost in front of the deli and plodded up the steps. Again, I nodded at the cameras installed on the landing, but when I reached the top of the stairs, the door was already open.

I stamped my feet to rid them of some of the muck that clung to them, even though I was sure that Ricky would never notice such a considerate gesture. From the look of it, her floor had yet to make the acquaintance of a mop.

"Hi." Her sallow face was lit only by the Vu screen as her hands flew across the text pad. "Come see."

I stood over her as I peered at the screen. There was only one chair in the whole apartment, and Ricky was already sitting in it.

"These are all genetic studies," she said, "but there's something wonky with them. They were super-encrypted. Big fat Darmes thumbmarks all over them."

I knew better than to ask how she knew that. "What's wrong with them?"

They were the same kind of complicated schematics that had been in the files I'd pinched from Gerrity's office, except that these appeared to be even more labyrinthine. Ricky scrolled down the screen rapidly as she talked.

"Okay, you start out, these are standard. Typical characteristic transmission, blah, blah, blah — but then — here." She stopped the dizzying scroll. "Something happens here and I don't know what it is. Some sort of catalyst was applied, and then the algorithm develops in a totally different way. A way it's got no business developing."

I looked at the section she was pointing to. It looked like complete gobbledygook, strings of alphanumerics and icons descending and branching and, for all I knew, doubling back on themselves. And then it all resolved itself at the bottom of the screen with a single symbol. A circle with an arrow jutting out from it.

This was far more complicated than the stuff I'd liberated from Gerrity's office and I struggled to understand what it meant.

"Am I reading this correctly?" I said finally. "It looks like the end product carries a Y chromosome."

"Yup."

"Is it possible that these are old?" I asked. "I saw something similar somewhere else, and someone told me they were archived studies."

Wordlessly, Ricky scrolled back to the top of the document. There was a date there. From two years previously.

"Holy shit."

"Indeed," Ricky said. "The holiest of shits."

Along with the dating info, the header at the top of the document also included the program title: "Project Bathwater." Alfie Longwell's fellow doctoral student Claire had been mining data from Project BW, according to her student records. They had to be one and the same.

How had information like this ended up on a student Fone? This was information worth protecting. My mind spun, trying to process the implications.

"So it looks like somebody's figured out a way to make little boys," Ricky said.

"At least on a theoretical basis. Is there any way to tell from this whether or not the theory has actually been put into practice?"

"No. But if you'd figured this out on paper, wouldn't you be dying to find out whether or not it really worked?"

She was right. Especially if what Jo Hines had said was true and as a species we were headed for an evolutionary dead-end. The scientists would be working overtime trying to make this work. And the government would be providing them with whatever they needed to do it.

If they were successful, the political implications would be immense. If our government — and it had to be government, no one could keep a program like this under wraps without the cooperation of the government — had been able to engineer a method of reproduction that no longer relied on the rapidly dwindling banks of existing genetic material, whoever controlled the process would control the world.

"The questions just don't stop asking themselves, do they?" Ricky said. "But my first would be, what happens after this?"

"What do you mean?"

"From what I've been able to figure out, the charts follow the process through to the point where there's a desirable end product. But that's only one generation. The acid test would be whether or not the end result is, in turn, capable of sustainable reproduction. I mean, that was the big stumbling block with cloning, wasn't it? It was pretty much a one-shot deal."

"And there were too many problems, even with the first shot. They'd have to make sure that didn't happen again, wouldn't they?" I said.

"There would have to be clinical trials, for sure. With real humans. After all, they thought they had all the bugs worked out of the cloning thing, but then they realized that you can't just test everything on rats."

"Wait a minute," I said. "What about Mighty Mite? Even if the male reproduced, wouldn't everybody still keep spitting out girls?"

She shrugged. "Yeah, but so what? The object of the exercise isn't to reconstitute an entire male population. It's to make sure there's a population at all. You don't need any more than a few of them to do that."

She was right. Over a lifetime, one male could father thousands of babies. Millions, maybe. Of course there was still the Founder Effect thing to get around. But what if someone had been able to mess around with the hormone thing and produce a male who could then be treated with gene therapy to screen out the worst of the inherited genetic abnormalities? Was it possible to pass on the new, improved DNA? I didn't know.

And the question — for me, anyway — wasn't really how it was done, but how it had led to Alfi Longwell's death. Her colleague Claire had been allowed access to at least some of the data from Project Bathwater because she was the star pupil of the Men's Studies course. Alfi was a good student too, according to her parents. Had the two been in competition for the position of research assistant that Alfi had been so excited about? And did the position have anything to do with Project Bathwater?

Just for a moment, I wondered if the story the Darmes had given us about Alfi's death was true. That Claire Sullivan had, indeed, pushed Alfi Longwell from a third story building in an attempt to eliminate the competition for a plum job. But Alfi's injuries didn't fit the story, not even to my untrained eyes, and certainly not according to the medical examiner.

I wasn't even sure why an academic like Gerrity would be involved at all in something that was, essentially, a mad scientist experiment. Unless the experiment had been successful more than once. If you're going to cook men up in a test tube, I suppose you'd need to know what to do with them after that. And Gerrity, with her lifelong study of the psychology and sociology of men, could well be one of the few people who would know.

"How many of these charts are there?" I asked.

"A bunch," Ricky said. "At least twenty."

"And is there any indication of where this document originated?"

"Other than Darmes files, no. It's pretty anonymous. Other than the date and the name, there's none of the usual stuff — no author, no credentials. There aren't even any parameters that I can find. Somebody could've just made it up, except that stuff people make up doesn't usually get super-encrypted."

"Is it possible that the author's name is Bathwater?" I asked. It seemed an odd thing to call an experimental program.

Ricky laughed. "Oh MacHenry, you are so slow. Didn't your granny ever tell you not to throw the baby out with the bathwater? Except in this case, they're hanging on to both."

I couldn't believe that hadn't occurred to me. Whoever had named the project had a really warped sense of humor. But then the whole thing was warped, if what I suspected was true.

"Somebody wiped this Fone, didn't they?" I asked. "Everything but this program?"

"Yeah. They disabled the leash and everything, but they couldn't do anything about the encryption program or the files it contained. You have to have special software. It's an added security feature."

I didn't ask her how she knew that. She probably wrote the program. What I did need to find out was whose Fone this had been. It couldn't have been Alfi's, or Hana's either. No student would have information like this, all sewn up in a Darmes file. I wondered if one of them had stolen it. If it had been Alfi, she may well have been killed because of it. And maybe by the Darmes. The thought sent a chill through me. The Darmes are spooky and furtive, but would they really bump somebody off to protect a state secret? And yet this thing was deep, deeper even than Ricky realized. What had I gotten myself into?

"Well," I said, "this certainly gives me some avenues to explore." Which was the understatement of the century. My back was sore from the crouched position I'd been in and I groaned a little as I stood up.

"Want some painkillers?" Ricky asked. "I've got lots. Anything you like."

"Nah, I'll be okay," I said. "So, what do I owe you?" I usually paid Ricky in credits, but my finances were at an unusually low ebb just then, even for me. I wondered what else she would take. If she had a stash of painkillers, the answer was probably almost anything at all. I'd file that piece of information away for someday when I needed it.

"You?" she said. "You get off easy. I haven't had so much fun in a long time." Without taking her eyes from the screen she reached down and plucked an old envelope from the teetering pile of papers to her right. She held it over her shoulder so I could take it. "It's my shopping list. I hope you can read it."

I don't know what I'd expected, but when I glanced at the scrawls on the back of the envelope, I realized that it was exactly as she'd said. "Tea. Kleenex. Bread. Marmalade. Eggs." The list went on and on. She was apparently out of everything.

"I'll bring it to you tomorrow after work."

She nodded. She'd loaded up a different set of files into her Vu and was engrossed in following a long string of code. "See ya."

I closed the door quietly on my way out.

Just as I stepped out into the street, I caught a glimpse of someone disappearing around the corner of the next building. I stood and watched for a moment, but whoever it was didn't reappear. It could have been an ordinary pedestrian, out for a midnight stroll. But it was such a filthy night, and something in the way the figure moved made me think of Nyguen.

CHAPTER 13

There was a party in progress when I arrived at the office the next morning. It was only a few minutes after nine, but a bottle of champagne had been popped open and was half drunk already. Diva Davis and her crack team of steely-eyed detectives had, according to her, solved the Tanaka Tyler kidnapping case. They were jubilant. Inspector Trent stayed in her office, turning a blind ear to the whooping and a blind eye to the drinking, as was her wont whenever something happened to make Division look really good.

Even though, as it turned out, it wasn't exactly any fancy footwork on Davis's part that had solved the case. The kidnappers had been stopped at the border. There had been something not quite right about the forged paperwork they carried. Further investigation revealed that the little girl matched the description that had circulated widely. Fingerprints were matched. The border guards' suspicions were confirmed when one of the kidnappers attempted to bolt. End of story.

Davis had set up one of the office Vus to play the latest newsfeeds, which were making the most of the successful conclusion of the operation. There was an interview with one of the border guards, who modestly stated that she had just been doing her job; with one of the child's parents, who was just thankful to have her baby home again; and with Davis. There were hoots and hollers and whistles when Diva's face came on the screen and claimed that it was the detailed description she had circulated that had been responsible for alerting the guards.

Coverage of the sensational case dominated the feed, pushing other news aside, but eventually everybody who could comment on the kidnapping had had their say, and the announcer went on to election coverage.

In a dramatic about-face, Prime Minister Miller Singh announced today that trade talks with SouthCentral Zone will resume next week. At a supporters' rally last evening, Singh confirmed that negotiations regarding the contentious GeneShare Treaty will be included in the talks. Issues regarding GeneShare have formed a major roadblock to reaching an agreement to date.

"We are now open to the possibility of exchanging currently existing reserves of genetic material with SouthCentral if it will facilitate a resumption of normal trade between the two zones," Singh was quoted in a soundbite. *"I have every expectation that SoCen will lift the embargo of their products in the very near future."*

Another cheer went up in the room.

"Kidnappers caught, chocolate back on the menu — how great is that," Diva crowed.

"Oh I see, you're responsible for the chocolate too, are you?" I shouldn't have said it, but I couldn't resist.

"Mac thought I should be looking for big bad kidnappers out in the DK," she said, to more raucous laughter from the rest of her team. "In the DK. Like anybody out there has the wits to pull off a kidnapping. Maybe we should have been searching the DK for hot chocolate and coffee as well." She snorted and slugged back another mouthful of champagne.

I ignored the shot. Instead, I tidied up a little paperwork and then left for the university to continue my pretense of cataloguing the contents of Professor Gerrity's office. I'd have a good look for information on Project Bathwater, but I was sure that it had long since been scoured from the files. I had a suspicion that the paper on hormone wash theory was directly related to the charts on the Fone, but the only reason I'd found that was because it had been put in the wrong drawer. Even with Gerrity's chaotic filing system, there was unlikely to be anything more.

At some point though, I was going to have to present Gerrity with an inventory of some description. It wouldn't have to be accurate, just reasonable. Apparently she didn't know what she had in there anyway.

While I rode along, my mind kept going back to what Davis had said about the DK, and the ability of its inhabitants to kidnap. Davis was correct, if it came to a regular snatching. There were just too many security measures in place. Border guards, security cams, fingerprints, a paper trail. The arrangements had to be pristine, and that would require a well-organized and well-heeled organization. But what about the little girl I'd seen with the sakers? Or the baby that had yet to be born? For the moment I set aside the question of where those children had come from, and thought about how vulnerable they were. Even if Jo Hines's conjecture about their mothers being recent converts was true, none of the usual protections were in place to keep them safe. Sakers didn't fingerprint. They didn't register. They didn't report crimes to the police. The kids were sitting ducks for anyone who had a mind to pick them off, and it would be surprising in the extreme if someone didn't decide to take them.

I'd suggested a kidnapping bandit group to Davis just to wind her up and, with any luck, send her off in the wrong direction. But was it so improbable? If I was a bandit, and there was a stray kid or two floating around the DK, I'd certainly consider snatching it. It would mean big money, especially if there was little likelihood that the snatch would ever be reported. So how did the saker group ensure that it didn't happen? Because they were under Darmes protection, that's how, and that's why I'd been challenged by the cop posing as a crazy old woman. And the only reason I could think of for the Darmes to be doing that was if the saker group was being used for something. Was it possible that the settlement I'd found really was the "oriole camp" Claire Sullivan had referred to, and that the sakers were being used as test subjects for Project Bathwater? That part of Claire's post-doctoral field studies included monitoring the results of the project? That would explain why she knew that Alfi had been nowhere near the camp. Because Claire had been there herself.

I pulled my bike over at the corner of Eston and Brant when I realized that I had just narrowly missed running down a pedestrian. I just sat there, straddling the bike, while I turned the idea over in my mind.

In terms of keeping the project secret, the sakers would be an excellent choice. They kept to themselves. They lived in a place seldom visited by outsiders. They weren't registered anywhere, for anything. They hid whenever anyone came near. Station a few Darmes around, just to keep an eye on things, and it was unlikely that anyone would ever notice anything unusual. And even if they did, there were Darmes right there to take care of it.

That made sense from the point of view of whoever was running the project. What I didn't understand was what the sakers were getting out of it. Parents want children so they can raise them, not so they can be whisked off to some government facility and used for scientific experiments. If Project Bathwater really was generating little boys, it would only make sense to keep them in a high-security facility somewhere, not in a saker camp in the middle of the DK.

Maybe I had it all wrong. Maybe Hines was right and the pregnant woman I'd seen was a recent addition, who had gone through the regular Parent Program and had suddenly seen the light or found the holy spirit or whatever it was sakers did, after she'd been approved and was already pregnant. But if that was the case, I was back at square one, with not a single notion of where to go next. One step at a time, I decided. Just keep looking and maybe the pieces would start to fall together.

— 《》 —

Gerrity was in her office when I arrived. I nodded a greeting to her and went straight to the filing cabinets where I pulled a file at random and punched some meaningless numbers into my Fone. I would wait until I was alone before I started rummaging for more misfiled information.

I figured there was no point in trying to track down Claire Sullivan. She had been extremely upset the day I'd seen her and had been talking about changing the topic of her dissertation, but she'd had some time to calm down and I doubted that she'd gone through with her threat. It would mean a whole lot of hard work down the drain, not to mention the probable forfeiture of the research position. Chances were she'd had time to consider her options and decided to stay the course. I would be unlikely to get any information out of her, and just the fact that I'd been asking would no doubt alert the Darmes.

Alfi Longwell's friends were a different matter, if only I could find them. I'd looked for the brown-haired girl every time I'd walked across campus, but she was nowhere to be seen. I didn't dare risk fishing through uni records. Too many red flags would go up. I supposed I could get Ricky to crack into them, but I liked to keep the Ricky option for the big stuff. I should be able to figure this out on my own.

I wondered about the student choir that Alfie had belonged to. When I checked on my Fone, the club still listed Alfie's pod as the contact. Good. The Darmes still hadn't realized their omission. It should be safe to snoop around there.

The group's WirePage had a new photo up, taken by the student newsfeed at a concert the choir had given two days previously. It was slightly out of focus, the faces indistinct, so I clicked the Pix icon and some more shots came up, including a close-up of three singers caught in mid-warble. The girl on the end was unmistakably the same girl who had cried over Alfi Longwell's lost poems. And underneath the photo, a cutline with the names of the girls. She was Hana Banerjee Williams. Lux. Lux and luck. Just what I needed.

The rehearsal schedule was posted at the bottom of the main page. And there was one scheduled for that day at noon.

"How much longer are you going to be at that?" Gerrity asked. I jumped a little. I'd been so absorbed in what I was doing, I'd forgotten she was still in the room.

"Almost done."

"And is it getting you any closer to finding out who broke into my office?" She sounded exasperated.

"It's beginning to look like it was a student," I said. "Probably thought they could improve their grades by fiddling with the records."

"Well, that's just stupid," she said. "The marks are all recorded in the central pod."

"Well, some students aren't very bright," I said. "Of course, I expect you get the cream of the crop, don't you?"

"I only wish. Most of them are here because they figure it's a gimme grade."

"Oh gee, that must be frustrating. No up and comers?"

Gerrity smiled. "Every now and then you get some really brilliant students. And then it's a joy."

"What does one do with a major in Men's Studies?" I asked. "I mean, what are the employment opportunities? Teaching, I would expect."

"Well, yes, that would be the usual track, but there are some openings in the field."

"Really?" I said. "I hadn't realized that. Do many of your students go that route?"

"Well, just the post-grads. You have to have an advanced degree."

"And I take it there aren't many of those?"

Gerrity's eyes narrowed for a moment, uncertain at the turn the conversation had taken, then she stood up and began stuffing papers into the oversize tote that was sitting on one corner of her desk. "Oh, dear, I'm late," she said. "I'm sorry, I have to leave now." She leaned over to reach for a stack that she had piled to one side, and, as she did so, her elbow knocked the tote to the floor. Its contents spilled everywhere. The papers she had already collected skidded across the tile and in their wake, four or five pens, a couple of lipsticks, a handful of credits, two combs, a Fone, a bottle of aspirin and an ID tag on a chain.

She gasped and then bent over and began picking up the items. I rushed over to help. I jogged a handful of papers together, and in the process of gathering them, managed to push the ID tag under the desk. I shoved the papers into the tote, then grabbed a pen and a few of the credits.

"Oh, dear, I'm such a klutz," Gerrity said. "Thank you."

"Let's just make sure we've got everything." I said. "I think some things rolled away pretty good." I got down on my hands and knees and shoved my head under the desk.

The ID was not from the university. It was a swipe card from the Cedar Lake Center for the Control of Communicable Diseases. There was a picture of the professor, with a long identification number underneath and, off to the side, an issue date. It had been handed out two days after Alfi Longwell's death. I grabbed it, straightened up and gave it back to Gerrity.

"Oh my goodness," she said. "Thank you. I'd be in big trouble if I lost this again."

"I think that's everything," I said. "You'd better hurry — if you were late before, you're really late now."

She bustled off, still shoving her belongings into the tote as she went.

Cedar Lake. Alfi Longwell's home town. With a big research facility just north of it. A facility that Professor Gerrity had recently been issued a pass to. I went back over to the student records drawer and pulled Claire Sullivan's file. She had been given access to Project Bathwater data at the beginning of the semester, three, nearly four, months ago.

If Gerrity had been working closely with the project, she must have had security clearance long before the issue date on the card. She said she would be in big trouble if she lost her ID again, implying that she had lost at least one already. Maybe Alfi had nicked it. Nicked it and gone snooping. After all, she had the perfect excuse to be in Cedar Lake. Her parents lived there. Had she gone to the facility north of town and stumbled onto something she wasn't supposed to see? Something to do with Project Bathwater. If I were trying to hide something from the general public, I could think of no better place than a remote laboratory dedicated to research on communicable disease. No one who didn't work there would risk going near it. There could be anthrax or ebola or trench fever or who-knows-what floating around, just waiting to jump on you.

But if Alfi Longwell had been caught snooping through the Cedar Lake labs, it made sense to come to the conclusion that she had been killed by either the Darmes or the security guards at the center. Could either of them have been responsible for the carnage that had been inflicted on her? I suppose they could have been responsible for the gash in her head, but they certainly wouldn't have subjected her to the rest of the damage, or sexually assaulted her. It was such a brutal murder that, even if I could make myself believe that someone in authority had killed her, whether by accident or by design, I couldn't bring myself to believe that they had done it so viciously.

I shoved Claire's files back into the student record section under "M" and turned to the only two drawers I hadn't really gone through yet. The two bottom drawers of the middle cabinet. Nobody keeps anything they need very often in the bottom drawers. It's too hard to bend down that far. If Gerrity had misfiled any more information on Project Bathwater in either of these, it could well be years before she realized her mistake.

I found a whole lot of history, as I expected, but as I skimmed the file tabs, I realized that it was a history that I knew nothing about. *Sexual Exploitation of Minors in the 20th and 21st Centuries*; *The Role of Male Bonding in Gang Rape*; *The Psychology of Pedophilia*. There was paper after paper documenting unimaginable crimes: abduction, rape and murder of small children; multi-generational incest; rape as an institutionalized weapon of war; child pornography; bestiality; something called "snuff films," in which helpless victims were tortured and murdered in front of a camera, all for the gratification of some weird and perverted taste. It went on and on, case after case of nasty, twisted, sadistic violence. This went far beyond anything I had ever seen before or anything I could ever have imagined. It made the silly sex games at Sarong's club look like a kitchen party, fantasies played out by willing participants in games of make-believe, with no real danger, no peril, called off when everyone had had enough. The victims detailed in these files had not been willing, and at no point did they have the option to say "enough."

Jo Hines and I had looked for a monster to explain Alfi Longwell's death. I had just found it. The monster lived here in these old, dead files from a history we had all but forgotten.

I slammed the drawers shut and leaned against the cabinet for a few minutes to try and clear my mind of the horrific images that had been called into it. Men's Studies was a far darker and more complex topic than I had ever imagined. I wondered that a fluttery and disorganized creature like Professor Gerrity could have chosen a field that brought her face to face with such malignancy.

I abandoned the search of the filing cabinets and just sat in Gerrity's chair until it was 11:45 and time to leave for the auditorium. Then I pulled myself together and set off to find Hana Williams.

— «» —

There were already a handful of girls clustered around the stage, chattering away, and I waited until several more had filed in before I slipped into the room and took a seat at the back and well away from the central aisle.

As a very thin and smiling woman entered through a side door, the girls lined up on the stage, books in hand.

"Shall we try *Birth of the Universe?*" the woman said. She blew into a pitch pipe and held her baton aloft. The girls found their note and with the baton's down stroke, launched into the song. It was quite beautiful. I closed my eyes for a few moments just to listen to them sing, letting the music wash over me and rinse away the filth I'd found in Gerrity's office.

Choirs aren't popular, as a rule. I've heard musicians complain that choir music, particularly the classical material that was written hundreds of years ago, can't be performed well by an all-woman choir. There is a preponderance of soprano voices, with no one to take the deep bass parts that anchor the music. A friend of Georgie's had once played me an old archived recording from a zillion years ago, and I could hear what she meant about the low parts, but I pissed her off when I suggested that there was nothing to be done about the lack and she should just get over it and enjoy what's available.

Even so, a couple of the girls in this choir had quite deep voices which wove in and around the high notes. To my untrained ear, it sounded lovely.

The smiling woman tapped her baton on the stand in front of her. The girls stopped.

"I don't think the altos quite hit that A flat in the middle of the phrase," she said. "Let's try it again from the top." Again, she gave them the note and raised her baton, and again on the down stroke they began.

This time my eyes swept along the rows, looking for Hana Williams. She was in the back row, third from the right. I was sure it was her. I'd wait until the end of the rehearsal to see if I could get her away from friends and get her to talk to me. Then I closed my eyes again and let myself get lost in the music.

Three quarters of an hour later, the rehearsal ended and the girls filed out. A few of them gave me puzzled glances as they went by, but no one challenged my presence. Hana was among the last to leave. I stood up when she drew level with my row. Her eyes widened when she saw me.

"What do you want? Haven't I answered enough of your stupid questions?"

"Well, Hana," I said, "my question's not all that stupid. Where did you get the Fone you sold the other day?"

She gasped and glanced at the two girls she had been walking out with.

They both shot me questioning looks. "Are you okay, Hana?" one of them said. "Do you want us to stick around?"

"No, it's all right," she said. "You guys go on and I'll catch up with you."

They didn't like this idea much, but I could see that Hana didn't like the idea of them listening to what I had to say either.

"It's okay. Really," she said. "Go."

The friends reluctantly turned and left the auditorium.

I waited until I heard the door slam shut before I said, "Well, Hana? The Fone?"

"I... A friend gave it to me."

"No, she didn't."

"I ... I thought it was hers, but it wasn't."

"Look," I said, "I'm not a Darme. I don't give a shit whether someone gave it to you or if you stole it. I'm just trying to find out what happened to Alfi Longwell. So why don't you stop lying, because you're not very good at it."

"If you're not a Darme, then who are you?"

"I told you before. I'm Detective Carson MacHenry of City Police." I flashed up my badge.

"Why should you care what happened to Alfi?"

"Because I saw her dead body. It wasn't very pretty. Your friend Jazz is right. She was murdered and the Darmes are covering it up. I want to know why."

Tears welled up in her eyes. "All the stuff on *IMeMine* was gone. There were poems there that Alfi had written for me. I thought maybe she would have copies on her Fone."

"So you went to her room."

"Yes. I found it then."

"That's bullshit, Hana. The Darmes cleared her room long before they got around to removing love letters from *IMeMine*. So when, exactly, did you go to Alfi's room?"

Her eyes darted from side to side — in my experience a sure sign that someone was trying to fabricate a story that they figured would fly.

"C'mon, Hana — I really don't care why you took the Fone. Just tell the truth. For once."

She swallowed hard and looked at me. Now we were getting somewhere.

"Alfi said she was going home for the weekend, so I knew her room would be empty."

"And you had a key?"

She nodded. "I hated it when she went home. There was this girl that she talked about sometimes, an old girlfriend who still lived in Cedar Lake. I was pretty sure Alfi was still seeing her, all the time she pretended she was with me. I thought there might be some photographs or something. You know, of Alfi and this other girl."

A girl in Cedar Lake. An old girlfriend. Lisa-at-The-Market. Lisa, who was apparently a much better liar than Hana.

"This was right after Alfi left?"

"Yes. And then I found this Fone. A really spiffy one. It wasn't Alfi's — or not the one she used all the time, anyway.

She would have taken her regular Fone with her to Cedar Lake. I thought maybe it was the other girl's or something. I tried turning it on, but it wouldn't boot up because I didn't have the password."

"So who did you take it to?"

"Jazz. She's really good with electronic stuff. I was just going to have a look and then put it back in Alfi's room. I swear." Hana was snuffling by then, clearly upset that I might think she was a common thief instead of just a jealous lover.

"So Jazz got into the files?"

"Yes, but she wouldn't let me look at them. She said it wasn't Alfi's Fone and there wasn't anything there that was any of my business. She fiddled around with it for a while and then she handed it back and told me I should get rid of it. 'Smash it with a hammer and throw the pieces in a dumpster somewhere' was what she said. I don't know why. And then we heard that Alfi was dead." The tears started to roll down her cheeks in earnest then. "And then the Darmes came around and asked questions about a Fone that was missing and I got really scared."

Jazz must have disabled the leash and erased as much as she could when she was "fiddling around" with it. Otherwise the Darmes would have simply tracked it down from the signal rather than asking about it. She must have been puzzled by the encryption icon. I didn't think she could have opened the files — it would have taken someone with Ricky's talent and experience to do that — but I wondered if she had copied them to her own Fone. And what else she had discovered from the files that hadn't been so heavily secured.

"But you didn't destroy it like Jazz told you to," I said to Hana.

"You have to understand," she wailed. "Everything of Alfi's was gone. Her Vu, her books, her clothes. That was the only thing of hers I had."

"Knock it off. Jazz had already told you it wasn't Alfi's."

"I thought she was lying," Hana mumbled. "And when I turned it on again, I realized that it had been wiped. The only thing left on the screen was this weird icon. I thought maybe Alfi's texts were there. But I couldn't get them open."

"So you decided to sell the Fone."

"It was top of the line. I mean really, really good. Better than anything I'll ever have, but I didn't dare use it because the Darmes were being so nosy." She glared at me defensively. "I know, I should have smashed it like Jazz told me to, but it was a perfectly good Fone. I figured if Jazz couldn't open those files, nobody could."

"And you needed the money."

"Not for me!" she protested. "I was going to use it to put flowers on Alfi's grave." She began to cry hard then. "I really, really loved her and I figured it was the least I could do."

I ignored her sobs. "I need to talk to Jazz."

"She's not here," Hana blubbered. "She left yesterday."

"Do you know where she went?"

She shook her head. "I didn't talk to her. I've been kind of ... avoiding her."

So she wouldn't have to answer a direct question about whether or not the Fone had been destroyed, I'd warrant.

"Okay, what's Jazz's real name?"

"Talerian. She's Jessamyn Huerta Talerian. Listen..."

"If I figure out what happened to Alfi, I'll let you know if I can."

"No, what I was going to say is, do you have to tell anybody what I did?"

I shrugged and then she scurried away, blubbering into a Kleenex as she went. — «» —

The easy way to track Jazz Talerian would have been to access student records from the office, but I was unwilling to alert the Darmes to the fact that I was looking for her. Besides, I didn't have to. There's no point in having an advantage if you don't use it, so I walked to the central administration office and flashed my badge at the woman on the desk.

"I need to check a student record," I said.

This woman wasn't easily impressed by badges and barked orders, though.

"Which student, and with respect to what?" she asked.

"Jessamyn Huerta Talerian, with respect to the break-in at Professor Gerrity's office."

"Oh," she said. "I've just been processing her file."

I'd have preferred a chance to rummage around in a file room somewhere, to see what else I could find, but I'd take what I could get. I opened the folder the woman handed me. You've gotta love these uni packrats — everything has a paper back-up. Sure enough, just as Hana said, Jessamyn Huerta Talerian had left university, at least for the time being. I noted that she had left her options open, though, citing the intention to transfer to another institution.

And then I found her forwarding address. Cedar Lake. Well, well, well.

I thanked the woman and handed the file back. I walked outside, straight across the street to a café, where I ordered a pot of tea and sat back to think, annoying the couple at the next table by drumming my fingers on the tabletop while I did.

"Could you please stop that?" one of them said.

I'd been so deep in thought I hadn't realized what I'd been doing. I apologized, but I couldn't seem to stop doing it. Eventually they got up and left.

There were no other customers in the restaurant, so I flipped out my Fone, deactivated the ID and leash and dialed the number that had been listed in the records under Jazz Talerian's home address.

Someone picked up on the third ring.

"Is Jessamyn there?"

Hesitation, then, "Who's calling please?"

Not "Jessamyn doesn't live here," or even "Jessamyn's not home." Lux. Lux and luck.

"I'm calling from the administration office at the university. We have some transcripts that we need to send her, and I'm just calling to verify that this is the correct address." I recited the information that had been in the files.

"Yes, that's correct," the voice said.

"So if I send them there, she'll be sure to get them?"

"Yes, I'll make sure she gets them."

"Okay, thank you. You know students — they move around so much. Sometimes it takes months for things to catch up with them."

"If you send them here, I'll make sure she gets them right away," the voice answered. "Thank you." And then she disconnected.

I was puzzled. I had expected more prevarication. The woman on the Fone had made no attempt to deny that Jazz Talerian was reachable at that address. She'd taken off from the university, but she hadn't run far. She'd gone home. And if I could find her that easily, then the Darmes would most certainly be able to as well. I'd have to be very careful not to draw any attention to the girl. At least not until I had a chance to talk to her.

I entered "Cedar Lake Research Center" into a search window and the Wire spat out the facility's page.

The Cedar Lake Center for the Control of Communicable Diseases provides national leadership in public health through surveillance, detection, treatment, prevention and consultation services. The Center provides both direct diagnostic and treatment services for people with diseases of public health importance, and analytical and policy support to government and health authorities.

It was typical, non-specific, all-encompassing government speak. I clicked a few links at random and found a report of a salmonella outbreak due to the consumption of tainted shellfish, a media fact sheet on influenza epidemics, a report on the rising prevalence of Lyme Disease and other dangers posed by the increasing invasion of wildlife into populated areas, and a list of the adverse effects that could follow immunization for whooping cough. No mention of reproductive technology or genetic therapy. That, apparently, was not within the purview of the Cedar Lake Center.

It wouldn't be, of course. Those centers were in the cities, where they could be reached easily by those accessing their services. The one that Georgie and I had gone to had been downtown, right on the edge of the city center. I supposed it made sense to locate a facility that deals with dangerous and communicable diseases in a sparsely-populated part of the countryside, just in case something gets away from somebody. But it was also the perfect place to locate a secret government program. All of the laboratory equipment and specialized personnel would be right on site with a perfect excuse to be there.

Everything was leading me back to Cedar Lake.

Whatever was there, it was big stuff. Dangerous stuff. For a moment, I considered just letting the whole thing drop. After all, if I was going to be perfectly honest with myself, the only reason I'd taken things this far was in a fairly pathetic attempt to impress Jo Norris Hines. And even if I uncovered proof that there was some secret breeding program that used sakers as guinea pigs, who was I going to tell? Any agency I turned the evidence over to would promptly destroy it, and I would no doubt be incarcerated somewhere for a nice, long rest. Besides, I still had no real evidence that any of it had anything to do with Alfreda Lucas Longwell's death.

The café had been playing music — background noise that normally drove me crazy because it made it harder to think — but now the waiter switched the feed over to the news.

"If you don't mind," she said, grinning at me, "I just want to find out how soon we can get coffee again."

"Can't be soon enough for me."

"You got that right. We're a café, not a tearoom."

Prime Minister Miller Singh's about-face on the inclusion of the GeneShare Treaty in trade talks has resulted in a bump in popularity for her party, according to several recent polls, the newscaster said, *although it has left many in the current ruling government scrambling to provide an explanation for the abrupt departure from Singh's previous position. Opposition leader Littlecrow blasted Singh at a recent rally in Westtown, calling it a blatant and cynical move to ensure victory in the upcoming election.*

A sound bite followed, featuring Littlecrow calling on the electorate to reject the attempt to manipulate them. Lots of luck, I thought. All anybody really wants right now is a cup of coffee and a chocolate bar.

Consumers have demonstrated approval for Singh's stance, now that previously unavailable SouthCentral products will once again be shipped to NowZo. The Minister of Trade and Commerce estimates that imports will have reached their normal levels by the end of the month.

"Yeehaw," said the waiter. "I've missed the coffee crowd." She turned the feed back to the music station that had been on before.

It was easy enough to dismiss it all as just so much politics, but Singh's policy on sharing genetic material with anybody else had seemed pretty much set in cement up until then. It was odd timing. If it was a necessary ploy to win the election, I wondered why she hadn't realized it at the beginning of the campaign, instead of waiting until halfway through. Maybe she hadn't realized how unpopular the embargo would make her. Maybe she hadn't realized what a strong run Littlecrow would make. Or maybe something else had happened to change her mind.

I went to the site that stored archived newsfeeds and found the announcement from that morning:

"We are now open to the possibility of exchanging currently existing reserves of genetic material with SouthCentral if it will facilitate a resumption of normal trade between the two zones."

Current. Existing. Nothing at all about a potential new source. Something had happened in the last day or so to change the equation.

Everything was leading me back to Cedar Lake all right, but before I went chasing north again, I needed to check one more small detail. And that would take me back to the DK.

CHAPTER 14

I tried to call Jo Norris that night, but I kept being routed to her message pod. Nor was she available the next morning. She hadn't said anything to me about taking time off and wherever she was, she wasn't checking her messages. Or at least, she wasn't checking mine. I tried not to let it get to me. Ours was a working relationship. She wasn't accountable to me. If she wanted to go off somewhere for a few days, she was perfectly at liberty to do so. I kept telling myself this. It didn't do much good.

I didn't bother going back to the university. I'd gleaned more than I wanted from Gerrity's files. I'd assembled a half-assed inventory from what I had already. I'd hand it in to Inspector Trent as soon as I went in to work the next morning, so it would look like I'd done something.

As it turned out, Trent wasn't in her office. I left a message that the file was available in her private pod, then I grabbed my bike and rode out of the city.

I wasn't too worried about going into the DK on my own this time. I was reasonably sure that Nguyen would be close by. It was too much of a coincidence that she'd jogged through the park on the same afternoon that I'd met with Jo Hines. And I may just have been paranoid, but I was also sure that she had been waiting outside Ricky's that night. She was supposed to be working on the robbery case, not following me around, but she'd promised all too quickly to cover my back. Trent had ordered her to tail me. It was the only thing that made any sense.

I didn't bother trying to cover my movements either. There was no point. If I was right about Nguyen, she would tell Trent where I'd gone anyway.

When I reached the edge of the city, I had to stop for a moment and think about how I'd found Oriole Avenue the first time. The street I'd followed had been blocked by a mass of concrete, and I'd gone east, back toward the city for about a half an hour, until I'd cleared the wreckage. After a couple of tries, I found the street that fringed the city limits. At least I think I did. It was reasonably clear, but in the DK one wrecked building looks pretty much like every other wrecked building, and everything is so covered with vegetation that identifiable landmarks are scarce. It was taking me in the right direction anyway. I guesstimated where I'd turned north again and when I checked my locator, it confirmed that I was on the road that led me to the foot of Oriole Avenue. I followed it like I had the last time, riding as far as I could, then getting off my bike to push when the ruts and potholes grew too deep to ride safely.

I stopped when I reached the upthrust pillar that guarded the entrance to the saker camp, but I couldn't find the tunnel that would lead me in. So much of everything in the DK looks the same — concrete blocks collapsed on concrete blocks. Jagged rebar poking out everywhere. Piles of broken bricks that I was sure hadn't been there before — evidence of how quickly everything out here was falling into the ground.

Finally, I just stood and closed my eyes. My intention was to listen for signs of life. That was what had led me to the camp before. This time it wasn't my ears, but my nose, that led me to the right gap in the jumble of cement. The smell of smoke. I opened my eyes again and scanned the sky. A misty wisp of whitish-grey smoke was rising from somewhere behind me and to my right. I turned around, and there, just behind a mound of rubble, was the tunnel.

I pushed my bike through the narrow passageway and again found the clearing deserted except for three chickens pecking in the dirt in front of the campfire. I knew that dozens of eyes were watching from the shadows.

"I know you're there." I flashed up my badge and held my Fone in the air so they could see it. "I mean you no harm. I was here before. I want to talk to your leader — your elder."

I hoped that was the right term. It's so hard to keep the terminology straight with these religious groups.

I walked out to the center of the clearing. "I'm not leaving until somebody talks to me."

"She's not here." The voice floated out from behind a slab of concrete off to my right.

"Where is she?"

"Gone to God."

If that meant what I was afraid it did, I suppose it should have been no surprise. She'd looked old and rickety enough to have keeled over the moment my back was turned.

"Who is the new elder then?"

"There is no new elder."

I experienced the frustration I always felt whenever I tried to talk to these nutty groups. They spoke in riddles. What did this one mean?

"You must have an elder. Someone to lead you."

"She's gone to God."

I tried a different tack. "Where is the pregnant woman? The one I saw before."

"Gone to God."

"And the child?"

"The child is safe."

"The child is safe here?"

"The child is with God."

Great. It appeared that everyone I wanted to talk to had ascended to a higher plane or something.

"I'm sorry," I said. It seemed like a stupid thing to say, but what else was there?

"Do not be sorry. It is a holy child."

"Holy? In what way?"

"It is born of God. And God shall reign supreme as it is foretold in the holy scriptures.

And the beast came up and swallowed them whole and there was great lamentation and the fruits of the earth multiplied not, yet the children of God did not despair and stayed in the faith. And then God came down to the earth and called to the faithful to go ye forth and multiply in the way of the Lord...'

That was enough for me. Once these people got started with the quoting, they went on for hours, and it was all just more of the same. You only have to hear the first bit and you've pretty much got the message. I turned and wheeled my bike back through the tunnel, the weight of all those eyes on my back as I left. When I reached the other side, I stopped and rested my elbows on the handlebars while I tried to sort through what I had just heard, but it was all such a load of gobbledygook that I wasn't really sure that there was any meaning at all. If I'd arrived at the clearing and discovered the child and the pregnant woman pottering around happily in the midst of the chickens and the flapping laundry, my entire theory would have been in danger of falling apart. I would have concluded that the sakers had nothing to do with Project Bathwater, or the Prime Minister's abrupt change of policy, or with Alfi Longwell's murder.

I had really expected to be simply told that they weren't there. The sakers aren't given to providing much in the way of detailed information — but the fact of their absence would have been enough to tell me that I was on the right track.

But "gone to God"? Wasn't that a euphemism for "dead?" You heard that phrase sometimes, from the older folks who still attended church, except that they usually said "Goddess."

If the sakers were being used as guinea pigs and they'd all died, then something had gone sadly awry with Project Bathwater. But then why would the Prime Minister have changed her mind about the GeneShare Treaty?

My mind was spinning as I kicked my bike into gear and rode back along Oriole Avenue. Suddenly I heard someone yell. The sound bounced off the masses of concrete and echoed all around me. For a moment, I wondered if the saker group was under attack, but then, in spite of the distortion, I realized who it was.

Cazzo. I'd forgotten about Nguyen.

I initially thought that the noise might have come from my right, but the echo was deceptive. When I ran to that side of the road, I saw that, beyond the line of sumac that grew along the shoulder, the roadbed had completely fallen away, the asphalt and gravel tumbled down into the ditch below. Then she screamed again, and this time it sounded like it came from over on the left. I threw the bike to the ground and scrambled through the bank of bushes and grapevines.

Nguyen was sitting in the middle of what once might have been a parking lot, her bike lying beside her. She was surrounded by three people, who I figured, by their dress, must be scavengers. One of them had a Fone — presumably Nguyen's — and was gleefully pushing buttons. Another had taken her WhamGun and was pretending to threaten the third with it. I fumbled to flash up my badge.

"Back away." I reached for my own gun and held it at the ready.

The scavengers looked up in alarm. When they saw the badge they slowly backed away.

"Throw the gun down on the ground."

The Scavenger with the WhamGun tossed it at Nguyen's feet while the other hastily handed her Fone back. Nguyen scrambled up, brushing the grit from her trousers. Oh, Nguyen, I thought, no. Get the gun before you worry about your clothes. Didn't they teach you anything at Police College?

"What do you think you're doing, attacking a police officer?" I asked.

"We didn't know," one of them whined. "She looks just like everybody else."

"Why are you attacking anybody?"

"We just wanted to see. We weren't going to take it."

"Bullshit."

By this time, Nguyen had recovered her wits enough to get her gun in hand.

"Put your hands on your head," she ordered the group.

"Oh look who's the big tough cop now that she's got help," said the woman who had been fiddling with the Fone.

Nguyen would have gone after her with her WhamGun if I hadn't stepped between the two.

"That's enough out of you," I said to the scavenger who had spoken. "Now get out of here, and I don't want to hear any more of your nonsense."

"But…" Nguyen was wide-eyed and outraged.

I ignored her. "This is a warning. Now skedaddle."

Two of them shuffled off muttering, climbed over a pile of cracked cement blocks and disappeared. The third followed, but slipped at the top of the wall, affording a glimpse of a jean-clad leg.

"Why'd you do that?" Nguyen was fussing with her stained clothes again.

"Do you really want to march them all the way back to the city so you can book them?" I asked.

"Oh." She stopped and considered this for a moment. "I guess not."

"Besides, they aren't scavengers anyway." I bulled my way through the scratchy brush back toward where I'd left my bike. I had little reason to believe that it would still be there. Anything that isn't nailed down is up for grabs in the DK. I didn't know how I was going to explain how I'd lost it and I sure wasn't looking forward to riding pillion behind Nguyen all the way home.

To my surprise, there was a saker standing guard over it. I wasn't sure how much protection she would have been if anyone had come along determined to take it, but I appreciated the gesture. She stepped away when she saw me and floated toward the stone tunnel.

"Thanks," I said.

She turned to look at me. "Covet not thy neighbor's ass," she said vaguely, and then she melted away into the ruins.

— «» —

Nguyen was still looking pretty shook up by the time we reached the edge of the city, so I signaled her to pull over as soon as we came to a reasonable-looking rest stop. She scurried into the washroom to finish pulling herself together while I grabbed a couple of bottles of water from the take-out window. I sat on a nearby picnic table until she came out.

"So…" I said, handing her the drink.

"So, if they weren't scavengers, who were they?" she asked.

"Darmes."

"No way." Her eyes were wide. "How do you know that?"

"It doesn't matter how bold muggers are, they usually disappear as fast as they can when they see a cop."

"But they didn't know I was a cop," she protested. "I didn't identify myself."

"First of all, why not? But never mind. That's why they took your Fone and your gun. To check your ID without making it too obvious."

"But…"

"And the one that fell? She was wearing jeans under her desperado outfit. Designer jeans. I recognized the stitching along the side." Cazzo crap but the Darmes were sloppy sometimes.

"Oh," Nguyen said. "I noticed that too. It did seem odd."

It was cold, sitting outside, and I cradled my hands in my armpits for a moment before I spoke. "Why are you following me Nguyen?"

She had been about to take a sip of water, but she jerked a little and spilled some down her chin.

"I just … um … you know — want to make sure nothing happens to you."

"I think it's probably the other way around, judging by what just occurred," I pointed out.

She blushed. "Er … um … yeah I suppose."

"C'mon Nguyen, you've been following me around like a bad reputation. I'd like to think it's because you're enamored with my pretty face and scintillating personality, but not even I'm willing to buy a story like that. Give."

"But you are … you know … really attractive." And her face turned even redder.

"Knock it off. Trent sicced you on me, didn't she?"

"What makes you think that?"

"Do you know what I'm working on right now?"

"Well, not Accident, I know that," she said. "Something to do with the break-in at the university."

"And something more than that." I wasn't sure how much to tell her. It was a given that she was reporting to Trent, and I wasn't sure I cared anymore, but how much did she need to know? I didn't want to dump Nguyen into the middle of a Darmes case. If things went haywire it might mean the end of her career as a police officer, and I wasn't sure she had that much of one anyway.

"Okay, here's the deal," I said. "I know Trent has detailed you to follow me. I don't know why, but there's something really freaky going on. I'll make it easier for you." And for me, I thought, but that was beside the point. "Instead of scuttling around behind me, you can just come with me."

"Okay," she said, and it was almost all she could do not to wiggle like a happy puppy. Maybe there was something to the crush theory after all.

"But — and you'd better think about this — you do what I tell you, when I tell you and you don't ask questions. You can pretend to Trent that you're still tailing me."

"You know I have your back," she said. "I promised that day in the restaurant."

And somebody somewhere give her a pat on her little puppy dog head, she meant it. I just hoped she'd manage to stay out of the way, because my back was starting to feel like it had a big fat target painted on it.

"What did Trent say to you anyway?"

"Just that you were investigating a case kind of on your own, and she wanted to make sure you didn't get yourself into trouble."

So it hadn't been an accident that Trent had cleared the way to Gerrity's files. The question that was starting to bother me, though, was whether she had she set me up from the beginning, or was just taking advantage of how the whole thing had played out.

"Do you know anything about her?"

"The inspector? What do you mean?"

I wasn't sure what I meant. "Anything … personal? I mean we all know that she's a stickler for discipline and a neat freak and all that, but I can't recall having heard anything about her other than work-related stuff. Of course, I don't hang out much with the other cops, so I don't know what they say about her."

Nguyen shrugged. "Not much. We all figure she's a solitaire. I mean, you never see anybody with her, do you? And I don't know how you could be that fussy and actually live with somebody else."

Unless the somebody else was just as fussy as she was. I didn't like where this was going.

"What does this have to do with what you're working on?"

Good for you, Nguyen. You finally figured out one of the right questions to ask. That didn't mean, of course, that I was prepared to answer.

"I'm not sure. I'm not sure of anything. As soon as I am, I'll let you know."

I slurped back the rest of my water and put the bottle in the recycle bin. "Let's go."

CHAPTER 15

Jo Norris called the next morning.

"I got your messages," she said. "Sorry I was out of town for a few days."

"But now you're back."

"Yeah, what's up? You want to do lunch or something?"

"Why don't we just meet for a drink after work?"

"Sure." She sounded puzzled. Every other time she'd suggested a meal, I'd jumped at the chance. But I needed a day to sort out how much information I was going to share with her. I'd been hot to tell her about the files Ricky had sucked out of the stolen Fone and to ask her what they meant. Suddenly I wasn't so sure I wanted to share that intelligence with anybody.

I needed to regroup.

We named a place and a time and, when I buzzed out, I grabbed a pen and went looking for paper. Although there was a tremendous amount of paper in the Division office, it was all pre-printed forms. All you have to do is enter your data on a text pad, and there's a program that puts everything in the proper spaces. Then the printer spits it out. There didn't seem to be a single sheet of blank paper anywhere.

I grabbed the top layer of bike theft reports that I hadn't yet reviewed and signed off on. There was some faint, grayish printing on the back of them, but if I pressed hard, I should be able to read what I'd written. We did have two machines with word-processing capability, but I was pretty sure that everything that was entered on them was automatically uploaded to the Division's central site. I didn't think, however, that anybody had yet figured out a way to co-opt old-fashioned pen and ink. Besides, nothing would clarify my thoughts better than laboriously writing them out.

I started with the initial hurried postmortem and worked my way through the meetings with Jo Norris Hines. When I put it all down in black and white, her motivation for pursuing the case seemed flimsy and false. It had made perfect sense to me at the time. Maybe I'd just been blinded by the thrill of being noticed by a creature I'd admired from afar for so long. Sort of like Nguyen wanting to be seen at a bar with me. Pathetic, isn't it?

Whatever the actual mechanics of the genetic hocus-pocus, it seemed clear from the files I'd found that there was some kind of secret experiment that involved both the government and Professor Gerrity. Whether or not the sakers were involved depended, I supposed, on what the saker woman meant by "gone to God."

Gone to God. It is a holy child. It is born of God.

I stopped writing and entered "sakers" into Search on my Fone. Everybody knew about sakers in general terms, but, like everybody else, I'd never paid much attention to the specific details of their beliefs. I mean, they were crackpots, right — why bother?

There were three hundred and sixty-five pages of references. I went straight to the *KnowItAll* site. I hate to admit it, but that's where I get most of my information. Nothing in depth, but you couldn't beat it for a quick overview.

Sakers — the slang name given to a number of anachronistic religious groups, from the word "Forsake," after the signs they frequently carry during public demonstrations.

A history of the different saker movements followed, which I skipped over, instead going straight to:

Beliefs: These vary from sect to sect, but generally speaking most saker groups believe that the rise of the so-called "Mighty-Mite" virus, and the subsequent disappearance of the male gender, is a punishment from God. Saker groups eschew modern technology, claiming that it is the core cause of the calamity, and their followers are urged to "forsake" most common scientific applications and treatments. Only by doing so, they claim, can the earth be restored to its previous, balanced state.

A list of the different major saker sects included: *The Children of Eden, The World Coven of the Creator, The People of the True God, Heaven's Omen,* and *The Sisterhood of Serene Acceptance.*

I wasn't sure at first which sect my little band of dementos subscribed to until I read what followed.

The Children of Eden, The World Coven *denominations and* The Sisters of Serene Acceptance *follow the teachings of Saint Meerakaatakilla who (according to the sakers) predicted the fall of man and foretold the subsequent rebirth of the world. The prophecy that is most often quoted to substantiate Meerakaatakilla as a prophet is:*

"...and the beast came up and swallowed them whole and there was great lamentation and the fruits of the earth multiplied not, yet the children of God did not despair and stayed in the faith. And then God came down to the earth and called to the faithful to go ye forth and multiply in the way of the Lord..."

Multiply in the way of the Lord. Which, according to Saint Meeraka-what'sit was the only way you should be making a baby. The old-fashioned way. A man and a woman. And sex. But for that you needed a man. A handy little Y chromosome popping up somewhere in the family tree.

The Meerakaatakillian sects have diverged in their thinking over the last fifty years, as The Children of Eden *and* The World Covenanters *became less conservative and allowed their members to more fully integrate into mainstream society, although both sects continue to denounce modern reproductive technology.*

The most fundamentalist of the sakers, The Sisterhood of Serene Acceptance, *adhere most strictly to the basic philosophy, rejecting a modern way of life in its entirety. They continue to inhabit the outlying and decayed regions of urban areas, awaiting the time when God returns to the earth and calls to the faithful to fulfill the prophecy.*

Cazzo crap on a cracker. If you ever wanted a bunch of people to be the guinea pigs for a secret government program, you could hardly ask for anything better than *The Sisterhood of Serene Acceptance.* Secretive, isolated and convinced that they are on a holy mission. The sheer cynicism of it was enough to turn my stomach.

True enough, it was a willing participation, but there was also every possibility that the outcome would be as devastating as the cloning experiments had been. What would happen then? Would the *Sisterhood* be left to cope with the damaged results? Even if the project was a resounding success, what were they getting out of it besides some sort of religious validation?

Children to bring up in their wacky way of the Lord? I had assumed that the child I'd seen was a little girl, because, honestly, what else could it be? But what if it was a little boy — the result of "natural" fertilization and a good old dose of chemical soup? And the Darmes were there to protect him.

Then God came down to the earth. And I'll bet anything he landed in Cedar Lake.

After I'd written down everything I could think of, I wasn't sure what to do with it. Shredding it would have been the sensible thing, but I was reluctant to destroy the only record of everything I'd discovered. I folded the papers up and stuck them in my pocket, then I went looking for a Fone.

Nguyen had been pushing papers around on her desk, waiting for me to finish. As soon as I headed toward the door, she stood up and grabbed her coat.

"Let's cruise those shops again," I said. "That stolen gear should have turned up by now." I said this in a loud voice. Everyone else in the office looked up at the sound, then realized that it wasn't anything they needed to pay attention to, and returned to their paperwork.

Nguyen looked puzzled. "But I thought you were..." And then she caught herself. "Yes, let's check again."

Although I was officially assigned to Accident Investigation, I doubted that anyone would remember that. It just wasn't that important in the normal course of things, and everyone would assume that Nguyen and I had been partnered again,

We drove our bikes back to the seedy cluster of shops that we'd cruised the first time. I wanted to stay away from *Previously Enjoyed*, just in case the owner remembered that I'd already bought one Fone from her and questioned why I was buying another so soon. *Angel's* would be a good bet for what I wanted.

"Wait here," I said to Nguyen, and left her sitting with the bikes outside.

Angel rolled her eyes when she saw me and, as soon as I saw all the new stock piled on the counter, I knew why. We'd cased the shop once. She hadn't expected us to return quite so soon.

But all I wanted was a burner Fone. In anticipation of the fine that she knew was about to be levied, she overcharged me for it. I should have gone somewhere else. I was beginning to get a little worried at the amount of money I was spending on this case. Technically, I should have been able to claim it all from the Division's expense fund, but that always involved a lot of explanation and paperwork, and I usually didn't bother. Besides, it wasn't an official case and, in spite of Trent's informal approval, asking for money might raise too many questions about how I'd been spending it.

I slid the Fone into my pocket and studiously ignored the pile of goods at the end of the counter. I'd have bet even money that they were the stolen Vus we were supposed to be looking for. I'd make Nguyen's day.

"I think we have a bite," I said to her when I reached the corner where she was waiting. "Why don't you go in and make the bust. I'll sit with the bikes."

She'd been looking kind of glum when I'd rejoined her, but now her face brightened. Her stock would definitely go up with Trent if she recovered a cache of stolen property, even if we hadn't actually caught the thieves. Getting stuff back for people made the police department look good.

I waited until she disappeared inside the shop, then I dialed quickly.

She picked up on the first buzz. "Yeah?"

"Hello, Mother."

"Yeah?" Ricky was good at covering her tracks. She never mentioned a name if she didn't have to.

"Can you encrypt this number and call me back?"

"You got it."

Registered Fones were monitored routinely, and an important tool in any cop's arsenal was the ability to trace someone's movements through their calls. What most people don't realize is that burners can be traced as well, just not so easily. They aren't registered to a user, and by the time the monitor has caught up with the number, the Fone has been discarded. That should have been enough, but I wanted to go one step further, just in case. Ricky had a way to jam the signal somehow, and, to tell the truth, it wasn't the first time I'd asked her to cover my tracks. Maybe I was being unnecessarily paranoid, but it would make me feel a little safer. It would cost me, though.

The Fone buzzed a few minutes later.

"What do you need?" Ricky asked.

"Nothing right now. Just to know you're there."

"I'll be listening." And then she disconnected. For someone who spends so much time snooping, Ricky is a singularly uncurious character.

Nguyen had wasted no time nailing the shop owner. A few minutes after I got off the Fone, a couple of uniformed cops arrived to take custody of the goods. Nguyen emerged, smiling and excited.

"Good work," I said.

"Well, we still haven't got the thief. There was a name on the paperwork, but I'll bet it doesn't pan out."

"Doesn't matter. People will get some of their stuff back, that's all they really care about."

"Um," she shifted her weight from foot to foot, "I need to go back to Division to file the report."

I checked the time on my regular Fone. "You know what? It's close enough to closing time for me. I'm going home." If I could get her to leave, it would save making awkward arrangements in terms of meeting Jo Hines.

"Okay, see you." She had one leg over the seat of her bike and was about to push off when I said, "By the way, we're traveling tomorrow."

She looked at me, puzzled.

"Wear something warm. We're going north."

— «» —

Hines was late. I'd already drunk half my juice by the time she arrived, uncharacteristically flustered. I'd grabbed the bench seat so she slid into the chair across from me.

"Hi," I said. "Did you have a good holiday?"

She looked puzzled for a moment, then recovered herself. "Oh, well, you look forward to these things while you're working, then after you get there, all you think about is work."

"I've found it helps if you go with someone — you know, sightseeing is more fun if you have someone to make snarky comments to."

"Yes, well, I guess it would have been. I should do that next time."

She was such a lousy liar. She ordered a glass of white wine and we waited in silence for it to be delivered to the table. She seemed uncomfortable with the lack of conversation and fiddled with her napkin while I pretended to check my messages.

"So," she said, when the wine had arrived and she'd taken a sip, "what have you found out?"

"Absolutely nothing," I said. "I'm beginning to think that we've been on the wrong track all along. Maybe the Darmes were telling the truth and the Longwell girl got pushed off a building."

"But that doesn't make any sense," Hines protested. "What about the strange injuries? And the stuff you found in the professor's office?"

I shrugged. "Nothing seems to fit together. We may be at the end of the road here."

The look of dismay on her face warred with a look of confusion. "Does this mean you're quitting the case?" she finally asked.

"Probably. It's taking up way too much time." I downed what was left of my drink. "Well, sorry, but I've got to get going. I've got a lot of stuff I've been neglecting."

I threw down a credit that would cover both our drinks and then I walked out of the bar, leaving her to finish her wine by herself. For some reason, she didn't much remind me of Georgie anymore.

CHAPTER 16

Even though Cedar Lake was serviced by rail, there were only limited runs available, so it was seven o'clock in the morning when Nguyen and I climbed aboard a train that would put us in Cedar Lake around eight-thirty or so, while its residents were just finishing their breakfasts and had not yet departed for work.

I had warned Nguyen to leave her Fone at home and I wouldn't let her board the same car that I did, just in case someone noticed us. I was still a little rattled by the speed with which the Darmes had cornered Nguyen. They were watching very closely, even though there was apparently no longer anything to watch. I hoped they weren't keeping such close tabs on Jazz Talerian. They'd questioned Hana, but it had been easy enough to find out that she'd been Alfi's girlfriend. All the Darmes had to do was look on *IMeMine*. They'd also probably figured out that Jazz and Alfi were friends; after all, they were from the same home town and they had continued to more or less hang out together in the city, but the fact that it was to Jazz that Hana had taken the stolen Fone argued for the continuation of a close friendship. As far as I knew, that was information the Darmes didn't have.

They didn't know about Lisa-at-The-Market either. They'd followed up, but not as thoroughly as I had.

Even so, if Jazz was holed up at her parents' house, she would be keeping a low profile. "I'm not afraid of the Darmes," she'd claimed. But she'd wiped everything she could from the Fone Hana had brought her. She must have had some idea of how important those encrypted files were. The last people she would want to talk to would be the Darmes.

At every stop along the way a few more women got on, and here and there I could see some that had that cop-look that gives me away so often. I could see them eyeing me, wondering why I was there. This was a change from the last time I'd ridden the train to Cedar Lake. Their awareness had been heightened by something. That was okay. With any luck at all, they'd conclude that I was a new security guard.

I'd grabbed some more paper and a pen before I'd left the city, and now I pulled out the notes I had made. I scribbled down the date and the time and the fact that I was on my way to try to find Jazz Talerian. Then I added Inspector Trent's name and message pod. I wasn't sure why I did this. It wasn't as if I expected anything to happen to me. But if something did, at least there would be a record of my last sighting. I just wasn't sure what to do with the paper. Nguyen would stick to me like glue, and wherever I ended up, she was apt to be there as well. On the other hand, if by some strange chance she wasn't, she would take them straight to Trent. I still wasn't sure what role my boss was playing in all this, but she was still probably the best bet to extract me from whatever trouble I was about to get myself into.

Nguyen and I were the only people to get off at the Cedar Lake stop. Too early in the morning for anyone but those reporting for the day shift at the disease center. I stood on the platform and looked up and down, as if I was expecting someone to meet me. Nguyen went straight into the station. I didn't follow her until the train had pulled away.

As had been the case with Alfi Longwell's house, it took all of five minutes to find the Talerian place. It was along a side street that was that funny mix of retail and residential that you see in small towns. The house was a brick story and a half with a detached garage, set back from the road and nicely treed. It would be well-screened in the summertime, but with the last of the leaves already fallen, I had a clear view of the property.

There was a small park with exactly one bench just down the street from the house.

"Go sit over there," I said to Nguyen. "Pretend you're feeding the birds and watch the house."

"What am I watching for?" she asked.

"Anything. People leaving. People entering. People moving around."

"Where are you going?"

"To have a look at some art."

There was a small gallery across the road. It was still early and off-season, so the store was closed. I stood at the window and admired the pictures anyway. Local artists, I judged. Lots of trees and flowers and scenic views of the lake. Probably none of it very good, but to me the canvases all looked like the trees and flowers and lake views they were meant to represent, which was my definition of good art. I'm a philistine. I'll be the first to admit it.

It was close to nine o'clock when the side door of the Talerian house opened and an older woman came out carrying a paper bag. The gallery had one of those recessed entrances and I ducked into the doorway as soon as the door opened. I could see the woman in the reflection of the plate glass.

She looked up and down the street, but I doubted she could see Nguyen from the front of the house. Then the woman went to the garage, opened the overhead door and disappeared inside. A few moments later, she backed a car out of the garage and turned onto the main street. I ran to the corner just in time to see the car turn left at the intersection.

Crap. I had no way to follow her. Almost nobody has a car in the city — it's far easier to bike everywhere, or catch a streetcar — but here in the country it made sense to own one. A four-seater vehicle that was really almost a truck would be worth the expense if you had to deal with snow-covered roads and a lack of transit.

Nguyen left her post at the park bench and ambled over to where I was standing.

"A woman came out of the house," she reported. "She went into the garage. Then she left in a car."

"Gee thanks," I said. "I might have missed that." Nguyen's lips twitched a little. Was it possible that she actually had a sense of humor?

"What do we do now?" she asked.

"I'm going to find us some hot tea. You can go sit on the bench some more."

"Why? The woman left." She was shivering. The park bench hadn't been nearly as sheltered from the wind as my recessed doorway.

"But we don't know if she was the only person in the house," I pointed out, with what I thought was a great deal of patience. "There might still be someone there."

She rolled her eyes and stomped back to take her seat once again in the park.

It was a short walk down the street to The Market. Not only was it the best bet for finding a warm drink, but I was hoping that the clerk, Lisa, would be working that day. She hadn't exactly been straight with me the first time I talked to her. Maybe, armed with that fact, I could get a little more information out of her.

With the sort of luck that I wish I had more often, she was working. It was still early and the store wasn't open yet, but as I cursed and was about to turn back, a bike rolled down the street and disappeared down the alleyway that led to the rear entrance. The rider was so bundled up, I couldn't be sure it was her, but I raced after it and caught up just as she was climbing off the bike and removing her helmet.

"Do you remember me?" I asked.

She squinted at me for a moment before she recognized me.

"Yeah, you're..."

"Never mind," I said. "Have you got a minute?"

"Not really. I'm supposed to be at work."

"It won't take long."

She shrugged and leaned back against the wall of the store.

"You lied to me," I said.

"About what?"

"About Alfi Longwell. You said you hadn't seen her in months. That you went out with her for a while when you were seventeen, but then she dumped you."

"Yeah, so?"

"You were seeing her all along. You saw her just before she died."

She shrugged again. "Yeah, we sort of hooked up again. She asked me to talk to somebody I know about a summer job."

"Does this somebody work at the disease center? Is that where the job was?"

"It was just a summer intern position. Nothing special."

Nothing special unless you were looking for a way into the place. And unless you had a stolen ID that would get you past the front office.

"What did you think when you heard she was dead?"

She glared at me. "What do you think I thought? The whole point of the job was so that she could spend the summer here in Cedar Lake. With me. And now she's dead. Because of me." She fumbled in her pack and extracted a pack of cigarettes and a lighter. She took one and cupped her hand around the flame while she lit it, her head down so she wouldn't have to look at me.

I felt a wave of pity for this tough girl who was carrying such a load of guilt. "There's a whole lot more to it than that," I said. "It wasn't your fault. What did your friend tell you about it?"

"Not much. Just that Alfi did the interview and then asked where the washrooms were. That she somehow got lost and there was an accident."

"I saw her body. It was no accident. It was murder."

She looked at me then. "Murder? Who would want to murder Alfi?"

"That's the question I've been asking myself ever since I saw the body."

"But—" She leaned back against the wall again and took a deep drag on her cigarette before she said, "Was it really bad? Her body, I mean?"

"It's the worst thing I've ever seen."

I waited. I hoped her guilt over what had happened would propel her toward a decision to trust something for once. It did.

"She wanted to get into the place because she was looking for something. She wouldn't tell me what it was, just that if she found it, it would mean that she could live in

Cedar Lake. I thought she meant with me. But maybe that's just what I wanted to hear."

It would have made more sense for her to wait until she found out whether or not she'd got the internship before she went snooping, I thought, but then I realized that she was working under a time constraint. She would have only a few hours, a day or so at the most, until Professor Gerrity reported the missing ID tag. But even then, what was her hurry? She'd been in the running for the research position, she could just have waited until that was sewn up and she would have eventually found out everything she wanted to know. Unless she already knew that the position was going to Claire Sullivan.

"Did Alfi say anything to you about how school was going?"

"Not a lot," Lisa said. "Okay, I guess. She really liked what she was doing. But I didn't understand a lot of it."

Welcome to the club.

"So where do I find Jazz?" I asked.

"What do you want with Jazz?" She looked wary, her defenses up again.

"I think she's got another few pieces of the puzzle."

She chewed her lip while she debated. "Do you really think Alfi was murdered?"

"Positive."

"She's at the cabin."

"Where's that?"

"North of here, not far, but you have to drive around Otter Lake to get there. Turn left at the corner here."

The same way the Talerian vehicle had gone. The woman must have been on her way to the cabin. That was too bad. I'd have preferred to talk to Jazz without a concerned parent hovering over her.

"Go about four klicks, then make a right hand turn onto the crossroad," Lisa went on. "Two, three klicks along, you'll see another smaller road. Follow it until you see a laneway on the right."

"Wait a minute — a laneway? You mean like a gravel road?"

"No," she said. "I mean like a laneway. A dirt road, like a farmer drives a tractor on. Don't worry, you'll find it easy enough. You'll see a big granite rock and a tree that's been struck by lightning." She stopped for a moment to think about this last instruction. "At least, the tree was there the last time I was. It may have fallen down, I don't know. But the rock will be there. It's about a kilometer in to the cabin."

"Okay. I think I've got that. Now — where's the best place to rent a vehicle?"

She laughed. "In December? There's no place. Only bikes and only in the summer."

Great. It was far too far to walk. The train had been such an easy, anonymous way to travel to Cedar Lake. I hadn't realized that it would put me at such a disadvantage once I got here.

"Okay," I said, "in that case I'm commandeering your bike."

"What?"

"I'll bring it back."

"Wait a minute…"

"Is it all charged up?"

"Yeah, but—"

"Listen," I said. "If I'm not back by the end of the day, you can report it stolen. In fact, I'll give you a number to call." I reached into my pocket and ripped a corner off one of the pieces of paper I'd stashed there. "Inspector Trent," I wrote, "City Police," and included the number and password for her message pod. I handed it to her. "Don't worry, Trent will look after you." I hoped that was true. In any event, Lisa-at-The-Market was one of the few people who both knew Alfi Longwell and who had managed to slip under the Darmes's radar, and I briefly considered handing the whole wad of papers to her to hold onto, but something stopped me. She'd been a lot straighter than the first time I'd talked to her, but that didn't mean she'd told me everything she knew.

"Okay," she said. "But you'd better get your ass back here by the time I'm ready to go home."

Nguyen was still waiting on the park bench when I pulled up on Lisa's bike. Her face was pinched and white, and she was shivering.

"Where's my drink?" she asked.

"No time," I said. "C'mon. We're taking a scenic tour."

"On that?" she said, looking at the bike. "There's only one helmet. And I'm freezing already."

"You take the helmet. If we get stopped, I'll pay the fine."

She made a funny mewling noise that was half-way between a groan and a whine, but she got up and got on the bike. Good old Nguyen following orders again.

We rode back down the main drag and turned left, my eye on the odometer. Right at the four-kilometer mark there was a paved road that branched off to the right. Not far down this, I found a marked crossroad, just where Lisa had said it would be. I was a little relieved when I saw it. It had occurred to me that she might be sending me on a wild goose chase — a big city cop given directions that would result in her floundering around knee-deep in a swamp or something. I pulled the bike over to the side of the road.

"What are you stopping for?" Nguyen asked. Her teeth were chattering so much it was hard to understand what she was saying.

"Just making sure there's no one following us." This part of the road was flat and straight and I could see behind me for quite a long distance. No traffic passed. It appeared that the Darmes weren't on my trail. I wondered if what I had said to Jo Hines about giving up on the case had been overheard and reported, and, as a result, they had relaxed their surveillance. Either that or they were far better at running a tail than I had ever given them credit for.

I turned the bike onto the crossroad. This was a much smaller byway of patchy paving and gravel, full of potholes that had collected water and then froze. I had to slow down and steer around these, as the bike tended to skid across them, and there were deep ditches on either side of the road.

"Keep your eyes open for a big rock and a tree that's been struck by lightning," I shouted back to Nguyen. She didn't answer. She had tucked her head against my back and I could feel her shivering. My eyes were watering badly and my nose was running from the cold, but I didn't dare let go of the handlebars to wipe my face. Even so, the laneway was unmistakable, although at some point the tree had given up and toppled over. But right beside it was a huge, pinkish chunk of granite, deposited as a signpost by some ancient glacier.

I slowed the bike to a crawl. There wasn't even any gravel to smooth the surface of the lane, just a hump of grass in the middle, bracketed by frozen ruts. I stopped. "We're walking from here," I said. "I can't drive on this."

Nguyen climbed off the bike and stamped her feet in an attempt to return feeling to them. "How far is it?"

"About a kilometer. That's not far."

"Hmmph" was the only reply I got, but she tucked her hands into her armpits and began to trudge down the lane. I was slower. I had to push the bike, but it wasn't long before my nose picked up the scent of wood smoke. We rounded a turn in the lane and there was a cabin, a familiar-looking four-seater vehicle pulled around to the side.

The cabin was long and low, with a wide veranda to take advantage of the view of the small lake that stretched in front of it. Tall trees, pine I guessed, crowded close to the rear of the building. It was a cottage, built mostly for summer use, but evidently outfitted to accommodate the occasional winter weekend. There were no signs of any other buildings on the shores of the small lake, no docks jutting into the water, no chimneys or peaked roofs thrusting up into the sky. Jazz Talerian hadn't exactly gone into deep hiding, but neither had she wanted to be easily available. This place would have been impossible to find without directions.

"What now?" Nguyen asked.

"I guess we go knock on the door."

"Do you think they'll let us inside?"

"I dunno," I said. "Just let me do the talking, okay?"

An older woman answered our knock, a glare on her face as she opened the door. It was the same woman we had seen coming out of the Talerian house in town. Probably one of Jazz's parents.

"Who are you? What are you doing here?" she snapped.

"I'm Detective Carson MacHenry," I said. "This is Detective Susan Nguyen. We'd like to talk to Jazz."

"She's already talked to you twice. Why don't you read the reports? She has nothing else to say to you."

"I'm not Darmes, ma'am. I'm City Police."

Jazz appeared behind her. "Oh," she said. "It's you."

"Do you know these people?" the older woman asked.

Before Jazz could answer, I held up the Fone that Hana had found in Alfi's room. "I thought you might like this."

Jazz's eyes grew wide, and then she said, "Let them in."

The woman hesitated. I could see that she really wanted to slam the door in our faces, but in the end she bowed to her daughter's instruction and pulled it open further.

The interior of the cabin was rustic, a couple of old sofas shoved against the walls, a rudimentary kitchen, an old pine table with mismatched chairs, and a doorway that most likely led to narrow sleeping areas. In the corner that wasn't taken up by seating there was a pot-bellied wood-burner stove that was chugging out a wave of heat. Nguyen rushed past me to get to it.

"You'll have to excuse my partner," I said. "She's a little frozen." So was I, after the long open-air ride, but I remained standing in the doorway, just far enough inside to prevent the woman from closing the door again.

"Well, all right," she said. "Come in."

As I walked into the room, Jazz said, "Where did you get that Fone?"

"From a junk shop. Your friend sold it. I bought it."

An angry look crossed her face. "Freakin' Hana, right?"

"Freakin' Hana," I confirmed.

"I told her to trash it. I told Alfi to trash it too."

"Jessamyn," the older woman cautioned. Then she turned to me. "I don't understand why you're here."

"I'm sorry," I said. "I didn't get your name."

"That's because I didn't give it."

I shrugged. I had no jurisdiction here and this woman knew it.

"This is my mother, Sonja Park Talerian," Jazz said. "Sonja, this is…" She stopped. "I'm sorry, what was your name again?"

"Detective Carson MacHenry. Capital City Police."

"Anything you say to Jazz, you say to me, have you got that?" Sonja snapped at me.

"Absolutely," I said. "I'm glad you're here. It helps clear things up if there are any misunderstandings later." Although I would have preferred to talk to the girl alone, at least with Sonja there I would have another witness in case the shit started to fly. I walked over to the table and sat down. I'd have given anything to slump down on one of the sagging sofas near the stove, but it was important that Jazz and her mother could see the Fone while we talked. I laid it in the center of the table.

"It's Professor Gerrity's, isn't it?" I said.

"You don't have to say anything more," Sonja interjected. "Cop or not, you don't have to tell her anything. We can get a lawyer if we need to."

"She already knows about the Fone," Jazz pointed out. "Besides, it wasn't me who took it. It was Alfi. She wanted to find out if she was getting a research job that Gerrity had told her about."

"And she found out she wasn't."

"That's right. The prof had already made a decision. It was going to Claire Sullivan."

"Alfi brought the Fone to you because she couldn't get into it, right?"

"Yes," Jazz said. "I told Alfi what she wanted to know, then I gave it back. She intended to return it, you know. Just slip it back into Gerrity's bag."

"But she didn't. And then Hana took it."

"I couldn't believe it when Hana turned up wanting me to hack into the same Fone again. I wiped it and made sure it couldn't be traced, and then I told her to smash it and throw the pieces into separate dumpsters. I thought she'd agreed to that."

"You couldn't wipe all of it, could you? There was an icon you couldn't make go away, but you couldn't open the files either."

"No. I couldn't."

"You know," I said, "the funny thing about files is that they're a lot harder to get rid of than they are to make. Especially if you know the right people."

"How did you get it?" Sonja asked. "Were you following this other girl?"

"No," I said. "It was pure luck on my part. Detective Nguyen and I were investigating a series of break-ins. We were just cruising the second-hand stores. I saw Hana take it in. I recognized her as one of Alfi's friends from the university and I was curious, so I went in immediately and bought it, just on the off-chance that there might be something there."

Nguyen had thawed out enough to speak. "Croissant," she said. "You sent me for tea and a croissant."

I smiled at her. "Bad habits are useful sometimes."

"I stood in line for ages to get that croissant!"

"Anyway," I went on, ignoring Nguyen, "if I had a Fone that had been completely wiped except for an icon that indicated hyper-encrypted files, I'd have been curious as all get out, wouldn't you? Alfi got you to copy them, didn't she?"

Jazz was unapologetic. "Yes, I copied them. But I still haven't gotten them open."

"I couldn't open them either," I said. "But I knew someone who could. They're genetic studies, but very peculiar ones. There are some things there that shouldn't be."

"Let me guess," Jazz said. "A whole lotta Y chromosomes."

It was my turn to be surprised. "How did you know that if you couldn't get the files open?"

She heaved a sigh and cradled her head in her hands for a moment before she replied. "This is such a mess. I don't know where to begin."

"Begin at the beginning," I suggested. "I need to know what you know."

"What's going on, Jazz?" Sonja was bewildered. "What's all this about encrypted files and chromosomes? What have you got mixed up in?" Whatever Jazz had discovered, she hadn't shared it with her mother.

"It's to do with Alfi's death," she said. Then she turned to me. "Just tell me one thing. Why do you need to know?"

"Because I saw Alfi's body. I was at the autopsy."

Her face blanched. "Was it … bad?"

"The worst I've ever seen."

"So you were telling the truth that day on the lawn. You're not buying the Darmes's version of what happened?"

"I wasn't buying it then. I'm not buying it now."

"It's a wild story," she warned. "You may not buy mine either."

"Try me."

She took a moment to collect her thoughts, but when she began speaking, it came out in a rush.

"We've always spent a lot of time out here by Otter Lake," she said. "We own the whole thing, you see — the little lake and a lot of the swampy land that surrounds it. It was paradise when we were kids. Completely private, and we didn't have to fight with the tourists to get near Cedar Lake. And then, when I got older, my friends and I would come out here by ourselves. Most of the time we'd just swim and sunbathe, but every once in a while we'd get a little more ambitious and go for a hike. The country to the north is pretty wild. Not really mountains or anything, but quite steep hills, with tiny ponds and lakes in the little valleys. We'd climb around on the hills or wade in one of the ponds."

"To the north?" I said. "You must have been getting pretty close to the disease control place."

"They were building it the summer I was sixteen. We took binoculars and climbed up the hill to watch the crew working. You know, check them out, like girls do. Talk about their muscles and how tanned they were. Wonder if we could engineer some way to meet some of them."

She glanced at Sonja, who tutted a little, just like a parent was supposed to.

"And did you meet any of them?"

"No." Her brow wrinkled in thought. "In fact, we always made sure no one saw us. I was never sure why, except that it made us feel daring or something, and we didn't want to get chased away. Anyway, they spent most of the summer building it and then we went back home and off to school and everything, so it wasn't until late fall that we came back. There was a long weekend and the weather was nice, so we thought, why not get one last visit in? And, of course, we climbed up the hill to see if the construction workers were still there."

"Wasn't the lab finished by then?"

"It seemed to be," Jazz said. "It looked like it was done from the outside, anyway."

"I know they'd started to hire staff by then," Sonja interjected. "There were new people moving into Cedar Lake because all of a sudden there were jobs here. And, of course, the local people got work as well, although not that many of them were qualified for the more technical jobs."

Lisa's friend must have been one of the locals hired for the front office.

"You saw something else, though, didn't you?" I said to Jazz. "Something besides a newly-built research plant?"

She nodded. "Because it was fall, most of the leaves were gone from the trees. We could see right down into a part of the yard that had been hidden before. Of course, everything was enclosed with heavy fencing — barbed wire along the top of it and so forth. We didn't think anything about that — after all, the plant was there to do research on some pretty nasty stuff, and you can't let just anybody wander in."

She stopped for a moment, gathering the specifics of what she had seen. "One part of the yard seemed to be separate from the rest of the building, with heavier fencing. It was built right up against the side of the hill. There were no windows in the plant looking out on it. That struck us as odd. There are a lot of windows at the front and sides, but nothing in this back section. And there was a fence between this area and the rest of the grounds."

"Like an exercise yard?" I asked. They build yards like that in prisons.

"Exactly," Jazz replied. "I don't think it was there before — at least we didn't see it. That part of the hill is really steep, almost a cliff really, and we had to kind of hang over the top to get a really good look."

Sonja gave a little huff of exasperation at the mention of hanging over the tops of cliffs.

"We were just about to leave," Jazz went on, "when the door into this area opened. We hunkered down flat so we wouldn't be seen — again, I'm not sure why. First three women came out and looked around. Then they went back to the door. We couldn't believe what came out after that."

"What?" But I was beginning to think I knew the answer.

"A bunch of kids, mainly. Some of them looked to be around our age. A couple of them might have been older. The youngest was maybe four or five. We couldn't for the life of us figure out why there would be kids there, unless they'd caught some sort of horrible disease and were being quarantined or something. The adults tried to organize a game with a soccer ball, but the big ones kept taking the ball away from the little ones, and then some of them started fighting. The whole thing just sort of fell apart after that, and eventually they were all herded back inside, but not before a couple of them decided to widdle over by the fence."

She stopped, her lips pursed, a frown on her face.

"They just stood there and peed. They didn't squat. They just stood there and peed and the stream went straight out and splashed against the fence. I'd never seen anything like it. It was just weird. We spent some time trying get the hang of it. Eventually we got tired of getting pee all over ourselves and gave up. We concluded that these kids must have had some really mega strange disease." She shrugged. "And then we climbed back down the hill and went back to the cabin. I don't think any of us gave it much thought, really. You know, after the excitement wore off, we went back to talking about our clothes and our hair."

"And this was you and Alfi?"

"And Lisa."

"Lisa-at-The-Market?"

"Yes."

Inscrutable Lisa, who hadn't been entirely open with me after all. No wonder Alfi had gone to her to try to get into the plant. She knew that Lisa would believe her, and more importantly, wouldn't give her away. She knew that Lisa was still in love with her.

"So when Alfi found out there was a research position for a Men's Studies grad at the Cedar Lake plant, she already had a pretty good idea what it was all about," I said.

"She was maybe in the middle of doing her Master's when she got really obsessed," Jazz said. "I'd half-forgotten what we'd seen, but she said she'd found out what was going on. And then, at the beginning of this year, she said there was a chance she could work at the plant and that it would be the opportunity of a lifetime."

She was right, I thought. It would be like being able to study real live dinosaurs or mastodons or saber-toothed tigers. Quite a prospect for an ambitious girl like Alfi.

"So when you cracked into Gerrity's Fone and told her she wasn't going to get the position...?"

"She went nuts. She kept saying that it wasn't fair, after all she'd *seen* these things, and she was from Cedar Lake so she *deserved* the job, and that she'd have to find some way to change Gerrity's mind."

A very determined girl, her parents had said. Unlikely to stand by and watch someone snatch away such a prize.

"Did you know that she also stole Professor Gerrity's key card for the plant?" I said. "And that Lisa has a friend who arranged an interview for a summer job?"

"Yes. She went to the plant to try to get pictures of them. She figured if she could prove that she knew all about them already, then Gerrity would have no option but to give her the job. I told her she was crazy to try it. That she should just return the ID and the Fone and get over it. Find some other way. She got caught, didn't she?"

It was the most likely explanation. She'd slipped off to snoop around and had been intercepted by a security guard. She must have penetrated quite far into the complex, otherwise she would simply have been escorted back to the front door and politely seen off the premises, no harm done. But what exactly happened after she was caught? I found it difficult to believe that the guards had beaten her, smashed her head in and sexually assaulted her.

"The Darmes killed her, didn't they?" Jazz said. "Because of what she knew."

"Oh my heavens," Sonja said. "What have you gotten into?"

"No, I don't think so," I said, in answer to Jazz. "There's no question that it would have been a monumental breach of national security and that Alfi would have been in a whole heap of trouble — but murder? I don't have any starry-eyed notions about what the Darmes are capable of, mind you, but I'm pretty sure they wouldn't have done that to her. Something else happened."

We were all quiet as each of us tried to imagine what that something else might be.

"Why did you come home, Jazz?" I said, breaking the silence.

She looked shifty at this question, and shot her mother a sidelong glance. "Oh, you know, I needed to get away. Alfi's death and everything."

"Bullshit," I said. "You were going to finish what Alfi started, weren't you? With a little luck and a lot of time, you figured you could decrypt the codes. And then what? Get into the plant somehow and get some pictures just to back up your story? And then maybe you'd have enough evidence to prove that Alfi was murdered. Is that right?"

"Umm ... more or less. Except that I hoped I wouldn't have to get into the plant."

Sonja looked thunderstruck. "That's not what you told me. You told me the police were harassing you and you needed to hide here for a while to get away from them."

Jazz rolled her eyes. "Think about it, Sonja. It's Cedar Lake. Do you really think no one would be able to figure out where I was?"

"The cliff," I said. "That's why you came here, to the cabin, instead of staying in town. You've been trying to take pictures from the clifftop."

"What?" Sonja said.

"Sorry, Sonja, but the detective is right. That's exactly what I've been trying to do. Only it hasn't worked out very well. I haven't been able to crack the codes and I haven't been able to get the shot I need. I've climbed up that hill every day since I got here, but unless one of them decides to pee against the fence, there's no way to prove that they're not just a bunch of weird-looking girls. I mean, unless you can get a picture of the ... you know ... *thing*."

"Even if you had been able to, what were you going to do with the information?"

"I don't know," she said. "Confront Gerrity, maybe. Get her to tell me the truth. At the very least, I figured it would be enough to get them to send Alfi's body home. Let Alicia and Freddie have a funeral. They're like a pair of ghosts rattling around over there."

Even though she'd pieced together a great deal of the story, Jazz still hadn't realized how big it was. And how much trouble she would be in if she breathed a word of it, no matter how good her intentions were. Sonja wasn't so naïve.

"Now there's a really good question," she said to me. "Just who are *you* intending to tell? Is somebody going to come after us because of this?"

"I'll be honest with you, Sonja," I said. "I don't really know what I'm going to do, but don't worry, it'll be me they come after, not you."

"I know exactly what you're going to do," Nguyen said from over by the stove. "You're going to take the whole story to Inspector Trent."

It was as good a suggestion as any — after all, the inspector had practically catapulted me into the investigation. On the other hand, even though I was sure I knew most of the story, all the evidence I had to back it up was circumstantial. Fact after fact had piled up, all of it pointing in a particular direction. But the conclusion was so monstrously ludicrous that I would have difficulty getting anyone to believe it, much less launch an official investigation into Alfi Longwell's death. Like Jazz, I needed more than genetic charts and a wild theory.

I would have to go in.

"If you'll excuse me for a moment," I said. "I need to make a call."

"Just tell me one thing," Nguyen said, with a puzzled look on her face. "Those kids. The ones in the yard. Do you really think they were boys?"

CHAPTER 17

I walked out to the front porch to call Ricky. I still hadn't really warmed up from the long ride, and stepping out into the cold air again set me shivering, my fingers so cold they were barely able to connect with the keypad.

"Hey big ears."

"All the better to hear you with," Ricky said.

"Can you find any specs on the Cedar Lake Center for the Control of Communicable Diseases?"

"Specs as in what? Floor plan? Construction? Mandate?"

Sometimes Ricky was annoyingly specific.

"Um … floor plan for sure. Maybe security system?"

"Okay. I'm going to need about an hour. The info on a place like that might be locked down pretty tight."

"Okay. I'll call back around noon."

"Hey, can you bring me back a present?"

"Sure," I said, knowing it would be some sort of consumable.

"Some peanut butter?"

"Smooth or crunchy?"

"Smooth. A big jar. Talk to you later."

I entered the number for my work pod, just to make sure I hadn't been missed for some reason and that no one was trying to reach me. There was one new message. To my surprise, it was from Diva Davis. The text was brief and smirky: "Me and the gang thought you might like to see this. Looks like you've been led down the garden path."

And then an image began to fill the Fone screen. I was puzzled as it loaded. It looked like a typical election campaign photo-op taken by the newsfeeds, pols waving to the crowd, signs in the background. There was Kirsty Chin

Littlecrow beaming broadly at the cheering supporters in front of her. But then the camera panned across the crowd, to demonstrate how full the hall was, and, just off to the left of the stage, I caught a glimpse of two familiar figures. They were embracing, a big, happy victory hug in reaction to good news. The report was captioned *Littlecrow and crowd react to latest polls*. I checked the date. It was from the Tuesday just past, the day that Hines had been out of town and unavailable for calls. The day that Trent had been out of her office.

I'd had a suspicion, but seeing the proof made me feel like I'd been punched in the stomach. The inspector and the medical examiner? It sounded like the opening line of a naughty joke. Except the joke was on me, and Davis and crew were obviously enjoying a huge ha-ha.

I have always found it useful to try to compartmentalize my various levels of disappointment. I've had a lot of practice at it. First and foremost, I supposed, there were my personal feelings about Jo Hines. That had been a no-go right from the start, and deep down I'd known it all along. Someone like Hines would have little interest in a slobby, disagreeable cop who was unbeloved of anybody, not even her fellow police officers. That wasn't entirely true, I tried to tell myself. I had been beloved of Georgie once upon a time. And Nguyen, I was afraid, but Nguyen didn't really count, other than for the fact that she was more or less in the same boat I was. But I should have realized that Hines was committed. The signs had been there. Her reluctance to meet at either of our apartments, opting always for public places. Her efforts to keep the conversation professional and focused on the case whenever we were alone. And to be fair, she hadn't pretended anything else. She'd played the game for whoever was listening, but she hadn't done any more than that. Alternate interpretations were a self-induced hallucination on my part.

The big question mark was Inspector Trent. Setting aside any details regarding her personal life — and I could well imagine that the office was buzzing with the intelligence that the prim and proper inspector, whom everyone had assumed was virtually asexual, had, in fact, been in possession of the jackpot — I had to ask why a high(ish)-profile public servant was openly involved in an election campaign. And why she'd cleared the way into Gerrity's office, why she'd set Nguyen to follow me, why she'd failed to question me about my whereabouts or demand the results of my investigations at the university. And why, before she'd done all that, she'd recruited her partner to reel me in. What the hell was going on?

Just for a moment, I tried to persuade myself that I'd jumped to conclusions, seen something that wasn't there. Davis and her seedy little crew certainly thought there was something, but that didn't mean they were right. Maybe Hines and Trent just happened to support the same political party, and the embrace had been nothing more than excitement at seeing their candidate do well. Maybe.

I punched in the numbers for City Directory. There was an address listed for Hines, but not for Trent. Not unusual. When you're a cop, you don't advertise where you live. I called Ricky again.

"Hello, Ma."

"Nothing yet. Like I said, this may take a while."

"I know. I'm calling for something else." I gave her Hines's address. "Can you check to see if there are any unlisted numbers associated with that address?"

I could hear clicking in the background as she accessed her magic spell book. "Trent. Kathleen Tomas Trent." And then a pause. "Holy shit! Really?"

"Yeah, looks like it. Thanks, Rick."

"Who?" she said. "You must have the wrong pod." And then she disconnected.

Diva had sent the photo to mock me, I knew. For her, it was just one more opportunity to rub my nose in the dirt. But it had far more significance than that. It tied Trent directly to Littlecrow, whose support of the GeneShare Treaty had been diametrically opposed to the Prime Minister's stance. Until a few days ago.

Trent and Hines had set me up to discover what had happened to Alfi Longwell because they hoped it might lead me to something else. Something bigger. Something Littlecrow could use to help her win the election.

But things had changed in the last few days. Some event had forced the Prime Minister to do an about-face. Something had happened all right, and I was pretty sure I knew what it was. The question I couldn't answer was what it meant.

This was complicated, labyrinthine, Byzantine, Machiavellian — all of those adjectives that describe a plot that is dark and deep and sinister, and I was sorely tempted to walk away from the whole thing, refuse to be used as a pawn anymore. Except that, apparently, there was far more at stake than just my sense of outrage and I wanted to find out what it was. I needed to make sense of why I had been used.

Besides, I didn't exactly have a lot to lose. Not anymore. Georgie was gone and she wasn't coming back. Jo Hines was a fantasy. My career as a police officer was uninspiring. I had nothing ahead of me but a long stretch of Tiresome Tasks and empty evenings, falling asleep on the couch with a glass of wine and a bag of stale curd.

Bugger it. I'd see it through to the end.

— «» —

Sonja had set the kettle to boil while I'd been out on her porch wrestling with the larger issues of life, love and political machinations. As I walked back in and sat at the table, she set out four mugs, along with cream and sugar. The kettle was one of those old-fashioned ones that whistled when the water boiled, and as soon as it began to tweet, she filled the teapot and set it on the table to steep. Nguyen left her little nest by the woodstove and joined us at the table.

"You were out there a long time," she said to me. "I thought you were just going to make a quick call."

"It turned into a long conversation," I said, and then I turned to Jazz. "So — are you going to show me where this hill is?"

"Does that mean you're going to help?"

"No, it means I'm going to take it from here. All I need you to do is show me the way."

"No," Sonja said. "She's not even going to do that. She's going to stay out of this."

"Sonja! She's a cop! What could go wrong?"

"That's right, she's a cop," Sonja said. "She can walk in wherever she wants. So let her flash her badge at the front door. What does she need you for?"

"It doesn't work that way," I said. "Not when the Darmes are involved." I decided to level with her. "Look, I won't lie to you. I don't know what I'm getting into. But all I want Jazz to do is show me where to go. She can come home as soon as she's seen me on my way and then you can both pretend you never heard of me."

"You want to know what happened to Alfi don't you Sonja?" Jazz said.

Sonja caved. "All right, all right," she said. "But don't come crying to me if it all goes wrong."

"Who else would I go crying to?" Jazz said and made a smooching noise in the air toward her. "Anyway, there's a path, sort of, up the side of the hill. I'll climb with you to the top."

"Okay, take me as far as that, then you come home," I said.

"She shouldn't even be going that far," Nguyen said.

"And neither should you. I'll do this alone."

"I don't think so. I'm supposed to be tailing you, remember?"

"You come right back, Jazz," Sonja said. "Don't you dare go down that cliff with them."

"Nguyen's not going," I said.

"Yes, I am."

I was getting dizzy from the competing arguments. "Whoa! Who's in charge here anyway? You can both go as far as the hill, but I go the rest of the way alone."

"Okay," Nguyen said.

"Okay," Jazz said.

They both gave in far too readily. Sonja poured tea into one of the mugs, but her hands were shaking and she slopped a little onto the table. "Here, let me do that," Jazz said. "Don't worry. It'll be okay."

I hoped she was right.

— ‹› —

It was just coming up noon when I buzzed Ricky again.

"Hello, Mother," I said.

"Got it." My Fone screen began to fill with a schematic drawing of the Cedar Lake Centre.

There was no wall Vu in the cabin that I could see, and the schematic was too big to see clearly on my Fone screen. "Do you have a Porta-Vu I can use?" I asked Jazz.

"Yeah." She disappeared into one of the rooms at the back of the cabin and returned a moment later with a Vu that she placed in front of me, and then hovered behind me while I transferred the file.

"So?" Ricky said.

"Hang on, I'm still looking at it."

"There's only one good way in. Otherwise there are two fences to get over."

"The enclosed yard with the steel door at the rear of the building?" I said. "Yup, I already figured that out and I know how to get that far. I just don't know what happens at the fence."

"I can disrupt the alarm. For three minutes."

I sat there, calculating. Three minutes to climb the fence, cut the razor wire, cross the yard and get in the door.

"I don't know," I said. "I'm not sure three minutes is going to do it."

"You haven't heard the good news yet," she chided. "Three minutes off for the fence. Three minutes off for the door. Three minutes off for the door beyond that and so on and so on. If I run the disruptions sequentially, they'll probably think it's a glitch in the power system."

"Won't the alarms sound when the power kicks back in?"

"Only briefly, and by then you'll be in. There will be a little burp each time, but it should draw security away from that back door and into another part of the building. There are only a couple of access doors between the back section and the rest of the building, so even if they all come running at first, there should be a couple of nice little bottlenecks to hold them up."

"What about cams?" I asked.

"There are a couple on the fence, but they're pointed at the yard. Shouldn't be a problem unless somebody happens to be looking at the exact moment you run across. There's one at the back door, but there's a blind spot on the hinge side. Get right up against the wall and you should be okay. Get through the door as fast as you can when it unlocks. There's another one in the hall just inside, but there's a closet right there. Duck inside and, with any luck, everybody's attention will be somewhere else by then."

With any luck. Luck and lux, that's what I needed.

"You know, this is the strangest set-up I've ever seen." Ricky sounded puzzled. "It's almost like they designed it so nobody can get out and didn't give much thought to anybody getting in."

"Okay, this is doable," I said, after a few moments of staring at the Vu screen and wondering if I was completely crazy. "I'll signal with the Fone when I get to the fence. It'll be a couple of hours anyway."

She giggled. "I've got it all set up and ready to initiate. All I need is the word. There will be about a five second delay, then you should be good to go."

"Thanks pal."

"Don't forget my peanut butter."

Two expectant faces and one extremely disapproving one were turned in my direction as I buzzed off.

"We're going to need some wire cutters," I said.

"And a rope," Jazz added. "At least then you won't fall down the cliff."

"Good idea. Nguyen can lower me down."

"I'll help," Jazz said.

"No you won't," Sonja said. "You'll be on your way back here."

"Oh right," Jazz said. "I forgot." Sonja glared at her.

"Maybe I should run back into town to get the things I need," I ventured. "Unless you have wire cutters and a rope handy."

"There's a set of garden shears," Jazz said. "Would those do?"

She walked over to a kitchen drawer and pulled out a pair of secateurs with long, curving blades.

I was doubtful.

"You don't have time to go back to town," she pointed out. "It's going to take nearly an hour to get up to the hill and I don't know how long to get down the cliff. You're going to start losing the light."

She was right. December in the temperate zone. It started getting dark at four o'clock in the afternoon.

"The shears will have to do," I said. "What about a rope?"

"Shed," Jazz said. "There should be something with the kayaks. I'll go see what I can find."

She was back in a few minutes with a collection of ropes of varying lengths and strengths. "We don't have anything very long," she said, "but I did find these." She held up a combination plier/cutter. "It was with the fishing tackle."

"I'll take anything I can get," I said. "But I don't think any of the ropes are long enough."

"No problem," Nguyen said and began joining them with deftly-tied knots. She saw me watching her. "I grew up near a lake. We had boats. Don't worry, they'll hold."

"I'm impressed," I said. "I got kicked out of the Explorer's Club long before we got to knot-tying."

Not only did Nguyen show a surprising facility with ropes (I must remember to introduce her to Sarong, I thought — now there was someone who would appreciate a well-tied knot), but when she'd finished linking them all together she asked Sonja if there was such a thing as a knife sharpener in the cabin. When Sonja located one that was part of an old carving set, Nguyen used it to put an edge on both the cutters and the shears.

"I can probably only manage one of them," I pointed out.

"You won't be able to manage it at all," she said. "Not by yourself. You'll need help cutting the wire. And who will spread the strands after it's cut? You can't climb over the fence and hold the wire at the same time."

"I'll figure it out," I said.

"In three minutes?" Nguyen had a knowing, skeptical look on her face. I guess she'd worked with me just long enough to know how often I flew by the seat of my pants. It explained why I was so disheveled most of the time. However, I knew when I was outgunned and since there was apparently little I could do about the current mutiny other than hogtie her and leave her in the back of the car, I gave in.

"Okay — but you," I pointed at Jazz, "you are staying at the top of the cliff, and you," I pointed at Nguyen, "are staying outside the fence. Got it?"

They both nodded.

"And both of you," I glared at them, "have to be ready to boogie on out of there as soon as there's any sign of trouble."

"How can there be any trouble?" Nguyen said. "Don't you have a plan?"

There was no putting it off any longer — we were ready to go. Sonja loaded us up with toques and extra mittens. "It's freezing out there," she said, and then she turned to Jazz. "You show them where it is, and then you come back, you hear?"

"I may just wait there for a bit to make sure they get down the cliff all right."

"If you're not back by dinnertime, I'm calling the police."

"I don't think it will do you any good," she said. "I'm with the police."

Nguyen snorted.

"Don't worry," Jazz said, her voice softened. "I'll be back."

We walked out into the yard in front of the cabin. "Cazzo crap," I said. I'd forgotten about Lisa's bike. "Can you do me one more favor, Jazz? If we load the bike into the back of your vehicle, can you deliver it to The Market?"

"Oh, of course — you talked to Lisa, didn't you?" she said. "That's how you found the cabin."

I was beginning to appreciate the advantages of small towns. You didn't have to explain much, because everybody figured everything out anyway. We slung the bike into the bed of the vehicle and then, finally, we set off for the hill.

We followed the laneway for a hundred yards until Jazz led us over a ditch and across a rail fence. Beyond this lay a small path, which led through a field and skirted around the bottom of a hill before it took an abrupt turn upward.

It was tough going, a steady climb along a rudimentary path that snaked from rocky ledge to rocky ledge, switching back and forth across the side of the hill in search of the easiest route. My feet slipped on patchy mud and loose gravel, and several times I was saved from tumbling down the path again only by grabbing a handhold in the scrubby bushes that had rooted themselves in the cracked rock.

Halfway up, we paused to catch our breaths at a flattish piece of exposed granite, another glacial memento that would someday loose itself from the softer surrounding rock and go tumbling down the hillside to join its sister at the end of the lane. The lake below nestled like a small jewel between the hill and the marshland of golden grasses that grew on the other side. I could just see the village of Cedar Lake beyond this, the occasional roofline reflecting the low-lying sun.

"It's beautiful," Nguyen said.

Jazz smiled. "Yes. Especially from up here."

"Has your family owned it for a long time?" I asked.

"It belonged to my other mom. She died a few years ago."

"I'm sorry," I said. All the harder for Sonja, I thought. Her partner gone, her daughter spinning away from her.

Jazz shrugged. "It was a tough time for us both. But you go on. And we should too. It's getting late."

I was panting heavily by the time we reached the cliff. Okay, okay, I know — too many greasy hamburgers and sugar-laden coffees. I was beginning to have serious doubts about being able to climb down, even with the help of the rope that Nguyen had spliced together.

I stepped gingerly to the edge to see what I was up against.

"I don't know how stable that is," Jazz said. "Erosion may have undercut the lip."

To my relief, I realized that it wasn't really a cliff. I had been expecting to see a sheer rock face, the sort of vertical elevation that mountaineers find challenging, but this was just a very, very steep slope covered with a tangle of stunted trees and scrubby bushes. At the bottom was the Cedar Lake Center for the Control of Communicable Diseases, and, as the plans of the facility had indicated, there was a single stretch of chain link fence that butted up against the foot of the hill. They must have figured that the hill itself was an adequate second barrier and that no one would ever try to climb down it. And then I remembered what had puzzled Ricky. Security had been designed to keep people from getting out, not in. No one could make it up the cliff without the help of a rope.

And the fence didn't look like it was going to be that big a problem. It was chain link, with four strands of plain old barbed wire across the top — far easier to cut through than razor wire, especially in the space of three minutes. Not only that, but the wire sloped inward, toward the yard. To keep people in, not out.

Nguyen tied one end of the rope around a pine tree that stood about five feet back from the edge of the cliff. "We'll take some of the weight as well, just in case," she said. And then she looped the other end around my waist. Jazz looked at the arrangement dubiously.

"Are you sure you want to do this," she said. "If you fall, the rope will save you, but I'm not sure we'd be able to pull you back up."

She was probably right. I was no climber and in terms of mountaineering gear this was rudimentary at best. Again, it occurred to me that any sane person would have gone home, smashed the Fone, burned all the papers and had a beer. I wasn't sane just then. All the time I had been climbing up the hill my anger at being played for a fool had grown.

"I've come this far," I said. "I'll see it through to the end."

"Okay," she said, "but I don't think you should have the shears in your pocket while you're climbing. Just in case, you know, you fall or something."

Good point. I wouldn't be much use at the bottom if I had a bloody great pair of garden shears sticking out of me.

"I'll lower them down after you."

I pulled them out of my pocket and realized that I still had the wad of papers that I'd written everything down on. I handed them to Jazz along with the shears.

"Hang onto these for me, will you?"

"What are they?"

"Everything you don't want to know. If it looks like the shit is hitting the fan, call Inspector Trent and give them to her. Her number is on the bottom of the last page."

She nodded and shoved them into her own pocket.

I took a deep breath and slowly lowered myself over the lip of rock. It was a good thing I was attached to a rope because as soon as I went over the side my feet hit a scree of loose rock. I kicked at nothing for a few moments, but then the rope tightened and I was able to jam my foot against a tree root to stop my downward momentum. I had to wait for a few minutes to let the adrenalin stop pumping before I dared the next step. But then, after another couple of heart-stopping skids, I found a rhythm. Let the rope take my weight until I found a tree or a rock or a bush to steady my descent. Consolidate my position, then trust the rope again.

The cliff really wasn't all that high, but I was panting by the time I reached the bottom. I'd made it down. I was pretty sure I'd never make it back up, even if I managed to get out of the building.

At the foot of the cliff there was a jumble of rock and uprooted vegetation. Here and there I could see whole trees that had given up their tentative holds and plummeted to the bottom. I ducked behind one of these, just in case someone in the building was watching, although Ricky had assured me that there were no cams trained on the hill.

I untied the rope and Jazz pulled it back up to the top. A few minutes later Nguyen came scrambling down. She had a little more difficulty finding a foothold at the top, being so much shorter, but after that she scampered down the rest of it far more easily than I had.

After Nguyen untied herself, Jazz pulled the rope back up, wrapped it around the pliers and shears and slowly lowered them down. I stuck the shears in my pocket and wondered what I was going to do next.

"Do you think I could just run across the wire and jump it?" I asked Nguyen. "Use the top wire as a springboard?"

"You won't know until you try," she said, "but it beats trying to cut it. Just make sure your pant legs are tucked into your boots so they don't catch on the barbs."

She was right. And there would be no stopping in the middle. I'd never be able to keep my balance if there was any sag in the wire. Provided I even made it that far. The chain link mesh was far too fine to offer any toeholds. I would have to haul myself up to the top of the fence, and I would have to do it fast.

"Okay, I'm going to give it a try," I said. "You get yourself back up the hill."

"No," she said. "If you get hung up on the wire, I might still be able to cut you free if I'm here. I can't do that from the top of the hill."

"I thought you were going to do what I tell you."

"Not if it doesn't make any sense."

"Okay, but as soon as I land on the other side, hide yourself somewhere. You can climb back up later when you figure no one's looking."

I tucked the cuffs of my jeans into the tops of my boots. And hesitated, unsure that I had enough upper body strength to pull myself to the top rail.

"Do you think you can give me a boost?" I said to Nguyen. "My big fat toes won't fit through the chain link."

"Maybe." She sounded as doubtful as I felt. And then she said something brilliant. "What if we used one of these trees?" She pulled at a small cedar that looked fairly fresh, a recent victim of the elements that battered the hill. "You can just climb up the branches. Like it's a ladder."

"Will it hold my weight?" It wasn't that big a tree.

"Just make sure you keep your big fat feet close to the trunk. When you're ready to go, I'll drop it on the fence and steady it while you climb."

I helped her haul it upright. I didn't know if it would work, but the idea wasn't any wackier than any other part of the plan.

Nguyen held it at the ready. I called Ricky.

"We're at the fence," I said.

"I know." She was giggling. "I've got your leash. I overlaid it on the schematic."

Sometimes I thought Ricky was the most dangerous person on the planet.

"Okay," she said. "This'll take a minute. Don't go until I give you the word."

I stood poised to climb, like a runner waiting for the starting gun.

"Go," Ricky said.

I shoved the Fone in my pocket and leapt at the tree. Halfway up, one of the branches cracked under my foot, and I almost fell, but by then I had a grip on the rail of the fence and was able to haul myself the rest of the way. I teetered on the top rail for a moment, then stepped forward. The first strand of barbed wire sagged under my weight slightly and nearly threw me off balance. *Keep going, keep going.* I skipped the next two strands and jumped to the top wire, which sagged even more. I catapulted into the yard, landing less than perfectly, but was back on my feet in a moment and ran for the door. Just as I slammed against the wall, there was one farting blast of alarm that stopped nearly as soon as it started. Then suddenly Nguyen slid in beside me. Against orders, she had climbed the fence and crossed the yard after me.

"Go back," I hissed.

"No. I'll never make it back up the hill."

I didn't have time to argue with her. I just glared while I pulled the Fone out of my pocket and clamped it to my ear, waiting for Ricky's next instruction.

"Go."

There was a faint *click click* as the locks on the door released. We scrambled inside. We were in a foyer, with a corridor just beyond it, and a door to my right. The closet. I tried the handle. It opened easily. There was a rack of jackets and hats and white lab coats hanging neatly inside. I pulled Nguyen into the closet behind me, and we stood panting and listening to the alarms sounding, first at the door, then off in other parts of the building. None of them built into the usual wail, just hiccupped one after the other. It was the perfect recreation of a fluctuating power failure.

We heard footsteps pounding down the hall and held our breaths when they stopped at the back door. Whoever it was tried the handle, but the door had locked itself again when the power was restored. Then the steps faded away down the hall.

I dumped my hat and mitts on the floor and chose one of the biggest lab coats to slip on over my winter jacket. If we managed to get out of the place again I figured we would need our warm coats for the long walk home. If.

Nguyen followed suit.

"No," I hissed.

"What do you expect me to do, wait in the closet?" she whispered back, and she followed me as I stepped back into the foyer.

We made a strange couple of lab technicians — the white coats were a pretty good disguise, but the winter jackets underneath made us look bulky and round. I hoped that if anyone was picking us up on the security cam they would think we were a couple of fat employees drawn to the back door by the alarm, but I hoped that they couldn't see our feet. Our mud-caked winter boots were leaving smears on the floor.

We turned down a long corridor that led to the right. The outside door had been set at the left hand side of the enclosed yard, so it stood to reason that whatever part of the building it served was located behind the rest of the yard. There didn't seem to be anybody else around. I hoped that many people had congregated somewhere else to investigate the strange malfunction in the security system. I hoped.

I opened the first door I came to. It was an office with a desk and a chair and a row of cabinets. A clipboard was lying on the desk. I took it. It would make me look more official, should I happen to meet anyone. There were no security cams in the small room.

"Stay here," I said to Nguyen.

"What? You want me to just sit here?"

"No, I wanted you to just sit by the fence. Or on top of the hill. Or better yet, back at the cabin. But you're here and now I want you to stay put."

"But what am I supposed to do if somebody comes in?" she asked.

"I dunno. Pretend you're filing, or hide under the desk or something."

"But—"

"No buts. Stay put. I'll be right back."

The next door on the right was another office. I took a quick look around, but there didn't seem to be much to see, so I went back out into the corridor. Just as I closed the door, I became aware of banging noises, as though something metal was being thrown against a wall. As I ventured further into the interior of the building, I could hear that the noise was punctuated by shouting, although I couldn't make out any of the words. I hoped it had something to do with the alarms and that it would be enough to keep everyone occupied for a while.

The rooms on the right-hand side of the corridor had yielded nothing of interest, so I opened the first door I came to on the left. To my surprise, it was occupied. A young woman with intricately-braided hair was lying in a hospital type bed, cradling something that was swaddled in a blanket. A young child of perhaps three or four sat on the end of the bed, coloring a line drawing of a flower with a scribble of orange crayon. I couldn't be sure, but the woman looked like the young saker I had seen, the one who had been heavily pregnant and had scooped up a child who was surely the same one that now sat on the end of the bed.

The woman looked alarmed when she saw me.

"Doctor Rodriguez has been in already. It's not time to go yet is it?"

"No, no," I said, looking officiously at the papers on my stolen clipboard. "I just came in to see how you're doing."

"I'm all right, I guess," she said. "I didn't realize this would be so hard."

"I know," I said soothingly, although I had no idea what she was talking about.

"It was so different with Janey," she sighed, indicating the child at the foot of the bed. "I knew she'd be with me forever. But this one is perfect, and I promised God. It's just so hard, when you know what it's like to be a mother." She smiled at Janey. "She's the joy of my life."

"I expect she is," I said. I was a little confused. I had been sure the child was a boy. Just then, Janey reached for a different colored crayon, and I noticed that there was an extra finger on her right hand.

I looked down at the clipboard again and made a couple of ticks in some non-existent boxes. "I wonder if I might do just one last check on the new one, just to make sure."

The woman unwrapped her bundle to reveal what appeared to be a very new baby. Under the blanket, it was wearing a soft cotton shirt and a diaper. It was so fragile-looking that I was afraid to touch it.

"If you could just..."

"Of course," she said and unhooked the tabs that held the diaper in place. And there, between the legs of the newborn child, was something I'd never seen before. It was an unprepossessing little dangle of flesh. It looked so innocent, resting there on its two mounds. This is what all the fuss was about? This doodle, this tiny little squib of tissue? I could see nothing particularly special about it.

Just then, the little worm started to waggle and a stream of pee shot out, spraying wildly. It was like watching an out of control fire hose. The woman clapped the diaper down over it again.

"Well, everything there seems to be in working order," I ventured.

She smiled. "Yes, it does that. It's the oddest thing."

"Do you think it's finished?"

She peeked under the diaper. "Yes, I think so."

"I wonder if I might just ... document?" I held out my Fone.

She frowned. "They've taken a lot of pictures already," she said.

"I'd like to get one more before you go."

She pulled the diaper aside and I snapped three quick shots with my Fone, two of the baby and one that managed to include the saker woman.

"Well, that should do it. Thank you, now I'll just be on my way."

"Could you do me a favor?" the woman said. "Could you just look in on Rachel? This is her first time and she's probably feeling pretty scared. I know I was the first time. In spite of how much they tell you about it, meeting God is kind of ... spooky."

"Of course."

I left the room and scurried down the corridor to where Nguyen was waiting.

I opened the door and there she stood, her WhamGun at the ready.

"Sheesh, watch where you're pointing that thing."

"I didn't know it was you," she said.

"So you were going to shoot your way out of here?"

"It occurred to me."

"Hold that thought. We may have to yet."

"So, did you find anything?" she asked.

"Big time."

I now had all the proof I needed that the government was conducting clinical trials on members of *The Sisters of Serene Acceptance*. There had been some initial problems with the chemical cocktail they were using, I guessed. The little girl with the extra finger was proof of that. The woman seemed to indicate that she had been allowed to keep the little girl. *"I knew she'd be with me forever."* And sure enough, there she'd been, playing in the rubble when I'd first visited the saker camp. "But this one is perfect," she'd said of the new baby, "and I promised God." The little boy was being taken away.

And then there was "Rachel," waiting, scared and alone, for her turn to meet God. "They've gone to God," the saker had said, when I'd gone to the clearing the second time.

"God" was one of those little boys Jazz, Alfi and Lisa had seen in the yard, now grown up and sexually mature. How easy it must have been to persuade the young women of the saker sect that this was what their God wanted. What Saint Meerakaatakilla had foreseen. The faithful going forth and multiplying. Making more little sakers to follow in their footsteps. And, quite probably, their only chance to have children, never mind the condition.

They could keep whatever girls they produced, the discards, the didn't-quite-work-outs. The boys were too valuable. They would stay with God. The manipulation was criminally cynical.

And where did Trent and Hines fit into all this? I'd been sent along this path for some reason, but I still wasn't sure what the final destination was. I decided not to worry about it just then. I'd focus on getting us out in one piece, then I'd decide what to do with the evidence I'd collected.

"So what do we do now?" Nguyen asked.

I really had no idea, unless Ricky could manage a reverse security meltdown. I hadn't thought that far and Nguyen's presence was going to make it twice as hard to remain undetected. I hoped Jazz had done as she promised and cleared off the hilltop as soon as we made it inside the building, but I found myself hoping that she had left the rope in place, something I realized just then that I had forgotten to mention.

"Well," I said, "I guess we send some messages, and then we scram."

I opened my Fone and retrieved the pictures I'd taken. I'd send copies to myself and, just for insurance, to Ricky.

"Look what I found," I keyed into the text box. And then I hit send. Nothing happened.

I entered the numbers again. Nothing. Then I checked the juice bar. Low, almost depleted. Cheap, crappy, throwaway Fone. Shit.

I turned to Nguyen. "You didn't, by any chance, disobey a direct order and bring another Fone with you? This one's dead."

Her look was pure venom. "So now we can't get your friend to unlock the door again. Terrific." It seemed that the shine of hanging around with Maverick MacHenry had worn off somewhat. Nguyen was looking distinctly peeved.

"So how do we get out of here?" she asked.

I brought up the schematic of the center that Ricky had sent to me. It was almost unreadable on the tiny Fone under optimal circumstances, and now the screen was starting to grey out. I peered at it and was just able to see, as Ricky had pointed out, that there were only a couple of points of egress into the main facility. The right-hand way led deeper into the windowless complex, toward the shouting I had heard earlier. If we went left, the corridor eventually led to a set of doors that opened into the main section of the facility. Left it was.

I would have to get to those doors and somehow get through them. It was an unlikely escape route, especially since the point of all the locks seemed to be to keep people inside the private compound. There were also likely to be far more people on the other side of those doors, and I wasn't confident enough in my lab coat disguise to believe that it would get me past them. But I didn't see any alternative.

I poked my nose out into the corridor. The way was clear.

"Let me go first," I said. "Count to twenty and then follow. If you hear anybody coming, duck through a door — these seem to be mostly offices along here. If you hear anything that sounds like big trouble, go to the back door and hide in the closet."

I scurried down the corridor at a very fast walk, my head down, as if I were studying the papers that had been clipped to the board I carried. I soon arrived at the double doors and slipped into a corner that I was reasonably sure wasn't covered by the cameras. Next to the door there was a security scanner that required an ID swipe card and a numerical password.

Nguyen joined me a few seconds later. I pulled her into the blind spot.

"Hmm. More locked doors," she said.

"Gee thanks, Nguyen, I might have missed that."

"Could we just blast it open?" she asked. "Is a WhamGun zap strong enough to disrupt the electric locks?"

"Wow, you really are trigger happy, aren't you?" But I looked at her with a new appreciation. For someone who generally followed the rules, she was showing some innovative thinking. Too bad it wouldn't work.

"The problem," I said, "is that even if we get it open, it will probably set all the alarms ringing. And it's a hell of a long way from here to the front entrance."

"What about the back door?"

It would be a better bet. Even if the alarms went off, we might have enough time to get to the fence before security arrived. But in order to get over it, we would have to cut through the barbed wire at the top. And then there was the cliff. It had taken at least ten minutes to get down it. It would take longer than that to get up, even if Jazz had left the rope in place. Too long. If we managed the fence without getting caught, we would have to hide ourselves in the brush and hope that no one thought to search it.

"Let's go back to the office. At least there are no cameras there. Count of twenty again, then follow."

I scurried down the corridor again. We were starting to resemble lab rats, I thought. Caught in a maze. It seemed an incredibly appropriate metaphor for the pickle we were in.

"Okay," I said, when Nguyen joined me once more. "You're finally going to get to shoot your gun off. Try it on the keypad first, then the swipe pad, and then the door, if it hasn't opened. If it works, get outside and run for the fence as fast as you can."

"What are you going to do?"

"Provide a diversion. I'll go try to open the big double doors. That should set something ringing. There haven't been that many people in this section the whole time we've been here, so I'm guessing it's going to take a couple of minutes for a security team to get here and I'm guessing they'll stop to check the double doors first. That may give me enough time to follow you."

"And if none of this works?"

"Then I'll think of something else."

"Why am I not comforted by that?" she asked.

It was a lousy plan, but I didn't have anything better, which meant that in reality I didn't have anything at all.

"If you get out, get Trent," I said. "Okay, so, count to fifty, then hit it, okay?"

I left her, gun drawn, as I half-walked, half-ran, back down the corridor. I didn't bother trying to dodge the cameras. I just walked up to the scanner and swiped one of my business cards through it, then I jiggled the door handle. As I expected, the wail of an alarm filled the hall. As I ran to the rear door, another alarm sounded, so I knew Nguyen had timed her blast well. I just hoped it worked. It hadn't. The keypad was smoking a little and the light on the scanner was flashing crazily, but the door remained firmly locked. She directed the next shot directly at the handle, but, as I expected, nothing happened.

It also took the security team far less time to reach the initial source of the breach than I had anticipated. I could hear a thunder of footsteps coming down the hall. Nguyen slid into the closet.

"C'mon!" she hissed.

Instead of joining her, I slammed the door in her face, then ran down the corridor to the right. I knew the guards would hear me, running as I did in my heavy boots, but at least that might draw them away from Nguyen.

I galloped past the offices. There was no point trying to hide in any of those — they were so small it would take about thirty seconds to search each one. I had no idea of the layout of the halls and rooms ahead of me and I expected at any moment to run into another set of locked doors. Sooner or later I was going to be caught, but at least Nguyen might be able to dodge security long enough to find a way out.

Suddenly a door on my left opened and the small child with the extra finger stood wide-eyed as I went past. Then — someone, somewhere give her a pat on her little saker back — she toddled out into the hall. I risked a look backwards. She had stopped right in the middle of the corridor and the security detail had to slow down so as not to run her over. I deked into another hallway that I hoped might lead me out. It was a mistake. There was only one door at the end. I skidded to a halt and tried the handle. It was locked.

Then a miracle occurred. There was an audible clank as the bolt slid open. I yanked at the handle again and slid through the door, slamming it shut behind me. I was in a lab of some sort. There were three or four people working at various counters and tables in different parts of the room. Their heads shot up as I entered, but I ignored them and ran straight through the lab to the door I could see on the other side.

This, too, was unlocked.

Just as I disappeared through it, I heard one of the lab workers say, "Hey, you can't—" but the rest of it was lost as the door crashed shut behind me.

I figured I must be in the heart of the complex. A short hallway led to two sets of double doors with only about six feet between them. Major security. I opened the first set. Then the second set burst open and four or five people piled into a bottleneck in the space between. One of them crashed into me and I went down. I covered my head with my arms, hoping to protect it from flying feet. As I watched from the floor, one of them finally got enough clearance to open the doors that led to the lab and then the others started pouring through, straight into the security detail that had been chasing me.

Howls of pain and protest filled the air as, without hesitation, the guards began firing their WhamGuns. I reached for mine as well, then stood up and elbowed my way through the second door. I stumbled straight into a uniformed guard. I threw her a good hard body-check, and she staggered to my left. A mob of a dozen or so people had crowded behind her and now they surged forward, shouting in their effort to get through the door. I kicked the first body I came to and shoved a couple of the others out of the way. Just as I broke free of them, a second guard made a flying leap at me. I pulled my right hand back fast enough that she was unable to get a secure grip on my arm, but she hit me hard enough to knock the gun out of my hand. Instead of finishing the job by taking me down, the guard chased the WhamGun as it skittered across the floor. She was apparently more concerned about securing the weapon than she was about stopping me.

I could see another door to my right. I desperately tried to remember how the facility was laid out. Surely, I thought, a door on the right would lead me back to the corridor of offices. If I could get through there, I might yet be able to double back to where I had started and reach the exit door that led to the yard. If the interior doors had opened all by themselves, maybe it had too.

I ran along the wall to the door at the end and yanked it open. The thud of my heavy boots on the floor attracted the attention of three of the mob, who ran after me. I burst through the exit and slammed the door, trying to hold it shut against them long enough for the guard to catch up. With any luck, she would concentrate on herding them back to the others and give me time to get away.

I couldn't do it. They were big, bigger than I am, and the combined force of the three of them was too much. The door flew open, knocking me to the floor.

I rolled into a ball with my arms over my head, but, to my surprise, they ignored me. Instead they ran down the hall and disappeared into a room to the right. There was a scream, then another, and then a high-pitched non-stop shriek filled the corridor.

I ran to the room. The three who had followed me were in a struggle to subdue a girl. A girl with a twisted mass of braids. Rachel, I'd bet, the saker girl who had been waiting to meet God. One of them gripped her arms, the second had her left leg pinned to the floor with his knee, and was trying to control her flailing right leg. The third was lying on top of her, one hand around her throat, the other fumbling with her beribboned dress. I ran across the room and kicked the one who had her leg pinned, then tried to pull away the one who had her by the throat.

I couldn't get him off her. And then the knee-pinner came at me. I dodged to the right to avoid his swinging fist, but he kept coming and his second blow found its mark. His fist smashed into my face and I felt the bones in my nose crack. I fell heavily and yelled as the garden shears in my coat pocket drove themselves into my right thigh. Another blow smashed my teeth into my tongue, and then what little breath I had left was knocked out of me as my attacker jumped on me, digging a knee into my abdomen. He'd had a snarl on his face when he first came after me, but now he began to grin as he aimed another shattering blow at my face.

So, this was how Alfi died, I thought, as the blows rained down. This was what happened to her. She must have gotten this far undetected, and somehow these things had found her, had slipped past the guards and got her alone. And when she struggled, they had taken what they wanted anyway. I didn't want to end up like Alfi, a battered and torn body lying dead on an autopsy table. But I wasn't going to be able to take much more.

I swallowed down my panic and tucked my head to one side. I took a hard punch to my left ear while I wiggled my right arm free. My fingers pushed past the rucked-up hem of the lab coat and found the pocket of the winter jacket underneath. I pulled out the shears that Nguyen had honed to a sharp edge. Then I swung my arm upward as hard as I could.

It was a move born of desperation, but I got lucky. The tips of the saber-like blades slashed into his neck. He rolled off me, his hands clutching at the wound. The blood bubbled through his fingers and down his shirt. His mouth was open and I think he was screaming, but for some reason I couldn't hear him very well.

And suddenly, inexplicably, Nguyen was there. She burst into the room, brandishing her gun in all directions. She said something to me, but I couldn't hear what it was. Then she went for the two who had completely ignored their friend's difficulties and were continuing their attack on Rachel. Nguyen zapped the man who was lying on the girl. As soon as he saw the gun, the other jumped to his feet and ran cowering to the corner.

Nguyen leaned in closer to me. "Are you all right?" she said. I had to turn my head to hear her. My left ear didn't seem to be working.

"No," I said, "I'm not all right." The pain from my nose was excruciating. "Where did you come from?"

"I just ran toward the noise," she said. "I figured if there was a ruckus going on, you'd be at the center of it. And then I heard you yell so I ran faster."

I was starting to grey out a little. Just like the Fone screen, I thought. I'm out of juice. I fought to hold on. "I told you to run," I said.

"And I told you I'd watch your back. Are those men?"

I struggled to focus on where she was pointing.

The man she had zapped was lying on his back, his peculiar appendage exposed. Unlike the baby's, it was an ugly-looking thing. The one I had stabbed was still on his knees rocking back and forth, his hands to his neck. At least the blood was no longer pulsing out of the wound, so I figured I hadn't killed him. The man who had retreated to the corner still cowered there in fear, his hand thrust down the front of the loose pants he wore.

"Yup," I said. "Nice, huh?"

"Who's the girl?"

Before I could answer, security guards came pounding down the corridor and into the room. One of them ran immediately to the saker girl. Another stood just inside the door and waved her gun menacingly at the sorry-looking trio of men. The third marched over to us and held out her hand. Nguyen meekly deposited her weapon into it. I gestured toward the bloody shears on the floor.

"That's all I had," I said.

"All right. Stay where you are."

I was happy to oblige. My head felt like it had been cracked in a vise and I thought I was going to throw up.

The guard patted Nguyen down and confiscated the cutters that were still in the pocket of her jacket. Then she frisked me and extracted the Fone. I hoped there wouldn't be enough juice left in it for her to view the pictures I had taken. Maybe I could get it back before she thought to charge it up again.

"Get up," she ordered.

I rolled over onto my knees, but I got a bad case of the spins as soon as I tried to rise any further than that.

"Help her," the guard said, and Nguyen took an arm and heaved me up.

The guard marched us down the hall to the suite of offices by the back door. I was hobbling badly, and had to lean heavily on Nguyen.

"Did you fritz the security system?" I whispered to her as we staggered along.

Nguyen shook her head. "I don't know what happened."

"What?" I still couldn't hear clearly.

"Shut up," the guard said.

She stopped at one of the offices, opened the door and shoved us inside. "Sit."

We meekly sat while she leaned against the door frame, her gun held at the ready.

"What happens now?" I asked, as if I didn't know.

"Shut up."

My nose was killing me, and my eyes and lips were starting to swell, so I was just as happy to shut up right then. My arms, my legs, my back — everywhere hurt from being manhandled. Funny, I'd never understood what that word really meant until then. Manhandled.

"Do you think I could see a doctor?" I asked.

"Shut up," the guard said again, and then I leaned over and vomited. Most of it went into the nearby wastepaper basket, but a portion of it splashed on the floor and spattered her shoes. Her nose wrinkled and she looked at the mess in disgust, but she made no attempt to clean it up.

And there we sat for the next hour, until the Darmes arrived.

CHAPTER 18

Nguyen and I were separated for interrogation, each of us taken to a different office with a different Darme. That was pretty standard when there were two suspects. You want to make sure they don't have time to concoct a story between them. That way you can see if the information one gives jibes with what the other is saying.

I wasn't sure how much of it Nguyen really knew anyway, and I hoped, for that reason, that they wouldn't be able to charge her with anything really hideous. Besides, she was under Trent's direct orders to follow me. I just didn't know if that would cut any ice with the Gendarmes National Security Corps.

She should have run when she had the chance. I couldn't say I was sorry to see her galloping to my rescue when she did, but the security guards would have arrived eventually. There might even have been something left of me by the time they got there.

I didn't tell the Darme much. I left Trent and Hines out of the story entirely and instead concocted a tale about investigating kidnappings and being suspicious that the sakers were somehow involved, except that it wasn't nearly that coherent at the time I told it. It was painful to talk so I answered with only a word or two when I could. The Darme's interrogation technique was in no way enhanced by the fact that I kept asking her to repeat the questions. The hearing in my left ear was starting to come back by then, but she didn't know that, and it made a pretty good delaying tactic.

I knew she wasn't buying the story, but I figured all I had to do was sit tight and wait for Trent. With any luck, Jazz or Sonja would have contacted her. At the very least, Lisa-at-

The-Market might have called to complain that I'd stolen her bike. Even with no luck at all, eventually someone would be bound to notice that two of the city's finest were missing in action.

In the meantime, my face continued to swell and I was becoming convinced that a bone in my arm was broken. I also vomited again, the most effective delaying tactic of all. After that, the Darme finally called for the plant medical officer, who bustled in, gave me an icepack and a painkiller and then left again.

Eventually I was marched out to a waiting car and taken somewhere. I didn't know where, exactly. It wasn't back to the city, but to a holding facility where I was unceremoniously dumped into a cell. It was there that Trent finally caught up with me.

She waited, standing just inside the doorway, until the guard had locked up behind her and departed.

"You look like shit," she said.

"I feel like shit. It's a matched set." It was the first time I'd ever heard Boss Tweed unbend enough to utter an obscenity.

"You know, I had the night off. I was having a nice, quiet dinner until my Fone started to buzz. I got a lot of calls this evening."

"Oh yeah?"

"Yes. First I was called by someone named Sonja who chewed me out because one of my officers had involved her daughter in a dangerous police operation. Then I was called by someone named Lisa who chewed me out because one of my officers had taken her bike and had not returned it. And then I was called by an inspector from the National Security Corps, who chewed me out because one of my officers had broken into a federal institution and stabbed somebody in the neck. For some reason, I had no trouble believing that they were all talking about the same officer."

"Jazz Talerian didn't call?" I asked, puzzled.

"Oh yes, she called. But that was later. She didn't chew me out either, which was something, given the way my evening was turning out."

"Where is Nguyen?" I asked.

"Detective Nguyen will be released shortly. I verified her story that she was merely following my orders, which were to keep track of you," Trent said. "As a result, she can scarcely be held accountable for where you led her."

"I told her to run. She didn't. She could have gotten away and no one would have been any the wiser."

Trent stepped further into the tiny space and leaned against the wall. "You know, detectives are a funny bunch," she said. "You have to go with their strengths. Nguyen's strength is that she will always follow orders."

"She didn't follow mine," I pointed out.

"No, she followed mine and I outrank you. Nguyen made absolutely the right call and obeyed the orders given by a superior officer. That's why I chose her to babysit you — I knew she would stick to you no matter what." Trent pursed her lips and stared at the floor for a moment before she looked up at me. "You, on the other hand, can be counted on to ignore orders, procedure, protocol, and anything else you figure you can get away with. That's why I chose you to do what you did. I don't have any other officer on my staff who could have tracked this case down the way you did. You're like a bulldog. You grab hold and you won't let go, no matter where it takes you."

"You could have just told me what you wanted me to do."

"No, actually, I couldn't have. First of all, the information I was after was highly sensitive. Secondly, I wasn't sure it was even there at all. I needed to set you loose before I could even begin to assess what I was dealing with. It could have been nothing at all. I am sorry, though, that it seems to have brought you a great deal of trouble."

"So how long have you and Jo been together?" I asked.

"Ah, so you did figure that out. I wondered, when you said you were quitting the case. Jo and I are coming up on our twenty year anniversary." She looked at the floor again and sighed. "I knew you admired her — almost everybody does — but I hadn't anticipated any sort of real involvement, if you know what I mean. In all fairness, Jo wanted out as soon as she detected the signals."

It was a good thing that my face was so bruised, otherwise I was sure Trent would have been treated to the sight of me blushing bright red in embarrassment. Said out loud, even in such a diplomatic way, the whole thing sounded pathetic. What an idiot I am.

"It's okay," I mumbled. "She's pretty much out of my league anyway."

Trent smiled. "Yes, she is. She's out of mine as well. I'm a very lucky woman."

Oh, cazzo crap on a cracker. Time to change the subject before we started to talk about my feelings or some other kumbaya-tic bullshit.

"Did Jazz turn the stuff over to you?"

"Yes, she did. Fortunately, she neglected to tell her mother that you had used her as a depository. I'm sure it would have been burned otherwise. Or else I would have been. Sonja was extremely annoyed."

"And the Fone?"

"Yes, I retrieved the Fone. You did well, Mac. Your evidence has given me all the leverage I need."

"To do what? That's the one thing I can't get a handle on. I know what happened. I know how the Longwell girl died. I just can't figure out why you set me up. Why you set anybody up."

"I'm sorry, I can't tell you just yet. For now, I have to leave you here. Apparently, you're going to need some surgery on your nose and getting over that should keep you occupied for a few days. After that, I'll see what I can do to get you out. But I'll promise you one thing — one way or another I'll come back and tell you everything. Can you trust me on that?"

"Of course not," I said. "But I don't have much choice, do I?"

She laughed. "You are smart."

— «» —

If you deliberately set out to torture me, you probably couldn't come up with a better plan than to coop me up inside with nothing to do. I was taken somewhere to have my nose fixed and for a few days I was totally wigged out on painkillers, but after that I didn't have much to do except lie there, drum my fingers, and think.

I went over and over what I'd found out, what I'd seen, tried to fill in the gaps and come to terms with what had happened. I was lucky that Project Bathwater was such a hush-hush government operation, otherwise I figure I'd just have been charged with whatever they were going to charge me with, after which I would be tried, convicted, fired from the police force and thrown into a proper prison instead of a holding cell. But no one offered to find me a lawyer. No one even read me my rights. I wasn't offered a Fone call so that my loved ones could be contacted. Of course all of my loved ones already knew what had happened to me. Ricky, Nguyen, Jo. Pretty pathetic list, wasn't it? I wondered if Georgie might at some point hear that I'd disappeared and make inquiries, but that was a bit of a forlorn hope. I was pretty sure she didn't care anymore.

It was a cold comfort that Jo Hines felt bad about leading me on. Except that she didn't. I led me on, and the sooner I put all that behind me, the better. But sometimes in the small hours of the morning when I couldn't sleep, which was most nights, Georgie and Jo Hines would get mixed up inside my head and I'd start to forget which one said what, which one had which mannerism, which one had that certain tone in her voice when she was teasing me. Stupid, I know. But that was me. Stupid, about both of them. Just in different ways.

I'd do my best to steer my thoughts away from that unwelcome subject, but that would only lead me to think about what kind of trouble I was in. My career as a police detective was at an end, that much was clear. I figured they had me on break and enter at the very least — I wasn't even sure what you get charged with when you break into what is supposed to be a secure government research center. I wasn't sure if anybody knew about the university break-in. They might be able to put two and two together and figure it out, but I doubted they could prove it. It didn't matter. One conviction was all it would take and not even Trent could save my job. Beyond that, who knew what they would come up with and what they would do with me because of it. If, by some strange chance, I got away with a slap on the wrist, I wondered what I could do as a civilian. There are lots of jobs in NowZo. I'm just not good at any of them. I could be a private detective, maybe. Go into partnership with Ricky. Except that Ricky didn't really need me. She can find out whatever she wants to without leaving her room. Maybe Lisa-at-The-Market would get lucky and land a job at the disease center. Then I could move to Cedar Lake and be a cashier. Now there was a depressing thought.

Sometimes, I'd think about the saker girl — not the one with the baby — the one waiting in the other room. I hoped she was all right. She had taken as much punishment as I had. I wondered if she'd ever really understood what she was getting herself into, or if she had just gone along with it because she was told to. It was her first time. It hadn't been the first time for the men. They'd been to that room before, not all together, of course, one at a time and strictly supervised I hoped. But as soon as they'd gotten past the locked doors, they'd rushed to where they hoped a woman might be waiting. Poor Sister Rachel. Meeting God wasn't all it was cracked up to be.

I expect it never was. Incredible, the price women pay just to keep the human race going, even if they didn't buy in to some wacko's ravings about being in communion with God and restoring the natural order to the world. Even without men, it's a messy business. With men, it's messy with extra added violence. But those thoughts would just lead me back to Georgie. And Jo. Jo and Georgie. The one I couldn't have and the one I'd let slip away.

Daytime was a little easier, with its routine of meals and showers and medical check-ups, the changing of shifts. After the fourth or fifth day — I wasn't sure which because I'd lost track — a guard brought me a cup of real honest-to-gosh coffee.

"Supplies are starting to get through," she said as she handed me the mug. "You may even have something chocolate for dessert tonight."

Ironically, it was the worst coffee I've ever tasted, badly brewed and they'd used cheap beans to make it with. Even so, it was a small luxury that I was grateful for.

The same guard was inclined to be friendly and got permission to bring in a Vu. I wasn't allowed a Fone, of course. I was far too dangerous for that. Sometimes she'd even sit in the cell and watch a video with me. But I soon discovered that there were only so many of those you could watch before you got sick of the same old jokes and started picking holes in all the plots. There were books on the Vu as well, but they were all current bestsellers and not very appealing.

The only things that held my interest for long were the newsfeeds. The headlines were dominated by coverage of the impending election and the progress being made in the trade talks, punctuated by the usual celebrity drivel and soppy human interest stories. I kept expecting to see at least a cursory reference to the disturbance at the Cedar Lake Control Center, but it wasn't mentioned on any of the feeds that I watched. Of course, it might have been reported earlier, when I was still stupid from painkillers and didn't have a Vu. It would look like a minor break-in, I suppose, and not worthy of much in the way of follow-up. A blip on the screen of the day's events. Either that or the Darmes had managed to shut the story down, in the same way they had covered up Alfreda Longwell's murder.

In fact, now that the Tanaka Tyler kidnapping case had been cleared up, there was little in the way of crime news, just the usual assortment of burglaries, minor domestic disputes, saker demonstrations, and traffic accidents. If there was a silver lining anywhere in the dark cloud of my incarceration, it was the fact that someone else, hopefully Diva Davis, would have to file reports for all of those Tiresome Tasks.

And then, just three days before election day, the newsfeeds went berserk. Prime Minister Singh suddenly, and with no warning, resigned, both as the leader of the Northwest Zone and of her party. The entire election campaign was thrown into disarray. She gave no reason for her decision. There was just a statement that she was calling it quits, with no successor designated, and no suggestion as to how her party should proceed.

Nothing like this had ever happened before, and no one was entirely sure what should happen next. Singh's supporters, of course, tried to get the election postponed, in order to give them time to regroup and decide on another candidate. They even went to the courts, asking for an emergency ruling, but the judge found against them, arguing that the democratic process must proceed regardless. In lay terms, her response was "tough shit." The party's outrage struck me as pretty funny.

When election day finally rolled around, the outcome was predictable. Littlecrow leapt into the lead early on. At least hers was a recognizable name. After all, nobody wanted a pig in a poke, and, at the end of the evening, she was elected with quite a margin to spare.

But what was the most interesting to me was the coverage of the two campaign headquarters on election night. Prime Minister Singh's crowd were gloomy, some in tears, all of them howling about the unfairness of the proceedings. Littlecrow's were jubilant. And as she gave her victory speech, there, in the crowd right in front of her, were Kathleen Tomas Trent and Jo Norris Hines.

— «» —

The post-election coverage went on for days with interminable analyses of the results, speculation as to who would be appointed to Littlecrow's cabinet, and in-depth panel speculation about what had caused the Prime Minister to resign.

They should have asked me about that last one. I knew exactly what had happened. Trent had taken the information I had provided, and Littlecrow had used it. It was blackmail, pure and simple. Get out of the way or we go public.

I don't really know what exactly would have happened if they had made good on their threat. I don't have a lot of political savvy. I'd never paid that much attention to the posturing and positioning that goes on. But even I could see that all hell would break loose if it became known that there was a secret government program that was manufacturing men.

There would be an instant and loud demand for access to them, or at least to their genetic material, especially if it became known that a wingnut group like *The Sisterhood of*

Serene Acceptance had been allowed to get in there first. There would be a clamor to make a supply available to anyone who wanted it. But I knew that Project Bathwater wasn't ready for that yet. The little saker girl had at least one extra finger. I don't know what else was wrong with her that I hadn't been able to see. It promised to be like the cloning mess all over again, with disastrous outcomes followed by bitter recrimination and demand for compensation. The government could claim that they had moved a little more cautiously for that reason and had kept the news to itself while it sorted out the problems, but I doubt that would have been enough to dampen the outrage.

In the short term, I could see nothing but mayhem. Protests, demonstrations, work stoppages, demands from the newsfeeds for pictures and interviews with the inmates, harassment of the saker sects — in short, a veritable explosion of Tiresome Tasks to be dealt with, reported on and filed. A detective's nightmare.

In the medium term, I suppose the other Zones would quite rightly insist that the formula for the procedure be included in the GeneShare treaty — after all, theoretically, there was now a limitless supply — but unless strict protocols were included in the agreements, I could see no way to control how any of the other Zones proceeded. They would be able to use it any way they wanted, whether the results were a success or not. And there weren't so many successes that anyone could afford to squander them. There had only been twenty or so people in the big room I had crashed into at the Cedar Lake plant. Twenty men. After forty years of experiments. Not a huge output in terms of volume.

And in the long run, I suppose, there were the men themselves. They were being used like animals, their only purpose in life to inseminate. As far as I had seen, they *were* animals, with little understanding of anything beyond a primal urge to mate. But sooner or later, some do-gooder somewhere was going to point out that they were human beings.

CHAPTER 19

Inspector Trent kept her promise and came back to explain, but it wasn't until a couple of weeks after the election.

By then, the majority of the guards had decided that I wasn't really the dangerous desperado they had been told I was, and the woman who led the inspector to my cell didn't even bother locking the door behind her. Nor did Trent stand in the doorway this time. She walked right in, handed me a take-out coffee, sat on my cot and slumped back against the wall. She seemed tired and preoccupied.

"Well Mac, you'll be one of the first to know. I've just been appointed Chief Inspector of the National Security Corps."

I had been expecting a pronouncement of this sort, and I'd already worked up a good head of self-righteous steam. Just to make my point, I set the coffee on the floor and ignored it.

"Congratulations," I said. "It's nice to know that I've been sitting in jail for weeks in the interests of your career advancement."

"That was an announcement," she said. "Not an explanation."

"So explain it to me."

"Have you been watching the newsfeeds?"

"And how is your friend Prime Minister Littlecrow? Do be sure and say hi for me."

"All right," she said. "So you know what's happened. But you don't know why. Did you know that I started out as a history major?"

Her statement was such a non sequitur that it confused me, and she went on before I could think of anything snarky to say.

"I subsequently transferred to law enforcement because there didn't seem to be much 'career advancement,' as you so aptly put it, in the field of history. Sooner or later you end up teaching, whether you want to or not. I didn't, much as I loved the subject. It has, however, given me a little more perspective on the current situation than most career police officers would have."

I still didn't reply. I wasn't sure where she was going and I wasn't about to commit myself in any way until I got a better sense of what she was getting at.

"As you know, our former Prime Minister was never in favor of the GeneShare Treaty," she said. "So everyone was pretty surprised when Singh abruptly changed her mind and agreed to negotiate. All of the pundits think it was politically motivated, because everyone was so fed up with the trade sanctions. But you and I know better."

"It was because of the baby boy," I said. "The one I saw at Cedar Lake."

"Yes. He's a very special little boy. Project Bathwater had been only marginally successful in terms of producing males up until that point. It was never designed to produce more than a few. And each one of them still required a certain amount of gene therapy in order to get around the problems associated with the Founder Effect. But the baby you saw was a milestone. He is the first of the second generation."

"So it's father had been produced by Project Bathwater?" I still couldn't get the hang of the masculine pronoun. It just wouldn't slide off my tongue.

Trent nodded. "Yes. His father was produced by the project. And the baby bred true. He inherited the benefits of the therapy received by his father. There had been problems prior to this birth — you saw the woman's little girl. If the formula fails to produce a male, the end result is a flawed female. But the scientists kept tweaking the formula until they produced a perfectly normal boy. No indication of any of the syndromes or diseases that have been so troublesome in recent years."

"And what about Mighty Mite?"

"Mighty Mite isn't licked yet. Untreated, the fetuses are all female."

"But that's not the point, is it?" I said, echoing what Ricky had realized. "We aren't trying to replace an entire population of men, we're just trying to ensure the continuation of the human race. And we only need a few of them for that."

"Exactly," she said. "And what you may not know is that NowZo has far more genetic material banked than all of the other Zones put together. There is some speculation that supplies in SoCen are at such a critically low level that there would be little advantage to us in a straight swap. And yet, there would be enormous economic benefits if an agreement could be reached."

"So, knowing that there was going to be a steady supply of the good stuff, Singh gave in on GeneShare in order to bolster her popularity, win the election and guarantee that we have enough coffee and chocolate to keep us from killing each other," I said. I'd had a lot of time to think about this and had already figured a lot of it out. "But the announcement mentioned only 'current stocks.' That means only the old crap would go to GeneShare, right?"

"That's correct," Trent said. "The chemically improved stocks would be for the use of the Northwestern Zone only, and the process for producing it would remain a closely-guarded secret."

"Not closely enough," I said. "In my opinion, Darmes security was pretty sloppy. You might want to do something about that now that you're in charge."

A wry half-smile. "I'll take that under advisement."

"So with your help — pardon me, that would be with my help — Kirsty Littlecrow found out about all this and used it to force Singh out of office."

"You're right, security was lax. She had heard rumors."

"Whispers," was how Ricky had put it. "Just whispers and hard to track down."

"Littlecrow came to me a year ago and asked for help in trying to figure out what was going on," Trent went on. "We're old friends, so I agreed, but it seemed hopeless at first. There was so little hard information. But then the Longwell girl turned up dead and the Darmes muscled in as fast as they could, which was suspicious in itself. But even then, I might not have realized the full significance of her death if it hadn't been for Jo telling me about the injuries she sustained."

Of course. A little pillow talk, a sucker detective and, before you know it, you're head of the Darmes. Cute.

"So what happens now?" I said. "You do the right thing, the fair thing, and tell the whole world that we've figured out how to make men?"

"That's exactly what Prime Minister Littlecrow is not going to do. And this is where knowing a little background could be useful."

She appeared to be gathering steam for a lecture on the history of the world, so I cut her off.

"I read a lot of Professor Gerrity's files. I know where you're going with this."

"Really?" Trent actually looked impressed. "I hadn't expected that."

"I'm a bulldog, remember? I also have first-hand experience to go by. I was roughed up pretty good, and I hadn't thought that possible. I thought I was as tough as they come."

"That was the reason Professor Gerrity was seconded to the program in the first place," Trent said. "You and Alfreda aren't the first to be roughly handled. Singh was hoping that Gerrity might provide some insight on socialization. She wasn't very successful, but I suppose at the very least she was able to prepare the saker girls for the violence they might encounter." She sighed. "There's something that happens to men when they're in groups. They egg each other on and all their acquired civility flies out the window. It's just the nature of the beast." She seemed puzzled by this. "It's a power thing, I think. Much more highly-developed than in us and far more aggressive than we would ever think of being."

"You're right, woman are a lot sneakier about it," I said.

She grimaced. "Okay. I guess I deserved that."

"So, cutting to the chase here, what exactly does Littlecrow plan to do?"

"She plans to shut the program down."

That wasn't what I expected to hear. I had to give it a minute to sink in. Part of me wanted to cheer. I'd had lots of time to think about the ramifications of what I'd seen and I didn't like the way it played out. Not after I'd seen the files of nasty history that hid in Professor Gerrity's bottommost drawers. Not after I'd been whaled on so viciously for no other reason than because I was in the wrong place at the wrong time. Not after the way the saker girl had been so brutally attacked at the first opportunity. And especially not after Alfi Longwell had been so savagely raped and beaten to death the moment no one was looking. The men in Cedar Lake had done those things just because they could. Who wanted to run the risk of setting that kind of violence loose on the world again?

But one small part of me, one tiny, tiny part, felt sorry for all the Georgies out there, the women who grew so sad without children.

"So what happens to the men we've already got?" I finally asked. "Do we just kill them off?" I didn't like that idea either.

"Of course not," Trent said. "We're not barbarians. They will be looked after, cared for. They'll continue in their capacity as a resource, but there will be no more trials, no more mating with sakers, no more secret births. And the details of Project Bathwater will be destroyed."

"But..."

"I agree with Kirsty Littlecrow that we can't do anything else. If we continue with the project we lose control of the results, no matter how hard we try to keep it under wraps. Sooner or later, the other Zones would find out about it and demand the formula. And although that might seem like a reasonable demand right now, it leaves us wide open to a host of future problems."

"It can go wrong so easily," I said. "The little saker girl had an extra finger. If somebody gets sloppy we get the cloning disasters all over again."

"That would be only one of the problems," Trent said.

"And everybody would want boys. Just for the novelty of it."

"Yes, they would. We raise our daughters like little princesses. Can you imagine how sons would be treated?"

"Like little princes. Who would grow up to be kings. And before you know it, our daughters are back to being beaten and burned and set out on hillsides to die."

"You've got most of it," Trent said, "but there's at least one more thing. Humanity nearly destroyed the planet once. Resources were used at an unsustainable rate. The environment was compromised."

"But Mighty Mite took care of it," I added.

"It did. By reducing the population. It did what people themselves wouldn't do. Not willingly."

In spite of the fact that I was still angry with Trent, I had to consider what she was saying. And I realized that she was correct in her assessment.

"So if Bathwater Project somehow became wildly successful and everybody started having babies left, right and center again, we'd be right back in the same boat again. Eventually."

"Not the most elegant summary I've ever heard, but yes, that's correct."

My mind went back to Georgie, who had been willing to do anything for a baby. Even leave me. What would she have done if she could have had four? Or nine? Or twelve? She would have. I know she would have. And the world is full of Georgies.

"Okay, I'll buy all that," I said. "But what about the Founder Effect? Jo — Dr. Norris Hines, that is — told me that we're doomed if we keep using the same old stock all the time."

Trent noticed me stumble on the name, but she was diplomatic enough to pretend she hadn't.

"Oh, I doubt it will come to that," she said. "There will be continued improvements in gene therapy. Our population may fall a little more, but we're probably pretty close to the planet's carrying capacity right now anyway. The human race will survive. And the earth will continue to be a much cleaner and safer place than it was before Mighty Mite."

"So how do you keep this a secret?" I asked. "There are a lot of loose ends that have been left dangling. Singh, the sakers, me." Not to mention Jazz Talerian, who no doubt had sat and read every word I'd written before she decided to call Trent.

"Singh won't breathe a word. Would you want to go down in history as the leader who played politics with babies? That's why she stepped down in the first place."

"And the sakers?"

"*The Sisterhood of Serene Acceptance* have a number of female children in different camps scattered all over the DK. We'll continue to give them protection. But they'll be told that God has departed the earth again or some such nonsense — I'll have to leave that to someone who is an expert in theology."

"But what if they go public?"

Trent shrugged. "Who would believe them? They're kooks."

"And me?"

"Well, it's like this, Mac. We have you dead to rights on two counts of break and enter, and then there's destruction of government property. Assault with a deadly weapon."

"Garden shears? That's a deadly weapon?"

"In your hands, they apparently are. We could go on from there, you know — a case might be made for jeopardizing state secrets, maybe even attempting to overthrow the government."

"Okay, okay, I get it," I said. "But what about due process? I haven't even been allowed a Fone call."

"Oh, you could have a trial. It just wouldn't be public. And I don't see how you could deny the evidence. After all, you did all those things."

Up until that moment, I'd thought that Ricky Vanek Chan was the most dangerous person on the planet. I was wrong. It was the woman sitting on my bed. But there was an out somewhere. Otherwise Trent wouldn't be telling me all this.

"So what do you want?"

"I want you to work for me. You and Nguyen. If you agree, she'd like to come too. If you don't, she'll go back to Division."

"If I worked for you — and that's an "if," not an agreement — what would I be doing?"

"Initially, I'd put you in charge of cleaning up the mess. You'd start with security at Cedar Lake, which by all accounts was deplorable. And then you'd tidy up all the loose ends. After all, if you want to plug the holes, there's no better person to ask than the person who found them in the first place."

The Ricky argument. Cazzo, this woman was good.

"There would be a couple of conditions."

"I wouldn't expect anything else."

"Alfreda Lucas Longwell's parents need to know how their daughter died. I know, I know," I said, as Trent began to protest, "national security and all that. They don't need all the details. Just enough for some closure."

Trent considered this for a full minute, before she finally said, "Agreed."

"And Jazz Talerian needs to know that they know. Otherwise she can be dealt with by a simple non-disclosure agreement. She may have read my notes, but she doesn't have any evidence to back it up, and I'd deny everything if she ever decided to blab."

"All right," Trent said, and I heaved a sigh of relief. When Jazz handed the papers over she must have neglected to mention what she'd seen the year she was sixteen. Or that she'd copied encrypted files from a stolen Fone.

"I'll let you know," I said.

Trent rose then and walked to the door, but before she went through it, she turned back to me.

"You're a good cop, Mac. You'd be a great Darme."

"I'll let you know."

She nodded and left. As soon as I was sure she was out of sight, I dove for the coffee.

— «» —

It might have seemed like a no-brainer to anybody else, but it still took me a day to come to a decision. A day and one long, long night.

I could dig in my heels, get stubborn, refuse to cooperate, but what would it get me? Nothing but a jail cell. Besides, I didn't trust my natural inclination to be stubborn anymore.

But the whole thing stunk. Right from the start. Right from the first time anybody ever decided to see what would happen if she tried messing around with a fancy new hormonal stew. The intention was good, I could see that. Nobody meant to do any harm. But at the end of the day, Alfi Longwell was dead, the sakers had been used, and there were so many ethical ambiguities it made my head spin.

Poor Alfi. Determined, manipulative, designing Alfi. One might argue that she had been the author of her own misfortune, and, in some respects, that was true. She should never have tried to get into the Cedar Lake facility. But no one deserved to die the way she had. Just because she was ambitious. Just because she was anything. Not that way.

Trent had called it "the nature of the beast." I had seen firsthand what that nature was. The question was whether or not the beast could ever be tamed. If my experience was anything to go by, the odds weren't good.

Hyacinth Belo Bree became the hero of the Testosterone Wars when she brought about the downfall of the last stronghold of men at the Siege of Monte Castra. No matter what I chose to do, nobody was ever going to hear about Hyacinth Carson MacHenry, who brought about the downfall of Project Bathwater. It was just as well, I decided. We have enough little girls called Hyacinth as it is.

I also spent a lot of time thinking about Nguyen. I must admit I'd grown a lot fonder of her than I had been in the beginning. We'd actually made a pretty good team. She had promised to watch my back, and she'd done just that. It was more than anybody else had ever done for me.

Then, just as the numbers on the clock flipped over to five a.m., I made my decision. I'd give it a chance.

SIX WEEKS LATER

The biggest container of peanut butter I can find is a two-kilogram pail from a restaurant supply house. I throw in a couple loaves of bread and a package of toilet paper, before I schlep it all up the stairs to Ricky's.

I wave at the security cam on the landing and the door clicks open. Ricky is in her usual spot, in the single chair in front of multiple Vu screens.

"Took you long enough," she says, without turning around.

"I was detained," I say, truthfully enough.

"I'm not surprised. It looked like all hell was breaking loose in there."

"So it was you who opened all the doors?"

"Yeah." She giggles. "It was neat. I laid your leash signal on top of the schematic. Wanna see how it works?"

She enters a furious string of code and the floorplan of the Cedar Lake Center for the Control of Communicable Diseases pops into view. "You entered here." She points to the back door of the plant. "I saw you go down here..." She moves along the corridor to the offices and the care rooms. "Then you went to the double doors. Then to the back door again, and then everything started to move back and forth in a hurry. I figured you were in trouble, so when the alarms went off, I hit the release button on everything I could find."

"I should have known it was you," I say.

"Yeah, well, I thought maybe I'd blown it when I didn't hear from you for so long."

"We'd have been caught no matter what. But, thanks to you, I gleaned enough info to make a difference."

"Info is good," she croons. "Info is power. Thanks for the peanut butter." She keys in more strokes and Cedar Lake disappears from the screen.

"By the way, I'm not at the same address anymore. I've given up the apartment."

"Yeah I know," she says without looking up from the Vu. "Don't worry, I'll find you."

I leave her to it and trudge back down the stairs to where Nguyen is waiting with the car that's taking us to Cedar Lake. Maybe when we get there, I'll pay a visit to The Market. Buzz around the corner and see if Sonja is still pissed off at me. Drop in on Alicia and Freddie and hope there's another blueberry pie in the oven. Cedar Lake looked like a pretty nice place to live if you're into the quiet life. I could use a little quiet.

I guess I'm lucky, the way things worked out.

Luck. Luck and lux. Just what I needed.

If you enjoyed this read

Please leave a review on Amazon, Facebook, Good Reads or Instagram.

It takes less than five minutes and it really does make a difference.

If you're not sure how to leave a review on Amazon:

1. *Go to amazon.com.*

2. *Type in The Bathwater Conspiracy by Janet Kellough and when you see it, click on it.*

3. *Scroll down to Customer Reviews. Nearby you'll see a box labeled Write a Review. Click it.*

4. *Now, if you've never written a review before on Amazon, they might ask you to create a name for yourself.*

5. *Reviews can be as simple as, "Loved the book! Can't wait for the Next!" (Please don't give the story away.)*

And that's it!

Brian Hades, publisher

About the Author

Janet Kellough is an author and storyteller who has written and performed in numerous stage productions that feature a fusion of spoken word and music. Her published works include The Thaddeus Lewis Mystery Series (*On the Head of a Pin, Sowing Poison, 47 Sorrows, The Burying Ground, Wishful Seeing* and *The Heart Balm Tort*); two contemporary novels *The Palace of the Moon* and *The Pear Shaped Woman*; and the semi-non-fictional *Legendary Guide to Prince Edward County*. Janet lives in rural Ontario, Canada with a husband, miscellaneous critters and thousands of red cedar trees.

Need something new to read?

If you liked The Bathwater Conspiracy you should also consider these other EDGE-Lite titles:

The Milkman
A Freeworld Novel

by Michael J. Martineck

In the near future, corporation rules every possible freedom. Without government, there can be no crime. And every act is measured against competing interests, hidden loyalties and the ever-upward pressure of the corporate ladder.

Any quest for transparency is as punishable as an act of murder. But one man has managed to slip the system, a future-day Robin Hood who tests dairy milk outside of corporate control and posts the results to the world.

When the Milkman is framed for a young girl's murder and anonymous funding comes through for a documentary filmmaker in search of true art beneath corporate propaganda, eyes begin to turn and soon the hunt is on.

Can the man who created the symbol of the Milkman, the only one who knows what really happened that bloody night, escape the corporate rat maze closing around him? Or is it already too late?

Praise for The Milkman:

The Milkman won the Independent Publisher Book Award (IPPY) as the best science fiction novel at the national level. The novel was also a finalist in the Eric Hoffer awards, given each year for salient writing from small presses.

"Reminiscent of the novels of Michael Coney, Frederik Pohl and Cyril Kornbluth as well as Terry Gilliam's Brazil, although with less bitter humor and more outrage than those luminaries, the work is a reductio ad absurdum examination of the increasingly corporatized world in which we all live, an impressive demonstration of the author's skills."
-- Publisher's Weekly

"I have a fascination for the art of writing; this author grabbed me at the first paragraph, relating crimes to works of art. His creative use of dialogue, description, and plotline moved the story along smoothly. Thought provoking ideas added depth to this powerful dystopian tale of murder in a corporate world, but did not get in the way of this futuristic noir style detective story. With believable, sympathetic characters and page turning action, I highly recommend this fascinating thriller."
— Paul Fruehauf

For more on The Milkman visit:
http://tinyurl.com/edge2075

——— < > ———

The Genius Asylum

by Arlene F. Marks

The truth is out there...

Earth Intelligence and Space Installation Security each think Drew Townsend is working for them. They're wrong.

Sent undercover to set up a covert intelligence operation on Earth's remotest space station, Drew Townsend finds himself managing a crew of brilliant mavericks, making friends with the most feared warriors in the galaxy, and feeling more at home in the controlled insanity of Daisy Hub than he ever did on Earth. Then he learns the truth about his mission there, and it's time to choose. In the coming interplanetary conflict, which side will Daisy Hub be on?'

Like the clues of a cryptic crossword, each book set in the Sic Transit Terra universe contains a puzzle – perhaps a riddle, perhaps a maze or an anagram – and in each case, the answer to the smaller puzzle brings the reader and characters one step closer to solving a much larger and more important one. The Genius Asylum is '1 Across' – it initiates a multi-book story arc that addresses one of the great mysteries of life: Why are we humans the way that we are?

Praise for The Genius Asylum

"The Genius Asylum starts out on Earth as something that looks like a crime story, but it then quickly describes a world of interstellar travel and alien alliances. After the first act concludes, the story's complexity starts accelerating and

doesn't slow down, and you'll find yourself drawn into the world, needing to know what comes next. It is an excellently written story that provides the framework for the series that is to come, and I'm looking forward to reading the rest of it."
— Chris Marks, reviewer

I thoroughly enjoyed this Sci-Fi Brainteaser. Very well written with incredible plot twists and turns. We've got a very intelligent double agent as the main character and an intriguing support cast. I was thankful for the planetary history at the beginning as it was helpful in understanding the different organizations mentioned throughout the novel. The Author has a witty way of expressing viewpoints, clearly has put a lot of thought into the storyline and created edge of your seat suspense and mystery! Admittedly, I was confused about the title of the book until about halfway through reading it but it makes perfect sense now. I highly recommend this absolutely unforgettable installment and can't wait for the next.
— Stephanie Herman

For more on The Genius Asylum visit:
tinyurl.com/edge6013

——— <> ———

The Rosetta Man

by Claire McCague

Wanted:
Translator for first contact.
Immediate opening.
Danger pay allowance.

Estlin Hume lives in Twin Butte, Alberta surrounded by a horde of affectionate squirrels. His involuntary squirrel-attracting talent leaves him evicted, expelled, fired and near penniless until two aliens arrive and adopt him as their translator. Yanked around the world at the center of the first contact crisis, Estlin finds his new employers incomprehensible. As he faces the ultimate language barrier, unsympathetic military forces converging in the South Pacific keep threatening to kill the messenger. The question on everyone's mind is: Why are the aliens here? But Estlin's starting to think we'll happily blow ourselves up in the process of finding that out.

Praise for The Rosetta Man:

"The cover and synopsis had me expecting a light-hearted comedy. I didn't realize I was getting a geopolitical first contact thriller that somehow still managed to be a light-hearted comedy. I really enjoyed this book! The characters are rich and diverse. Estlin and Harry are great, Beth and Bomani made me cry. The story is fast paced and engaging

and again, completely unexpected. Great book for fans of first contact scifi, but also fans of thrillers and mysteries. And so well-executed that I give it a solid 5 stars."
   — Scott Burtness, author of Wisconsin Vamp (Monsters in the Midwest)

"This book ranks up there with many of the classic sci-fi "first contact" stories and Claire McCague's scientific background comes through in waves."
   — Cameron Arsenault, Amazon Reviewer

"A completely enjoyable read. Good action, lots of humor, and a global setting. Strongly recommended."
   — Diane Lacey, Amazon Reviewer

For more on The Rosetta Man visit:
tinyurl.com/edge6004

———< >———

For more EDGE titles and information about upcoming speculative fiction please visit us at:

www.edgewebsite.com

Don't forget to sign-up for our Special Offers

CPSIA information can be obtained
at www.ICGtesting.com
Printed in the USA
LVHW03s1705180818
587386LV00001B/142/P

9 781770 531642